# GRANDMAS NEVER DIE
## Their Wisdom Lives Forever

Judith Morton Fraser, M.A., L.M.F.T.
Marriage, Family Therapist

Heart of the Canyon Publishing
1st Edition

Heart of the Canyon Publishing
2386 Sunset Heights Drive
Los Angeles, CA. 90046
USA

First Edition
Printed in the United States

Cover designed by Mackie Osborn

includes questions for discussion and glossary

isbn ISBN 9780983535003

# DEDICATION

To my family who continue to shine light on the dark corners of my life, paint my thoughts with colors I didn't know existed and move me into realms that keep me stumbling forward into delightful possibilities. You are the creators of my Universe.

# TRUST

*Life is an adventure.*
*Each difficulty we overcome*
*is a rite of passage*
*that expands our compassion*
*for ourselves, others, and the world.*

*Our enemies are not external,*
*they are internal.*
*What we fear most*
*is to trust*
*that still, small voice*
*within.*

*Judith Morton Fraser, MFT*

# ACKNOWLEDGEMENTS

Inspiration for this book comes from words of wisdom my grandmother passed on to me.  Those words, along with the awareness I have gathered from friends, family, my Focusing and Therapist Community, I now share with you and my grandchildren.

I am also grateful to James H. Howard for his book SHAWNEE! The Ceremonialism of a Native American Tribe and its Cultural Background.

Chapter One

## FIONA'S TWELFTH BIRTHDAY

*Somewhere in time, in the Star World, twelve women from various ethnic cultures, dressed simply in their native costume, sit cross legged in what is called "The Circle of Light". Each of them rises -- then slowly steps forward to drop a pinch of sacred Kin.ni.kin.nick, a mixture of bark, dried leaves and tobacco, into a small fire that glows in the center of the circle -- before returning to her original place to sit.*

*Ho ya ne ho ya ne ho. The women chant as smoke from the tobacco, together with that from the wood, forms a picture of a young girl, Fiona Lonestar MacLean.*

"Clean up quick and get in here, birthday girl." Momma called out to me from the kitchen in that voice like a chirping bird she used when she was happy.

"I'll be quicker than you can say *alakazam*," I yelled back. Momma had laid my Easter dress out on Brucie's bed. It still looked brand new. I only used it for special occasions, like today. It's my birthday. I turned twelve at six o'clock this morning, June 16th. I slipped my arms through the long sleeves, pulled down on the pale blue skirt and reached back to bring up the zipper.

Every Easter Momma took us shopping at Penny's to buy something special for church. This year we got to buy twin dresses. A pretty blue one with a flared skirt for her and the same for me. Only, of course Momma's fit right away. Mine, I get to grow into. I tied the belt real tight around my waist and folded the sleeves up at the wrist to make it fit better. "I'm movin' up in the world," I whispered.

I walked over to the mirror and stood real close. My blue eyes stared back. I ran my fingers over my cheeks and down across my chin. I wasn't as dark skinned as my brothers, or my mom for that matter. People in my family aren't any one color.

*La-La-La-Lonestar, beautiful Lonestar, you're the only ga-ga-ga-girl that I adore,* Momma sang as she banged on the pans near the stove to keep rhythm. If Momma wanted she could be a professional singer just like her best friend Ann Marie Thorsby who sings at the Gaiety nightclub in downtown Detroit. Ann Marie and her husband Andy Joe live just up the street from us.

It was five-thirty. I peeked out of the door of the bedroom I shared with my fourteen year old brother Sean, and nine year old brother Brucie. They were sitting at the kitchen table. Momma stirred a pot at the stove. As soon as Father drove up Goldy would jump up from under the table and make some happy cries. That way I'd know he was here.

The drawer where Father kept his secret stuff was in his dresser just across the hall from our room. All I had to do was take a few quick steps and nobody'd know. Sean told me he looked in it last week and found some neat stuff, so since it was my birthday I figured it'd be okay if I took a turn.

I held my breath and made a run for it. "Blam, blam." My heart beat so loud I thought it was gonna pop out. I'd be the only kid at school with a gaping hole in my chest.

"Thou shalt not," screamed inside of me. "I'm not stealing anything," I said real soft like. "I'm just gonna look. *God punishes sinners. They cook in hell for a long, long time.* Words Preacher MacNeal said during church service jangled in my head. My hands started to shake as I pulled out on the wooden knobs of the third drawer down from the top. "God, Jesus, Great Spirit, *Kokumthena,* don't let me get caught."

God and Jesus are who everybody prays to at church. Grandma, that's momma's momma, is not so wild about those names. *God and Jesus are mighty powerful energies, but the meanin's gotten misused,* she said. *People use religion as a reason to war with one another. They don't understand that life is sacred. All life.*

Grandma told me that *Kokumthena* is The Great Spirit's helper, the one that does all the work. It's sort of like Jesus is to God. Only she's a she, not a he. I use all the names sometimes. That way, I'm covered.

I stopped to take a deep breath and listen. *You're the only ga-ga-ga-girl that I adore,* Momma sang again as her feet shuffled around the linoleum floor. Sean and Brucie joined in with the, *La-la-la-Lonestar.* I bit down on my upper lip. And peeked inside the drawer. A piece of red material covered whatever was there. Musty smells flew into the air. Sean was right. Father did have old stuff tucked away. Father never talked about his relatives. When we ask he jokes and says "I just sprung into the world full grown." He's such a joker.

I pushed the red material over to the right. A bunch of yellowed letters tied with string filled up one corner of the drawer. I leaned way in to see who they were from. "Dancing Feet, Route 5; Nashville, Tennessee," the return address read. That was a weird name. Was that a relative I wondered?

A vision of a woman leaped across the inside of my eyes as graceful as a deer. "Dancing Feet," she said. It made me smile. I liked seeing pictures in my head.

I carefully put the letters back where I found them and ran my fingers over the top of what looked like an old sketch book. Something an artist might use for special drawings. Sean told me Father had a special book, so I was sure this was it.

The book opened sideways. With the top flipped over it took up the whole length of the drawer. The drawing on top was a fox. Even though it was drawn in pencil, the eyes nearly jumped off the paper they looked so real. Scary too. Like he was about to eat me. Father's name was signed at the bottom of the drawing, Frank T. I've seen him sign papers that way. But no one but Momma seems to know what it stands for. She just runs her thumb and finger across her lips like she's zipping them up when we ask. Father never talks about drawing, "Hogwash and horse feed," he'd say if anyone mentioned doing, being or thinking about anything creative. Yet, here, hidden in his drawer, was evidence of the opposite.

The sound of car tires spitting out gravel in front of our house brought my search to a stop. I stood still and listened harder. My heart did it's loud pounding again. I turned and looked out the window next to Momma's vanity. But it was too late. Whoever it was zipped past. Not Father. Still, the sudden noise gave me the all-overs. Doing things you weren't supposed to isn't easy.

A photograph, about the size of my hand, slipped out of the sketch book and into the drawer next to some old buttons and stuff. I quickly closed the book and picked up the photo. It was a woman. She was wearing an ankle length dress belted at the waist. Her dark hair was set in two braids that fell over the front of her shoulders. She looked about Momma's age, maybe 30, but her skin was a deeper brown. Two children stood next to her, side by side. One looked to be about five or six, the other ten or eleven. They were a lighter color than she was. I wondered who they were.

"Lonestar, uh, Fiona, what in tarnation is taking you so long?" Momma called out again.

Oops! I took a deep breath and blinked my eyes to bring them back into focus. She called me Fiona. She only did that when Father was around. It's a Scottish name. Father's real proud of being Scot's. He doesn't like me to be called Lonestar. That's the Indian name Grandma gave me.

I slid the photograph back into the book. Pulled the red cloth back over everything. Closed the drawer. Shut the bedroom door and inched, shadow like, into the hall. "I'm comin'."

My hands were sweaty. I interlaced my fingers and put them behind my back. "Father here yet?" I murmured from the doorway. Sean shot me a suspicious look. "Where ya been?" He asked. I just titled my chin and ignored him as I hurried in and sat down at the table.

"Not yet, but any minute now." Momma curled up the corners of her mouth and winked at me then turned back to the stove. A pink checkered apron covered the front of her blue dress.

I tried to wink back. I couldn't do one eye, so I did two. "It sure smell's good in here," I said. "What's for supper?" Every burner on the stove had a pot on it. And something was cooking in the oven. Momma was too busy to answer.

Brucie was sitting next to Sean. They were cutting out stars from colored construction paper. Sean's were perfect, Brucie's were a little ragged on the edges.

Momma looked so pretty in her Easter dress. I loved it when we dressed the same. It made me feel like I was really a part of her. With her olive skin, blue eyes and black hair, she looked just like a movie star.

"You think I'll be as pretty as you when I grow up, Momma?" I asked.

"Pretty is as pretty does." She took a sip of beer, then went back to stirring the pots.

"Well I was thinkin' I might wanna be a movie star one day. So, I really need to know if I have a chance." Momma turned from the stove and fixed her eyes on mine for a second. If she thought I could be pretty, then maybe I could be a movie star. If she didn't think I could, I'd have to settle for being ugly, like a toad. She glanced at her watch. Then lickety split, ran into the living room, pulled back the drapes and looked out at the road.

I took a deep breath in, then let all the air blow out of my mouth like a balloon with a hole in it. Her not answering, meant I was a toad. I looked out across the living room and shouted, "do you think ..."

"Shush," Sean hissed pointing to the empty bottles of beer on the kitchen sink. "Don't ask for anything right now."

The wall clock made a clicking noise. I looked up. It was six o'clock.

"He's prob'ly working overtime again." Momma sighed as she turned away from the window and headed back towards the kitchen. Her eyes were glassy, like she was ready to cry. "You kids know how he is." Momma pulled out the chair at the end of the table and sat down. "If there's a piece of machinery not working 'Good 'ole Frank' will stay until it's as good as new. Thinks he's Superman." She let out one of her sharp laughs, the kind that's not happy, then drummed her fingers on the table and stared at the clock.

Brucie started chewing on his shirt collar like he does when he's nervous. I stood up, reached across the table and grabbed it out of his mouth like Momma told me to do. "Stop it," I said. Brucie gave me the *evil eye*, but he did like I told him.

"Sean open one of those beers in the ice-box. Let's start the celebration," Momma ordered.

Sean, sitting kitty corner to her right, shook his head. "You already started celebrating." Momma raised her eyebrows and gave Sean a look that could wilt flowers.

Sean jumped up from the table, dragged his feet across the linoleum, went to the ice-box, popped the lid and handed Momma a beer.

"Me and Jesus have a lot in common." Momma ran her fingers up and down the outside of the cold bottle. "Both born on Christmas Day." She lifted the bottle in the air, brought it to her lips, tilted her head back and let a good gulp run down her throat. When she was finished, she wiped off the top of the bottle with a cloth she had tucked in her apron pocket, grinned from ear to ear and handed the bottle to me. "Happy Birthday sweetie."

"You want me to drink this?" Even though we always had plenty of bottles in the ice-box, and nobody would care if I took one, I never thought about drinking one.

"You're the only birthday girl here," Momma answered.

I wrapped my hands around the outside of the bottle. It was cold and slippery. Careful not to drop it, I tilted the bottle up towards my lips, pressed them tightly against the top, closed my eyes and lifted my head towards the ceiling. The sour liquid ran down my throat like muddy water rushing down our Jackson Street creek. "Umm, good," I lied as I set the bottle back down.

"The taste grows on you," Momma said reading through my disguise. She took the beer, wiped it again with the cloth and passed it on to Sean. "When you're big, you'll like it."

"I am big." I sat up tall, but I didn't think growing bigger was ever gonna make me like the yucky taste of beer.

"Wow," Sean said acting smart. "Here's to my BIG sister." With a wave of his hand he brought the bottle up to his lips and chugged it like a cold soda. I rolled my eyes and muttered to myself. I hate it when he acts like being two years older than I am is such a big deal.

"Happy Birthday," Brucie said reaching out to Sean for the bottle.

"Oops, Brucie, sorry it's all gone." Sean set the beer on the counter behind him.

"Man-o-man, why's it you get to decide?" Brucie crossed his arms over his chest and slunk back into his chair.

Sean pulled his shoulders back and sat up tall, "Because I'm your BIG brother," he growled. I kicked Brucie's foot under the table, blinked my eyes and mouthed, "you didn't miss much."

A car horn honked just outside our front window. Goldy barked and ran to the door. Momma's face beamed as bright as a fresh red apple. I jumped up, pushed Goldy out of the way, ran to the front door and stepped out.

It was Harriet Helmsly from next door. I watched as she parked her car on the side road that divided our house from hers. Harriet's one of Mom's coffee buddies. They sit at the kitchen table Saturday mornings and gab about the news, relatives and anything else that catches their fancy. I gave her a quick wave, then looked hard up one way and down the other. Herby, Dickie and some of the other kids on the block were playing ball, but, no sign of Father. I went back and sat down in the kitchen.

Brucie jiggled in his seat. "Something smells good, can't we eat it?"

"Scotch pie," Momma muttered. She pushed her chair back, stood up and went to the stove. "Barley'n peas," she added lifting the lid off the pan. Steam flew out, followed by a sweet smell.

Brucie squished up his face and gave me his pleading look. Vegetables are like poison to him. "I'll eat them," I whispered.

"And strawberry birthday cake." She recounted the twelve candles on the counter.

"Umm." I licked my lips. I loved strawberries.

"No bread pudding?" Sean whispered as he put his hands together and looked up at the sky prayerfully. "What are we gonna do with all our stale bread?" Brucie and me covered our mouths trying not to laugh, but it didn't work.

"Are you three making fun of my cooking?" Momma said as she started to put the candles on the cake.

"No Momma. Your cooking's great!" I said. "Yeh, if you like pigs feet," Sean growled. "Yuck," Brucie made a face, "and cow's tongue." Momma shook her head and laughed. "You three don't know it yet, but you get to dine like royalty." She turned back to the cake, took a deep breath, then slowly made a circle with the candles.

Goldy brushed up against my leg under the table and whined. She didn't know we were just joking. I reached down and scratched under her chin. That was one of her favorite spots.

We sat quiet for a long time after that. The only noises in the room were the clock ticking, Momma's checking stuff, Goldy licking her chops and our stomach's growling.

Suddenly Momma hit herself on the side of her head, like something important had just landed there. "Sean, do you ..." Momma cleared her throat and sat back down, "think you could?" Her eyes shifted between Sean and the door, "you know?"

"Go up the street to Morrie's Bar?" Sean said looking her straight in the eye.

"Well, yes," she answered squishing up her face. "I hate to send you there." Her eyes got all soft and watery. "God knows it's no place for kids ... but, maybe he's not working late. Maybe he's ... umm ... dropped in to see some of his friends and forgot ..." Momma swallowed hard, glanced at me, then back at Sean, "the time."

"Of course I'll go," Sean said standing up. "And I'll give you odds, ten to one, I'll find him."

Usually Sean went to Morrie's by himself. Being the oldest he was always in charge of stuff like that. I hated it when he got to do things I didn't. We'd passed by the bar every time we went to church or the movies or anywhere near the shops around the corner. The windows were dark so you couldn't see what went on inside, but I could hear the sounds of people laughing, singing, or playing music whenever I was within a block of the place.

The screen door slammed as Sean headed out the door. His shoes made skipping sounds as he went down the steps. I thought about him going to that mysterious place again without me. It didn't seem fair. I mean, it was my birthday. Fire burned in my stomach. I leaped up and hurried over to where Momma was standing in the doorway. "Momma let me go with Sean?" I shouted.

"What are the neighbors gonna think?" Momma asked. It really wasn't a question so I didn't say anything back. "Besides, you're a girl. Girls don't go to bars."

"It is my birthday." I pleaded like I'd never pleaded before. "P-l-e-a-s-e?"

Momma took a deep breath, one that went from the top of her head to the tips of her toes. "Will you take care of ...?"

I nodded yes. Taking care of Brucie was something I always did. We grabbed three dinner rolls from the table, one for each of us, and ran out the door lickety split.

I yelled at Sean to wait up so we could walk together. He was all the way up to Ann Marie's house by that time, but he heard me. Brucie and I ran as fast as we could to catch up. I handed Sean his roll like it was a Cracker Jack prize. "You guys shouldn't be coming with me," he said, but he ate the roll anyway.

Ann Marie waved out the window as we gathered in front of her house. We waved back then headed up the street like we were just playing, not out on a secret mission. Even though

Ann Marie and Momma were best friends and shared lots of stuff, Momma still wouldn't want her to know she was letting us go to Morrie's Bar. "Never hang your laundry in public," Momma always says.

Chapter Two

## A *CEILIDH*

I peeked into the window of Mr. Johnston's shop at the end of Jackson Street, just to the right on the main road. He's the optician who helped straighten my crooked eye. I used to have one eye that went right while the other went left.

"A wanderin' eye for the boys," Father'd say. He'd raise one eyebrow, lower his chin, wiggle his shoulders and go into that Scots brogue of his. Momma says he jokes on account of he's just a big kid. I'm not so sure about that. He's a whole twenty years older than I am.

One of the kids at school teased me about wearing glasses. *Nana, nana, na, na, Lonestar's got four eyes like a monster from a slimy pit,* she sang in this stupid sing-songy-tweaky voice. It didn't even rhyme.

Grandma said when kids are mean it's because someone else is mean to them. *Turn around and walk away Lonestar. Meanness is contagious. Don't catch their sickness.* I wanted to "Nana, nana, na, na," right back, but instead, I did what Grandma said.

My stomach started to jump as we walked in front of Morrie's black window. I squeezed Brucie's hand. "Let's stick together," I said. Sean held the door open as we slipped into the darkness and noise of the bar. Once inside, Sean pulled us behind him. The jangle of the music and people talking rushed at me and blew right through my skin. "Fiddling music!" I shouted, trying to make myself heard over the noise.

"Those are *ceilidh* sounds," Sean shouted over his shoulder at Brucie and me.

"Kay-what?" I yelled.

*"Ceilidh* sounds," Sean said, talking into my ear. "It's pronounced kay-lee but you spell it *c-e-i-l-i-d-h*. It means big party. It's where everybody dances, sings or something. Part of who we are and where we come from." I hate it when Sean knows stuff I don't. Sometimes he sounds like a dictionary.

We walked around the dozen or so tables and made our way through people who were watching someone on the dance floor. We didn't see Father. We figured he must be part of the crowd facing away from us watching the entertainment, so we scooted over towards the back to wait 'till the show was over. Some people made room at the far end of the bar and motioned us over.

Brucie and me climbed up over the vacated stool and stood snug against the back wall, next to the framed head of an elk. I hated when animal heads were nailed on walls.

Sean plopped down on the bar stool in front of us. We tried to see what was going on, but it was hard. Besides the smoke, there were bright lights going on and off and people standing around blocking the view. Brucie's hand felt like a part of mine. "Don't let go!" I ordered as we shifted around trying hard to see what was going on.

"Look it's Father," Brucie squealed as he pointed into the crowd.

I lowered my head and looked hard towards where he was pointing. A quick chill whipped through me. It was Father all right. Dancing. By himself. In a kilt. He leapt from side to side. One hand on his hip and the other high up in the air. The silver pin on the front of his tam sparkled when the overhead lights hit it.

This morning I had snuck into his briefcase and put a note in the center of his tam. *Fiona's birthday*, it said. *Don't forget she wants a bicycle.* I didn't know he was going to put his tam on ... and dance. I thought he just carried it around in his briefcase in case it got cold. I had no idea where the kilt came from ... *that* wasn't in his briefcase.

I strained to catch glimpses of him as he moved around the floor. Sometimes I could see all of him, other times just pieces. "Wow! He's really good," I said.

"Yeh! He's good all right. I've only seen him dance like this a few times."

"Why didn't you tell us?" I snipped.

"Why? You'd just be mad because Momma wouldn't let you come to the bar," Sean turned to look up at me. "It's not a place for girls."

I rolled my eyes and let out a deep sigh. "Girls are no different than boys," I huffed. But, Sean was right. Momma only let me come this time because it was my birthday.

People started to clap and stomp, hoot and holler. The fiddling got faster as Father twisted and jumped, kicked and turned. His head bobbed up and down above the shoulders of the onlookers over and over again. Sweat beads gathered across his forehead and streamed over his high cheek bones. His face and hair became a blur of red tones. I tugged on Brucie's' hand and shot him a big grin. He beamed back at me. We must've looked like a couple of flashlights in the back of the room.

I looked around at all the grown-ups! They were smiling. Everybody loved Father, just like Sean, Brucie, Momma, and me. I swallowed hard. A part of me wanted Father to come home, but another part didn't want the show to end. I let go of Brucie's hand so we could start clapping and stomping along with everybody else.

"Heads up," some men over to the right of us yelled as they passed someone along through the crowd. "Here'e comes." The pants going through the air seemed familiar.

I looked down at Sean's bar stool. "Jeez," I stopped clapping and stomping and reached out again for Brucie's hand. Everybody else stopped too as they moved back to clear the way for...Sean. Hand after hand passed him forward like a surprise bundle.

Father stopped dancing and waved his arms. The fiddling music screeched to a halt.

"Well, what have we here then?" Father chided in his Scottish brogue, that quirkish accent he used sometimes. Dancing had shortened his breath making his words all crash together. His hair and cheeks had become a blend of red and pink.

My stomach tightened. *Was he going to be angry?* I wondered. *Were we all gonna get a strapping?* I watched closely trying to read his mind.

"Is it the little folk from the forest?" Father's words sounded playful, but that didn't mean anything.

"Father, you know it's me," Sean, boomed back with a slight crackle in his voice." *Was Sean scared*? I wondered.

"Now, is that a fact, then?" Father tousled Sean's dark hair with his big hand.

Brucie and me waited, trying not to make too much noise breathing while we stayed on top of the bar. My legs were kind of tired, but I didn't dare move.

Father looked at Sean, laughed and shouted, "Come dance with yer old Fa'er then. Show 'em how we kin do it together." Bubbles of joy exploded inside of me. He didn't see us, he wasn't mad and now we were going to see more of his dancing.

The fiddling music started again and quick as a wink Sean was standing next to Father, chin held high, one arm raised over his head and the other at his waist.

*"Bas no beatha*, life or death," Father cried. "Follow me."

The bar we were standing on began to shake. The elk head, on the wall next to us, trembled as if she were coming back to life. Oh! how I wish she could.

Sounds of clapping and stomping roared through the room. Our hands and feet moved right along with everybody else's as we watched Father dance, this time with Sean. "One day that's gonna be me," I whispered to Brucie. "I can feel it in my bones."

"Drinks all around...on me," someone yelled. The bartender started throwing beer bottles out like they were juggling balls. We'd been to the circus downtown Detroit once and sat up high in the bleachers, but this was like being *in* the circus.

After a while the music stopped. The clapping and stomping faded away. Father's chest heaved in and out. He stumbled forward. I stiffened against the wall. Was Father going to fall? Sean reached out to steady him. Once secure on Sean's arm, Father laughed, raised his head and turned to the crowd. "What da ya think?"

My tension eased. Everything was okay.

"Good for you kid." "Great *ceilidh.*" "Way to go Sean." "Just a chip off the old block." Happy words sailed through the air from every direction.

Father and Sean laughed as Sean led the way to the back of the room towards Brucie and me. I reached out for Brucie's hand again, this time ready to leave.

"Don't forget the sawbuck you owe me," a heavy man, sitting next to us said.

"Yeah! I'll cover it next week." Father's breath came out hard, like a horse on the way back to the stables. "I shoulda called you on your cards, but your sour puss is too good a disguise for me. I'm gonna work harder on my poker face so ole Lady Luck'll be in my corner next time." Father laughed so hard his belly shook. I liked it when he did that.

"A sawbuck's a funny way to say ten dollars," I whispered to Brucie. "Father likes to gamble. Sometimes he wins, sometimes he doesn't. I guess with this guy, he didn't." I slipped down onto the stool, then stood up and waited while Brucie did the same. We both stood real still.

Father wobbled toward us. He dabbed his sweaty face with a cloth. We stood real still. "Looks like I've got me whole clan here." Father looked at Brucie then me. The sweet-sour scent of beer came out with his words. The back of his white shirt was wet through. I squeezed Brucie's hand. "He's not mad that we're here," I said softly.

Brucie grinned then looked up at Father. "You are TRIFFIC," he blurted out.

"TRIFFIC, am I, Laddie? Now that's a new word for ya." Brucie blushed. He hated being teased.

"Will you teach me to dance like that, Father?" I crossed my fingers behind my back hoping against hope that he'd say yes.

Dad raised one eyebrow and peered at me through the sides of his dark eyes. "You want to dance like your old man?" I could feel my cheeks flush red as I waited for his answer. Father smacked his lips and made a sipping sound like he did when he was thinking. "Sure Lassie. I'll teach you one day."

My eyes glued onto his face as I struggled with the jangles of my inner fears. *Did he really say yes, or did I make that up? Would he remember tomorrow what he said today?* I crossed my fingers, took a deep breath and smiled.

As we started winding our way to the door people called out as we passed: "good-bye, fair-thee-well, cheerio," and "see ya next week." I wasn't sure where Father's blue suit was. That's what he wore when he went to work this morning. I didn't know where his brown leather brief case was either. That's where I put my note to remind him about my birthday, inside his tam, in his brief case. "Where's your ..." I tried to ask. But, the noise of people talking was too loud. He didn't hear me.

Sean started doing some dancing steps as we followed Father down Jackson street. Brucie and me copied him. Sean was pretty good. Maybe he had practiced with Father when I didn't know about it. All he'd done at Morrie's was mimic Father's steps, but now he was leaping from side to side like a grasshopper.

*Gin a body meet a body comin' thro' the rye*, Father bellowed as we passed Ann Marie's house. He was having such a good time that it was hard not to sing out with him, but I knew better. I didn't want Momma to be mad at me. She would have a tizzy fit if Ann Marie or any of the neighbors saw the MacLean Clan acting up.

Poor Momma, I thought. She made such a wonderful dinner that nobody got to eat. She even baked a special strawberry cake just for me. Now it was too late for dinner. Most of it was probably burned or dried up.

*Gin a body meet a body comin' thro' the rye, gin a body kiss a body need a body cry?* Sean's voice rang out right along with Father's. I shot an arrow stare in his direction, but he didn't pay any mind. He and Father just kept bellowing like wild cats right up and into our house. Momma was not going to like their shenanigans one bit.

Brucie ran ahead of me to catch up with Sean and Father. I stopped on the sidewalk out front, turned and looked into the sky, searching for the North Star in the Little Dipper.

"There you are," I said softly once I found it. No matter how many times we moved, knowing some things stayed the same made me feel good. I pointed my finger up high and drew the design in the air. A rectangle with the North Star in its crooked tail.

My foot stepped on something soft as I started to take a shortcut across the lawn. I couldn't see what it was in the dark, so I reached down and picked it up. It was Father's brown wool sweater. I shook it out and slung it over my shoulder. God, I hoped Momma wasn't throwing all of Father's clothes out like she does when she gets really angry. A few steps further my feet tangled on my birthday streamers. Then I walked over a shirt. Trousers. Shoes. And a pair of shorts. My stomach twisted into knots. She was angry all right. There must've been more stuff on the lawn than in his closet.

I started to walk up the front stairs when I heard Momma scream so loudly that her slurred words sailed right out of the house and filled the air all around me, "you're druunnk, Frank. You smell like beeeer ... and ... cheap per ... fume. I've had it with you."

I swallowed hard. The slur in Momma's voice pounded in my ears. She must've kept right on drinking after we left to fetch Father.

"Yer jis jealous a've friends'n you don't," Father yelled back.

"Gamblers, 'n drinkers 'n playboys aren't friends," Momma screamed back.

My breath caught in my chest. The sound of my heart beat wildly in my ears. God, I hoped my brothers weren't in the living room. I hoped they were in bed or hiding in the closet. Being around our parents when they were fighting was dangerous. Once Momma was so angry she hurled a frying pan across the room towards Father. It missed him and hit me. My eyes turned black and my head ached like crazy for over a week. Another time Brucie stepped on a broken dish. A sliver of glass lodged in the heel of his foot – blood gushed out like a broken faucet.

I stepped around the porch, leaned up against the house and dropped the clothes I'd been carrying. I couldn't go in.

The front door opened. The porch light went on. Momma pushed Father out the door. He stumbled onto the porch, then down the stairs. I hid in the shadows.

"It's yerr kid's birrr-thday and you didn't even re-mem-ber her bi-cycle." Momma hollered from the open front door. A suitcase flew through the air.

"I can-na help if I...forgot. It's yer fault Merle MacLean. Yer the one who makes birthdays so cock-a-mamie im-por-tant." Father shouted as he climbed up the stairs hanging onto the railing for balance. Momma beat her fists against his chest, but he grabbed her hands, pushed her into the living room and slammed the door.

Tears welled up in my eyes. I brushed them away with the back of my hand. Noises and grunts exploded from unknown places deep inside of me. I hated their fights...the hitting...yelling...breaking stuff. I hated it even more when the fight was about me.

Slowly, chest heaving, stomach aching, I forced myself to move backwards toward the street, careful not to drag any of Father's clothes along with me, clothes still hiding in the dark clumps of grass. Once off the lawn I started to run as if I was in a race that nobody could see. I passed the Jackson Street Creek where we caught spiders, tadpoles and frogs...past my best friend Donna's house...crossed over Ecorse Highway...and into the forest...the shortest way to Grandma's house.

"God...Great Spirit...keep Brucie and Sean safe," I mumbled as I ran. "And make all this fighting go away."

## Chapter Three

## RUNNING TO GRANDMA'S

Lungs aching. Head pounding. Legs burning. Stomach growling. I ran on towards Grandma's. The more I ran, the more I hurt, but the hurt was good. It was better to hurt on the outside than the inside.

"You forgot Fiona's Birthday," Momma yelled at Father. "You forgot her bicycle." I was sure he'd remember my birthday this time. Didn't he see the note I put in his tam? Maybe the note fell out before he put his tam and kilts on for the *ceilidh* at Morrie's Bar.

I was tired of the fights, tired of being forgotten. I was never going back.

A train whistled in the distance. The tracks ran through the middle of the forest, just past our club house, half way to Grandma's. I'd been there zillions of times. Just not in the dark.

Suddenly, something yanked me to a halt. A sticky bush grabbed onto the bottom of my dress. "Stop hanging onto me!" I pulled my dress away from its sharp thorns and stumbled backwards into the weeds.

"Where's that Great Spirit Grandma talks about?" I screamed. "Or the God the preacher says looks over us? Or Jesus. Or *Kokumthena*." Momma baked a strawberry cake, made Scotch pie with barley and peas and we were all gonna be together, one big happy family. But we weren't and we aren't.

Brucie and Sean were probably hiding in the closet and Mother and Father were breaking everything they could get their hands on. "Oh God, I hope nobody's hurt," I mumbled.

I pulled myself up, wiped my hands on my dress and moved forward, walking fast not running. After a while I started to hum-sing, like Momma did. It made me feel like I wasn't alone. *Eagles have wings...hum...they know how to fly, up to the trees and high up in the sky.*

My eyes got used to the dark so I could see outlines of things, but not the things themselves. The trees and bushes grew into monsters. A hand came up from the ground and tried to grab me. "Eagles have wings...they..." A purple eyed witch with glary eyes tried to snatch me by the neck. A jagged toothed vampire tried to suck all the blood out of my body.

"Everybody get away from me." I yelled, turning in all directions. I reached down, ran my fingers through the dirt, and found a big stick. I held it tight ready to swing. Then, eyes straight ahead, jaws clamped tight, I moved ahead again, in and around bushes and trees. Nothing was going to stop me from finding my way to Grandma's, nothing.

*Eagles have wings...hum...they know how to fly, up to the trees and high up in the sky.* I sang loud and strong trying to block out Momma's screams, Father's forgetting my birthday, worries about my brothers and every other cockamamie worry stabbing me in the gut.

Somehow I reached our clubhouse. I knew I should keep on going but my legs felt like jelly and my feet throbbed all the way to the tips of my toes. I put my stick down close by so I could find it again, sat down on our swing and pushed off.

Then I heard it. My name. Somebody called my name, "Fiona Lonestar MacLean". I slipped off the swing and grabbed my stick. The voice was deep and low. I held tight to my stick and waited.

"Ba, ba boom, ba, ba boom," my heart thumped. Could Momma and Father be searching for me? I wondered. Sean could lead them to the clubhouse with his eyes shut. Of course Father wouldn't call me Lonestar, he'd just say Fiona, but maybe Momma spoke up for me and said he should call out my full name. Maybe he was sorry he forgot my birthday.

I waited. My heartbeat got softer. Crickets chirped. A bird cooed. The wind rustled the leaves in the trees. No one came. "Imagination." That's what Momma says I've got too much of. I figured nobody was gonna come and get me; nobody even noticed I was gone. Still hanging tight to my stick, I headed for the railroad tracks, angry at myself for hearing things.

I edged along the steel rails as far as I could, then made a big jump into the meadow. The grass was soft and damp. The coolness felt good against my legs.

"I'm more than halfway there Grandma," I yelled. My words flew past the moon.

Something screamed in the dark. It, for sure, wasn't Grandma or somebody calling my name. It was a wild thing. I wanted to run, but couldn't. Tingles ran up and down my back like fingers tickling me from the inside out. But, nothing was funny.

I tried to hum-sing again, but what came out was just a stupid squeaky noise.

"S-C-R-E-E-C-H," that something screamed again. My head rattled like a tin bucket with a rock in it. When I ran away I didn't think about stuff going wrong. "Grandma, I wish you were here," I managed to mumble.

The screeching stopped. My knees jiggled. I stumbled forward careful not to fall into any holes or run into any bushes or trees. Danger circled around me. I could feel death's heavy breath on my back. It made the hairs on my neck stand up straight.

I'd never thought about dying before. Brucie and me put two spiders in a clay box and buried them in the sand at the Jackson Street Creek. When we went back to dig them out and opened the box, there wasn't anything left but legs. We felt real bad.

Grandma says, *nothing dies, it just changes form.* But, I don't want to change form.

"SCREECH," went that something again.

This time, I took a deep breath. Turned around. Looked into the shadows. And yelled, "HAYA!" Wings of blackness fanned my face with puffs of air, then disappeared. It was an owl.

I unscrunched my shoulders. Still looking up, I turned in a circle. Everything around me looked real big. I was so worried I forgot to look where I was going.

*Did I turn wrong at the clubhouse? Or was it just around the meadow after the railroad tracks?* Questions rolled through my head. I dropped my stick and sat down in the damp grass. Mosquitoes buzzed around my face, arms and legs. I swatted them away, but it didn't help. They nibbled on me like I was their dinner.

"HELP!" I screamed as loud as I could. "Somebody help. God. Jesus. *Kokumthena*. Great Spirit. This is me, Fiona Lonestar MacLean. Please send someone to find me. I'm real lost somewhere out here in the forest. I'm scared and tired and I want ... my Grandma." My chest heaved in and out.

I sat real still. The inside of my head sounded like the thumping of Momma's broken down old washing machine as I waited for my prayer to be answered.

After a few minutes I heard something far away. A different noise. Different than the branches blowing in the wind or night birds like that owl. I couldn't tell exactly what it was, but it sounded like someone yelling back at somebody, maybe at me.

"Yo...hel...lo," it echoed muffled like. Then it got a closer. And louder. Crashing sounds, like someone, or something, moving fast through the forest, started to fill the spaces in between the "yo...hel...lo's."

I squinted my eyes and searched through the dark. Grandma said that sometimes when you can't see with your eyes you can see with the inside of your mind. I tried to do that, but nothing came in except the gray and pink from inside my eyelids.

The sounds got louder. I didn't know whether to hide behind a tree, lay low on the ground, or get up and stand tall. The more I thought about what to do, the more tired I got. I finally stood up, dug my feet into the ground...threw my shoulders back...held up my stick...and tried to look big and tall.

"A'ho. Hakiiilhamo?" A shadowy figure headed towards me.

I swallowed hard...tried to say something ... but couldn't. I searched my head to see if I could figure out what the words meant. They sounded like some foreign language. Even though it was warm outside, I started shaking all over. My fist was clenched so tightly around my stick that I couldn't feel my fingers.

"Hello. Are you okay?" The voice said as the shadow moved to a few feet in front of me. "Someone yelled for help a while ago...so...I came running to see...if I could help."

This time, I knew what he was saying. He didn't sound dangerous, but Sean says *sometimes people sound real nice and rob you behind your back.*

"Are you out here all by yourself?" His breath came hard and heavy.

I'd called out for help, but now that someone was here I didn't know what to do. Thoughts raced through my head. *Was he going to hurt me? Did he want to steal something? How can you tell if someone's dangerous?*

I didn't have any money on me. There wasn't anything he could take away so I had to take the chance that he wanted to help while at the same time get ready to run like the wind.

"Who are y-you?" I mumbled. My eyes burned hot from trying to see in the dark while the rest of me continued to shake.

"My name's Johnny. Johnny Whitefeather," he said slowly. I peered up at him. After all the scary things I'd gone through it was hard to focus, but he looked kind of familiar.

"I live in a house just on the edge of this here forest," he went on in a kind of flat speaking way. "I was going home when I heard someone calling out for help, so I ran as fast as I could to try to find out who it was and what was wrong." A white feather dangled over his shoulder hooked to a piece of his hair.

"Johnny?" I swallowed hard as his honey colored face came into focus. He was Grandma's friend. The one she's known since she was a kid. Father doesn't like him, so we don't see him very often. My lip started to tremble. "It's me Lonestar." Tears raced down my cheeks. "I was going to see my Grandma and...I got...lost."

"Lonestar!" Johnny bent down and put his hands on my shoulders. "You...shouldn't be out here all by yourself. What...?" He stopped mid-sentence, nodded, shook his head, then asked, "isn't today your birthday?"

"Uh, huh," I nodded my head. He handed me a big hanky so I could wipe my face, then stood up. The hanky felt soft in my hands. I blotted my eyes first, then my cheeks. "Thanks," I said handing it back.

Johnny Whitefeather gave it a quick flip with his wrist then pressed it into the front pocket of his jeans. "We'll find your Grandmother together," Johnny said as he reached out for my hand.

I took a deep breath and put my hand in his. It felt warm and safe.

"I got lost when I was twelve years old," Johnny said as he led me forward through the darkness of the forest. "It was scary."

"Yeah! That's for sure." It felt good that someone as big as him was scared once too.

"My older brother took me hunting for berries in the forest near our house. I picked and ate 'till my skin turned blue." Johnny laughed.

His deep sounds flew into the sky like a flock of happy ducks. I laughed with him. My shakes lessened. Going in and out of trees felt safer now that I wasn't alone.

"Then it was dark. I couldn't find my brother. In my picking and eating, I'd forgotten where I was. Nothing looked familiar. I yelled his name and searched through the brush, but he wasn't there. He must've figured I started on home ahead of him."

I wondered if Sean and Brucie wondered where I was. Since we all slept in the same room they for sure would know I wasn't in bed. And, if they were in the closet, they'd know I wasn't underneath the shoes. I swallowed hard and took a deep breath. Whatever they're wondering, I hoped they were okay and not in any kind of trouble. I swallowed hard and looked up at Johnny, "What happened?" I asked.

Johnny laughed again. "I found me an old tree with a big hole in the bottom and crawled inside. Wolves howled in the distance. Owls hooted. Big things moved all around me. I wasn't sure what was real and what wasn't, but I pretty much figured that by morning I'd be somebody's dinner."

"Scary stuff." My head was still a bit dizzy from the scary things I'd run into. Going to Grandma's at night wasn't anything like I thought it would be.

"Yup. It's scary out in the dark all alone." Johnny squeezed my hand and stopped. He moved his head one way then the other as if he was listening for something. After a while we moved forward again.

"What happened? Did your brother come back...or your mom or dad?"

"Nope. No one came."

"Oh!"

"While I waited in that tree trunk making up stories about how I'd die I remembered something my father told me." Johnny let out a deep sigh and smacked his lips together. "My father said before you die you must write your own words and sing your own song. This will aid you in finding your way to the ancestral resting place."

"I've never thought about writing my own song before. All the ones I know I learned from someone else. Did you do what your father said?" I asked as we walked along.

"Nope. But thinking about it kept me from worrying about being lost." Johnny laughed his deep laugh again. "Now, when I think I have just the right song, it changes."

He didn't hurry me at all, instead of making me keep up with him, he was careful to take small steps and move at my slower pace. Even at that, after a while, my feet started to drag. It must have been way past eleven. I didn't want Mr.

Whitefeather to think I was a cry baby and get angry at me so I made myself keep going.

"When I was a kid my father used to play a game he called 'Horse.'" Johnny said. "Care to try it?"

Funny how he understood what I wanted when I didn't even ask. It must have taken a whole split second for me to throw my stick away and say, "yes". Johnny leaned forward and lifted me onto his back.

*Row-row-row your boat, gently down the stream, merrily, merrily, merrily, merrily, life is but a dream,* Johnny Whitefeather sang. I joined in after the first chorus. We played with the words as we moved along. Sometimes he'd sing first, then I'd take a turn. It was so fun it took my mind away from my parent's fighting.

We came out of the forest and stepped onto the edge of a gravel road sounding like songbirds. Johnny didn't seem to care if anyone heard or saw us. A few porch lights as well as street lights glittered in the dark.

"If you look to the right you'll see my house," Johnny said. "It's the one with all the lights on inside. When I heard your calls, I just took off."

"I'm glad you did," I sighed. "I thought I was a goner."

Johnny laughed. "A goner huh?"

Johnny let go of my legs. I slid down from his back and landed on my feet. They felt less wobbly after being able to rest for a while.

"And, guess what's just ahead?" Johnny said.

I looked up the road, a little woozy from everything that had gone on. A soft light shimmered along the top of the small shiny stones like tiny moon kisses. My eyes landed on a familiar porch, dimly lit, but one I knew well. "Grandma's!" I cried reaching up to hold onto my heart as it started to make that loud skipping noise it sometimes did. All the tiredness I'd felt before seemed to fall away like bark peeling off a tree.

I ran the next half block, Johnny close behind, then stopped in front of Grandma's house and looked through one of the front windows. Candles flickered across her living room wall casting shadows that looked like eagles in flight.

I hurried forward, stepped onto the porch, put my right hand on the door ringer and pushed hard.

Feet shuffled across the floor. The door opened a tiny crack...then swung wide open. *"Ahaw!* (hello) What's this?" Grandma said in that soft sweet voice of hers. She stood wide eyed, her hands clasped around the front of her robe. A narrow gray braid fell over one shoulder and stopped at her waist like a long rope – ready to pull me up – out of the darkness and into the light.

"I love you Grandma. I love you so much and I'm so glad I didn't die in the forest. Momma and Father had a big fight and we...didn't get to celebrate my birthday." I pushed my face against her warm body. My nostrils breathed in her smell. My mouth tasted the cotton in her robe. I was safe. I'd made it, and I was never going home.

Out of the corner of my eye I saw Johnny give Grandma a quick nod before he turned to leave. "My, my, my," she clucked, as she moved me into the kitchen. "Looks like the mosquitoes sure had a feast on you."

It felt so good to be with Grandma that whatever pain was there before, vanished.

When she was done cleaning me up and healing my bites with herbs, we made a bed for me on the sofa. Even though it was warm, she covered me with the quilt she made out of square patches from old family clothes. "Lives from the past are always part of our present," Grandma said. "Old clothes are one of the ways to carry family spirits forward and remind us that they live in our veins and in our hearts."

As I closed my eyes I wondered who all of those spirits of the past were and if I was ever going to meet them face to face.

*Life is a circle. A circle never ends. It reaches up to heaven, then down to Earth again,* Grandma sang as she sat in the big flowered chair across from me. The candle on the table next to Grandma flickered over my eyelids. The sweet smell of herbs filled my chest. I was safe. God, Great Spirit, let everyone at home be safe too, I prayed.

## Chapter Four

# GRANDMA'S BIRTHDAY PRESENT

"Time to wake up, little one," a voice echoed. "I want us to share the sunrise."

"The ... sunrise?" I opened my eyes and looked into the candle lit room. "Grandma?"

She gave me a big hug. "The Sun will be rising in another hour. Didja forget you ran all the way to my house last night?"

Grandma smelled like lavender. Her hair was freshly braided and twisted into a neat bun on top of her head. The olive color of her skin looked darker in the flickering shadows the candles made. A bright yellow apron, full of pockets, covered the front of her dress.

"I guess I did. In my dream, I was flying way up in the sky." I rested my head on her shoulder and relaxed into her strong arms.

"Where were you flying to?" Grandma stroked my hair. I loved when she petted me like I did our dog Goldy.

"I...don't know." I hadn't thought about that. "It seemed like I lost something. Or maybe I was just trying to find my way back...to you." I shivered as a train whistled on the track in the forest. It reminded me of Momma's screams.

"*E'ne*, yes, you've found your way to me all right," Grandma shook her head back and forth as the train got fainter. "I hate to think what could've happened to you if my friend Johnny Whitefeather hadn't heard you screaming for help."

"I'm sorry Grandma. I was...just...real mad. I wanted everyone to be happy...and to have a birthday party and...then...everything went *kerflooey*."

32

*"Kerflooey?* Hmmm. It sure did." Grandma spoke out of one side of her mouth while she held tobacco against the inside of her cheek with her tongue. "Well, we'll give your folks time to make up and get up, then we'll give'em a call from your Aunt Dawn's. She's the closest one I know with a telephone." Grandma patted my arm then stood up. "And if you can get your airplane motor runnin' again, we're gonna celebrate your birthday *now.*"

Grandma spread her arms like the wings of a plane and flew into the kitchen. I followed close behind making little engine sputters by blowing air out of my closed lips.

I dipped my hands into the bowl of warm water Grandma set out for me and washed my face. Then, I brushed my teeth with one of Grandma's extra brushes at the sink and slipped into my dress. Grandma must've washed it when I was asleep. It was clean.

"How are we gonna celebrate, Grandma?" I sat down on the red plastic chair at the wooden table and looked out the kitchen window. It was still dark. A tiny sliver of moon peeked out beyond Grandma's potato plant vines in the window sill.

"I have a birthday surprise lined up for you." Grandma twittered like a happy Robin.

"But, Grandma, yesterday was my birthday, not today."

"Today's close enough, Lonestar." Grandma clapped her hands like a little kid. "The week before and the week after your birthday are all mighty powerful times. Today is part of the week after." Grandma took a brush out of one of her apron pockets and ran it through my hair.

The strokes seemed to go through my whole body they felt so good. "What do you mean?"

"The days around your birthday are kind of a marker. A time to stop and think about how you came to be and who you are." Grandma put the brush down and led me out the back door.

"Where are we going?" I could hardly wait to see what was going to happen.

"To the far end of my garden," Grandma said. She tilted her head and gave me one of her sideways glances. "To the

Sacred Stone Circle to pray and to watch the sunrise." Grandma grinned, her words came out slow and deep.

My stomach clenched. That was Grandma's special place. The Sacred Stone Circle was something she kept for very special people at very special times.

Sean, Brucie'n me had seen it at the edge of the back fence. But we'd never gone inside. Fifty rocks, about the size of Momma's dinner plates made up the main circle. Smaller ones, the size of saucers formed a cross in the center.

The stars twinkled brightly as we made our way along the dark path. They looked like they were gathering for a party of their own and heading towards the moon. The crickets sang. Their night song exploded all around us with a pulsing rhythm, "caree-caree". There must've been millions of them, but somehow they all sang the same tune at the same time.

Grandma squeezed my hand, then let it go. I looked up. We were there. Happiness pushed so hard against the inside of me that I thought I might crack like an eggshell. Grandma wove her flashlight in and out of the circle of rocks. Her yard abuts a cornfield. Sometimes raccoons, mice, possums and other small animals hide among the rocks. We waited, watched and listened. Something moved. My breath quickened. Everything got very still, then a jack rabbit, the size of a small cat scurried out of the rocks and headed for the cornfield.

Grandma laughed. "Good sign," Grandma said. "The Shawnee call the rabbit a *trickster*." Grandma pointed the flashlight into the brush. Flashes of fur leaped away.

"Trickster?" That was a strange thing to call a rabbit.

"Rabbits come out of nowhere and disappear like magic. If you watch them, they zigzag in and out, around and about. You see their furry bodies, then you don't." Grandma chuckled. "When you see a rabbit for real, or in a dream she's calling on you to reverse your thinking."

"You mean the rabbit would want me to see that Father didn't forget my birthday?"

Grandma nodded. Her gray head moved up and down against the dark sky. "Or maybe rabbit would want you to see

34

that your father forgetting your birthday had nothing to do with you. It had to do with him.  Maybe he has other things in his life he wants to forget."

"What would he want to forget, Grandma?" I hated secrets.

"Everyone has to speak for themselves, Lonestar.  I can't say his words." Grandma set the flashlight down pointing towards the center of the circle.  Light streamed along the Earth and bumped up against the stones.  Shadows spun out and around the circle like gray spider webs.

Grandma took my hand. "Our Indian ancestors created special places to connect to the Great Spirit, the wisdom of the universe that runs through all things. This is my special place."

"But, I'm not a full blooded Indian Grandma, and neither are you."

"No, you're not and I'm not, but that doesn't prevent us from connecting to the part that is.  I'm part Shawnee, part Scots, part Irish, and part mystery.   I respect the rituals and ceremonies of all religions when they're used in a positive light – as I hope you will one day."

"I will Grandma.  I promise." I knew what Grandma believed was always good.

Grandma smiled, took my hand, led me to the center of the circle, then let go.  She reached into one of her pockets, brought out a metal tin, opened it and took out a pinch of Kin.ni.kin.nick mixed with other special things she always gathered in the forest. I watched as she rolled it between her fingers, held it up to the sky, then dropped it on the ground. The pungent smell danced around our heads like an invisible veil.

"Grandfather Sky, I call on you to hear my special prayer." Grandma reached for my hand and brought our arms up to the sky. "Guide and protect Lonestar as she walks her life path," she called out. "Be with her in the darkness that we all must learn to endure.  Lead her to the light, that her life may be filled with the knowledge that cannot be found in books."

A tiny breeze blew a kiss across my face.  No one prayed as powerfully as Grandma.   Hers was a knowledge and wisdom not found in books. Grandma wanted that wisdom for me; I knew I'd try to find it.

Grandma brought our arms down towards the ground. "Grandmother Earth," she cried out, "hear my prayer. Be with Lonestar as she learns to grow straight and tall with strong roots that reach deep into your rich soil."

With the sound of Grandma's words I could feel my feet being drawn firmly down into the Earth. A rich musty smell circled around my whole body.

"Lend her your strength that she might rise above life's difficulties, strong and keen like the Golden Eagle, and learn to see the gifts in those challenges. Ho." Grandma lowered our arms, took a deep breath and nodded her head while still looking up.

My heart swelled up so big that I thought I might burst with joy.

I watched the sky 'till black turned into...deep blue, then lavender, orange, pink ... and finally a softer blue. Little puffs of air burst out of me like messengers of joy. I'd watched the sunrise before, but this time, standing next to Grandma was way different.

"All these wonderful colors of the sunrise," Grandma said, "are *in* you, and one day you'll be able to *see* 'em." Grandma's dark eyes flashed with a light of their own. "Gifts of all kinds will visit you, Lonestar — messages, visions, a knowingness. When they come — be grateful. The more you acknowledge this wisdom, the stronger it becomes." Grandma took another pinch of *Kin.ni.kin.nick* from the tin and dropped it to the Earth. *"I gwi yen,"* (I am grateful). She closed the tin, put it away and led us out of the circle.

"So many gifts, Grandma," I said. "How will I know when messages, visions and a knowingness come?"

Grandma laughed. "You'll know," she said. "It's different than thinking about things, or figuring out how to deal with a problem. It's something you hear from deep inside your heart, an image you see that others don't, or a strong knowing that rises from your solar plexus."

"Like you have about things?"

"Yep, and others." Grandma took a deep breath.

"Momma said she found a bird in the pantry a day before Grampa died, and ever since then, when there's a bird in some weird place, she thinks it's there to warn her she's going to lose someone she loves."

"The knowing comes to different people in different ways." Grandma pursed her lips together and nodded. "I remember how upset she was when she found that bird. My husband, your Grandpa, died when she was just starting high school."

"Well, I hope I understand when the knowing comes to me." I playfully kicked the dirt just outside the Sacred Circle with the toe of my shoe.

Grandma smiled. "You will. I promise." She scanned the stones in the circle as if she was searching for something. The morning light made some of them sparkle as if they held hidden treasures.

Grandma reached down and picked up one of the smaller stones and cupped it in her hands. She blew air on one side, turned it over, then blew on the other side. "This is for you, Lonestar. A keepsake from the Sacred Circle." Grandma pressed the small gray speckled stone in my hand. It was about the size of my thumb.

The stone felt cool. I rubbed my hands together to warm it up. "Thank you. You're the best Grandma in the whole world." I tucked the stone into my dress pocket and wrapped my arms around her waist.

Grandma laughed. "I'm the only Grandma you have. At least on Earth."

I stretched my arms out to my sides like an eagle and zigzagged my way up the path. Grandma spread her arms out and flew right behind me. We raced up the back steps like we were taking off into the sky.

Once inside Grandma bent over the kitchen chair to catch her breath. "Not as young as I was once," she said.

"Me neither," I kidded.

"Funny girl." Grandma put her hands on her hips and bent way back to stretch.

Chapter Five

## AUNT DAWN'S GIFT

After breakfast Grandma opened her eyes real big as she looked up at the clock on the wall. We sat opposite each other at her small kitchen table. Empty dishes of what had been filled with pancakes covered with syrup lay in front of us. "Goodness gracious is it eight a.m. already?" Grandma asked in disbelief.

I turned around and looked at the clock. It was one of those questions that wasn't a question, like Momma asks sometimes, but I answered anyway. "Yep! Eight."

"We'd better wash up real quick and make that phone call at Aunt Dawn's. Your folks'll want to know where you are." Grandma picked up our plates, dropped them into a bowl of soapy water, then walked back to the table with a wet cloth in her hand. "After the ruckus you all went through last night they're probably sleepin' 'till at least 10:00, but when they wake up they'll be worried. They're gonna want to know where you are." Grandma wiped down the table.

I looked up at Grandma, I wasn't so sure my folks would want to know where I was, or even care. They never seemed to worry when my brother's and I disappeared into the forest for a whole day. I wanted Grandma to let me live with her. I wouldn't take up much room.

The path to Aunt Dawn's ran through an open field behind a poultry farm. As we rounded the final turn, Grandma found a turkey feather and stuck it in my hair. We ended up doing The Turkey Trot on up to Aunt Dawn's front gate.

The entrance to Aunt Dawn's house has three signs that form an arch over the gate. The one in the middle reads LITTLE AXE. That's her last name. The one on the right reads PRAYER FEATHERS. People come to buy the feathers for the cemetery nearby. It's a way for them to bury a prayer with their loved ones. Aunt Dawn gathers the feathers from the fields next to the poultry farm that Grandma and I just walked through. She dyes some of them different colors: red, blue, yellow, green, purple. Others she leaves natural.

The sign on the left reads TALISMAN STONE READINGS. Aunt Dawn's readings tell people their future. The talisman's are small stones in different colors and animal shapes like cats, fish, turtles, birds. Aunt Dawn collects them on her walks.

Reading stones is big business and Aunt Dawn's a whiz at it. When she was born, there was a thin veil of skin covering her face, that's what gave her better powers than most. Before I was born, Aunt Dawn told Momma, "A blue eyed, blonde haired girl is waiting at the gate of the Milky Way to come through you." Nine months later, I arrived, just like she said. They were kind of surprised because most of my cousins have dark hair and cream colored skin. Father says I take after the Scots part of him (even though I don't have his red hair), but Mom has some lighter mixture in her ancestors as well.

Grandma opened the gate and waited for me to come through. My legs wobbled a bit. I stopped, took a deep breath and tried again. A giant hand pushed down on the top of my head. It made me dizzy. Grandma, the gate, Aunt Dawn's house, the signs, all turned into one big whirl.

When I opened my eyes I was lying flat out on the grass. I must've fainted. Grandma was running her hands over the outside of my body like she was smoothing out invisible wrinkles.

"Stay still, your Aunt Dawn and cousin Zane are coming to help us." Zane's fourteen, like Sean, and real nice. "All this running away and worrying must've been too much for you." Grandma's mouth tightened into a rosebud.

"I'm okay." I pushed on my hands to sit up. I didn't want Grandma to worry about me and I sure didn't want cousin Violet to have something to tease me about. Violet's older, but acts younger than me.

"Don't you move," Grandma warned. "You have to learn to listen when your body's talking." I put my head back down 'till Aunt Dawn and cousin Zane came to help.

"Where would you be without me?" Zane teased in that flat way of his as he helped me up. The dark green in his shirt made his hazel eyes look like they were peering out of a forest.

Dawn and Zane made me hold onto their arms while we walked up to the house.

Violet was right where I thought she'd be, sitting and sniggering on the railing of the front porch. Her dark curly hair hung in perfect ringlets around her face. Red suspenders stretched across a faded white blouse and clipped onto the waist of her flower sack skirt. She gives me the creeps. She makes everything I do wrong and always gets me in trouble. Momma says it's because her father died so she's jealous of every cousin who still has a father.

Aunt Dawn hurried to make tea after she and Zane laid me on the porch sofa.

"If you need somethin' I'll be close by." Zane picked up his bow and went down the steps. The slats in the wooden verandah creaked as Grandma made her way into the house to make that darned phone call. Violet cocked her head to the side, slid off the railing and walked over to where I was lying down. "Momma said yesterday was your birthday. Did you have a party?"

The word *party* made my head hurt. I slowly pulled myself up and leaned my back against the sofa arm. "I don't want to talk about it," I said biting down on the inside of my cheek.

"Violet, come get a cold rag for Lonestar," Aunt Dawn ordered as she pushed open the screen door with her shoulder, then swung around to set her tea-service down on the table.

"Jeez Louise, Momma, Lonestar's fine. Let'er get'er own rag," Violet moaned.

"Shush up now and run do what I asked," Aunt Dawn buzzed like an angry bee as she sat down and poured my tea. Violet dragged her feet across the floor and slunked into the house.

Once Violet was gone, I got up from the sofa, walked across the verandah and sat down at the table across from Aunt Dawn. Circular posts anchored the slats of yellowed wood that formed the lower edges of the verandah. Red squares of old linoleum nailed over bare tree branches served as an awning to protect us from the Sun.

"Good tea," I said after I took a sip. It felt soothing on my throat.

"Momma told me what happened last night Lonestar," Aunt Dawn said real worried like. "I guess it was pretty scary at your house, your folks fightin' and all." She reached into the front pocket of her faded patchwork apron. The charms on her bracelets jingled like sleigh-bells as she pulled out a small bag. The bright beads sewn on the outside of the bag made it look like pieces of the Sun breaking through the night, like the dawn Grandma and I shared.

"What's in the bag, Aunt Dawn?" I didn't want to talk about Momma and Father fighting all over again, or how we didn't get to celebrate my birthday. I didn't want to think about Brucie or Sean or anything bad. It made me feel sick to my stomach.

"That's where I keep my talismans," Aunt Dawn replied. She lifted the bag and spread a red cloth underneath. "I'm going to read them for your birthday."

"My birthday!" My heart started to thump loudly.

Aunt Dawn nodded. She took a candle out of one of the pockets in her full skirt and set it down in the center of the red cloth. "What happened last night?" she asked as she smoothed out the edges of the cloth.

I swallowed hard, I felt cornered into saying something, but I didn't want things to sound as bad as they were. "Momma made a special dinner, and...baked a cake." I ran my hands over the skirt part of my dress to smooth it out. "And...well then...Father didn't come home and well...it didn't work out like we planned." I tried to make my words come out easy, like I wasn't hiding anything. Momma wouldn't want Aunt Dawn to know about all the fighting.

Violet came out with the wet rag and handed it to me. I put it on the back of my neck. When she saw the talisman set up, her face turned beet red. She let out a painful sigh and went back into the house. My back stiffened. I felt like I was taking something away from her.

Aunt Dawn tapped her foot against the wood floor and waited for a minute. Then she turned back to me. "Of course, I didn't know I'd give you the reading today. I just knew it was something I wanted to surprise you with for your birthday." She took some matches out of her pocket and lit the candle. Then, she reached back into her pocket again, took out a tiny box, opened it, took out a pinch of *Kin.ni.kin.nick* (a mixture of bark, dried leaves and tobacco) and dropped it in the flame. The candle sputtered a bit. Puffs of smoke flew up from the fire. They smelled like damp bark that's fallen away from an evergreen tree. I liked the smell, but it made my eyes water. I squeezed them shut and pushed the heals of my hands over my eyelids .

"You never smoke sacred tobacco," Aunt Dawn said. I opened my eyes and nodded like I knew. But, I hadn't thought about it until now. "It's ceremonial," she said.

Aunt Dawn picked up her beaded bag, held it next to her heart, closed her eyes and prayed. Her words came out slow and rumbly. "Great Spirit speak to me. You who hold the answers to questions large and small. Let me see through your eyes and hear through your ears. Let my voice echo your words. Ho!"

I sat there breathless, afraid to move, wondering what would happen next.

Aunt Dawn opened her eyes and nodded. "Shake the bag and say your name seven times, Lonestar." She reached across the table and put the bag in my outstretched hands.

"Why seven, Aunt Dawn?" The bag was lighter than I thought it would be.

"Seven is a spiritual number. It has many meanings, but the one I use it for is completion. God made the world in seven days. It might not be the twenty-four-hour days we think of, but it still gives us boundaries; a beginning, middle and end."

"A beginning, middle and end?" I asked.

"Yeh! It's good to know that no matter how difficult things are, they will level off, then end."

"I hope that's true," I said. "I have some endings already in mind." Like ending all the fights at home, I thought. I shook the bag like Aunt Dawn told me to do. "Fiona Lonestar MacLean, Fiona Lonestar MacLean," I said over and over, until it added up to seven.

Aunt Dawn spilled the stones onto the red cloth. They spread out forming a kind of trail. She stared at the stones, nodded her head and mumbled as if she was talking to somebody who wasn't there, like Grandma does sometimes.

"You're gonna have quite a life," she said in that far away voice again.

I leaned forward and looked closer at the figures, curious about what she'd found. The Sun peeked through the lower branches on the trees just beyond the verandah and added a pinkish yellow color to the table.

"Says you're gonna travel...and see lots of tall buildings. You'll live near the water. 'Course in Michigan it's hard to get away from it, but this says you'll go from coast to coast."

I looked toward the front door to see if Grandma was standing near enough to hear the good news, but the doorway was empty. *She must be in the kitchen,* I thought. *That's where the cockamayme phone is.*

Aunt Dawn folded her hands together, prayer like, and let her long fingers rest on her mouth for a minute. "Says your gonna dance too. Maybe that's part of the traveling."

My heart jumped when she said that. In the darkness inside my head, I saw myself twirling across a stage. My friend Donna and I practiced dance steps on her lawn all the time and after seeing Father dance at Morrie's Bar I knew I wanted to be able to move as gracefully as he did. I looked toward the doorway again, but still no Grandma to share my good news with.

"Your Earthwalk is filled with great adventures," Aunt Dawn said.

"What's an Earthwalk?"

"Well, you see, we're reborn into human form to learn lessons. Not just the kind you have in school. Life lessons. Yours aren't too bad." She looked down at the stones again, moved her hand over the top of them and tilted her head from one side to the other. "The main thing is to understand the difference between helping and sacrifice, between doing and being."

"How will I do that?"

"The stones can't tell me that. No one knows the choices you'll make along the way."

The train whistled in the distance like it always does as it makes its way through the forest. This time it wasn't scary, it made me smile. For a second, I could see myself sitting inside as I traveled from state to state. "Thank you, Aunt Dawn," I said. But words weren't enough. Nothing I could give her seemed as large as what she'd given me.

"Thank you, Great Spirit!" Aunt Dawn faced the palms of her hands toward the sky, then brought them together in front of her chest with a loud clap. My reading was over.

I jumped up, excited to share my good news. Since Grandma hadn't been standing in the doorway I figured I'd have to go inside and find her. "Grandma," I cried as I opened the front door. "Wait 'till you hear."

"So, Lonestar, are you gonna meet a tall, handsome stranger," Violet taunted as soon as I walked in. Her dark curls bounced against her cheeks like a mattress spring.

"Where's Grandma?" I asked, crossing my arms and tightening my jaw.

"Grandma's in the kitchen," she said in that high squeaky-door voice she put on sometimes. "She called your house and your father answered and man-o-man are you in trouble."

I knew Grandma was calling my house. I knew I'd get into trouble. What I hated was the sarcastic way Violet said it all.

"Grrrrr," I lunged forward and growled. I wanted to push her over, but I didn't.

Violet ran around the living room yelling, "Lonestar choked me," at the top of her lungs. Aunt Dawn swung open the screen and stood in the doorway; Grandma hurried in from the kitchen; cousin Zane clunked up the porch steps and stood next to his mom.

"Stop that screaming, Violet, and come outside right now, you hear," Aunt Dawn ordered.

Violet slunk past us and went outside. Grandma and me followed right behind her. "Lonestar tried to kill me." Violet sobbed and sniveled. Real tears dripped down her clown face.

"What did you do, Lonestar?" Aunt Dawn wiped Violet's tears away with a hanky.

"I think I scared her, but I didn't touch her. I just growled and put my arms up like a bear." I looked down at the cracks on the wooden porch. Violet was such a good actress she could have been in the movies.

A car raced up the dirt road, honked two times, then came to a stop in front of the house. It was Father, driving his second-hand Frazer-Manhattan. A bottle of beer was tied to the front of the hood. My stomach fluttered.

I spat on my hands and brushed my hair back behind my ears. Even if Father was mad at me for running away, he'd believe me when I said I didn't choke Violet.

"What in tarnation's going on here," Father demanded rushing up the stairs — seeing how upset everybody was.

"Lonestar, tried to kill me," Violet whined.

"You mean Fiona," he snapped, sucking in all the air on the front porch. "Call her, Fiona." His green eyes, still blood shot from the night before, skidded from face to face like a cat deciding where to pounce.

"Violet, you do anything to Lonestar?" Grandma questioned.

"Nope. I was just sittin' in the living room doin' nothin'."

"Wait 'till I get you home, Lassie, you've got a lot of explaining to do." Father jerked on my arm. His heavy eyebrows squished together in a frown.

Thinking he might believe Violet without even asking me what happened made me feel like I was lost in the forest all over again.

"She didn't do it," Cousin Zane said flatly. "I was tightening my bow just outside the window. I saw it all. Lones ... , Fiona didn't choke her. She didn't even touch her."

I relaxed against Father's side, looked over at Cousin Zane and smiled. Thank God someone saw what happened. Then, I noticed Aunt Dawn's stones. They were still laid out on the table.

"Let's just go." I reached out for Father's hand and nudged him towards the stairs. He stopped near the first step. "Wha ... what's going on?" Father let go of my hand and headed towards the table.

"You've been brainwashing my daughter into believing in your hogwash." Father yanked up the red cloth and tossed it over the railing. The stones flew through the air.

My stomach twisted into a knot. Father was mad at me for doing Indian stuff again. Aunt Dawn crossed her arms over her chest. Zane shook his head. Violet's neck stiffened.

Grandma's eyes flared. "It's people, not things, that are important Frank. What are you so afraid of?"

"You teach my child nonsense and ask what I'm afraid of?" Father growled. "Old woman ... " His voice started to break. "I don't want her to have to feel the pain of being so different she doesn't fit in." His voice softened. "Or the dangers that come with it."

"I'm sorry about your mother, but you must know that ceremonies and rituals add richness to the pains of everyday life." Grandma's chest heaved in and out. She was good and mad. "You can't take away a part of Lonestar's bloodline. It's mixed and each part adds a richness to who she is. It's a part of who you are too, even though you want to forget it!"

*Father was afraid something bad would happen to me. Why? What does he want to forget? I wondered. What happened to his mom? He never talks about her ... never talks about anything in his past. It's against his stupid cockamayme rules.*

Father grabbed my arm, pulled me across the porch and down the stairs. Violet ran to the front edge of the railing and watched us leave. Her eyes glassed over. Maybe she was sorry for getting me into trouble. And, maybe she wasn't so jealous about me having a Dad anymore.

I watched Grandma and Aunt Dawn out the back window until their faces turned into specks of dust that Father's car left behind. They'd given me such great birthday presents, the Stone Circle, the Talisman Reading. Now, I bet Father was never gonna let me see them again.

"Seven," I mumbled. *There's always a beginning, middle, and end to everything,* Aunt Dawn had said. I wasn't sure what the middle was, but I was sure ready for the end to Father's fear about me learning Indian ceremonies. I reached inside my pocket and held tight to the small speckled gray stone from the Sacred Circle.

Chapter Six

## *BAS NO BEATHA*

The neighborhood baseball game came to a halt as we drove up Jackson Street and parked on the side of our house. Brucie and Sean made a beeline for the front door. Herby Romaine, our neighbor who always had a garage full of games and stuff, grabbed his bat and ball and scurried home to his grandmother's. He had everything we ever wanted, except a Mom and Dad. That's why he lives with his grandparents.

I was in big trouble. First I'd run away, then I let Grandma take me to her Sacred Stone Circle, and then I let Aunt Dawn give me a Talisman Stone reading for my birthday.

Goldy ran up to me and tried to lick my fingers to make me feel better. I pushed her away. I didn't want Father to be mad at her too.

"Just smile and zip up your lip, Lassie," Father murmured to me while waving to Dolly Duffield from the front lawn. "No need for her to know anymore than she already does about the MacLean Clan.

I turned the corners of my mouth up, but they felt rusty. *There's no way she could have missed all the commotion last night,* I thought.

Dolly Duffield was our across-the-street-neighbor. She waved back with her free hand. The other held tight to the rhinestone leash that kept her white fluffy dog, Fi-Fi, in tow.

"Top of the mornin' to you," Father called out, in his friendly way, to Harriet Helmsly next door as we made our way up the front stairs and onto our porch.

Mrs. Helmsly nodded, "thanks for fixing my washing machine, Frank. It works just like new." She beamed us a big smile then went back to watering her front lawn.

"Tis nothin' Harriet. I like figurin' out what makes things tick." Father opened the door, Goldy ran in while I dragged my feet forward. My insides felt broken — like pieces of glass.

"Sean, Brucie, clean up and come into the living room," Father ordered in that deep voice he used sometimes. The one that could bend nails.

Momma looked up from the back of the room where she stood ironing. Next to her was a basketful of crumpled clothes. Probably the ones she threw out onto the lawn last night.

I ran over and wrapped my arms around her waist. "It's dangerous running through the forest at night. What were you thinking?" She pushed me out and jerked my arms up and down. "Nothin's ever so bad that I wanna lose you." Dark patches of black and blue dotted her wrists like tattooed fingerprints. Red streaks ran through the whites of her eyes. She pulled me back into her waist and hugged me real hard. "I'll make you kids some Ovaltine later," she whispered.

"Don't coddle her, Merle," Father called out.

Momma let me go. Took a swig of beer. Then set it back down on the end of the ironing board.

Sean and Brucie ran out of the bathroom and stood at attention in front of Father.

"Fiona, get over here." Father cried as he pulled down the window shade.

I hurried over and stood between my brothers. Sean shook his head from side to side. "Stupid. I don't like it when you don't tell me when you're gonna dissapear."

"Me neither," Brucie muttered.

"Sorry, I didn't know...I just...got mad...and had to see Grandma." I swallowed hard. I didn't tell him that I wanted to move out – stay with Grandma forever.

"You know this is gonna hurt me more'n it does you?" Father's eyes skitted from face to face.

None of us said anything back. It wasn't really a question to be answered.

Father put his hands behind his back and paced back and forth in front of us. "If you were on the battlefield of Scotland, Lassie, you could've been killed, or caused one of your clansman to die because you didn't follow orders." The veins, on the side of his face above his ears, popped out. They looked like dried up rivers. Father turned his eyes on me, *"Bas no beatha*, is the battle cry of the MacLean Clan. It means life or death. Ye haf ta stick together. It's a dangerous world out there. Everything one of us does wrong all of us have to pay for."

I swallowed hard. "I know. I know." I hated when Father was mad. I hated it even more when it was my fault.

"No one is to run away, ever." Father unclenched his fists, stretched out his fingers and rubbed his hand over the stubble on his cheeks. His cuticles were stained black from all the work he did on cars. "And FI-O-NA. His red-green eyes flashed. "No Indian nonsense. Not now. Not ever. That stuff'll just get you into trouble, you hear." Father stopped. His body shook like something more inside wanted to pour out. Probably one of the things Grandma said he wanted to forget.

"She's just curious, Frank," Momma said from the back of the room. Father jerked his head up and puffed out his big chest. "Woman, you stay outa this. If it wasn't for you kowtowing to your mother, none of this woulda happened." Momma picked up one of Father's shirts from the basket, threw it on the ironing board and ran her hot iron over the collar.

My stomach tightened. "It's okay Momma," I said in a hushed tone. I didn't want Momma to get into trouble again just because of me. And I sure didn't want them fighting again.

"Fiona," Father boomed. "Your first, bend over."

I looked down at the rug and searched for a place I could crawl into. A tiny breeze blew across my cheeks. *Be with Lonestar in the darkness,* Grandma said. *Lead her to the light...that her life may be...filled with knowledge that cannot be learned in books.* I slipped my hand into my dress pocket and wrapped my fingers around the small speckled gray stone from Grandma's Sacred Circle. I needed something good to help me through the bad.

Father's belt made a dull thudding noise when it whacked across my bottom.

I clenched my teeth and fastened my eyes onto one of the roses in the carpet. *Lend her your strength that she might rise above any of life's difficulties strong and keen like the Golden Eagle,* Grandma said.

I stared at the rose and squeezed my stone as tightly as I could. *Whack.* The belt hit my bottom a second time. My fingers got numb and my eyes began to blur. *Whack.* The belt hit my bottom the third time.

Suddenly, a pulsing energy circled around my whole body. It lifted me up through the living room ceiling and high into the sky above our house.

The sweet taste of cool air drifted down my throat, into my chest and then out. My arms felt light yet strong – wing like. My whole body felt weightless, like I was being held up by some invisible force and carried by the wind.

"I'm an eagle," I whispered. I looked down through the roof and into the living room. I could see myself bending over, being smacked with a belt – but I couldn't feel it.

"Next," Father called out.

His words dragged me back through the ceiling and onto the living room floor. I landed with a thud, unclenched my teeth, straightened up, took a deep breath and looked at Father. His face was blurry. I rubbed the back of my hands over my eyes. *What was that?* I wondered. I reached back to touch my rear end. My bottom was warm, but I couldn't feel any pain. *My imagination's playing tricks on me,* I thought.

Momma let out some little choking noises, picked up yet another shirt, threw it over the ironing-board and like before – ran her hot iron over the collar.

I stumbled forward a few steps. Sean reached out for me. This time he didn't dig his elbow into my ribs. His hands held onto my arms. It felt good. After a few seconds he let go, stepped forward and bent over like a toy soldier.

Father's belt slammed against his rear. Sean's nostrils flared, but he didn't make a sound. *I wondered if he was being protected by the invisible energy too.*

"Next," Father called out.

Brucie looked over at me. The tip of his collar was totally gone, nervously chewed off. Tears rolled down his cheeks. I bit down on my lower lip. If there was any way I could help, I would. "Sorry," I whispered. He shook his head, bent down and put his hands on his knees. Father's belt made a thudding sound, but not as loud as it did with Sean and me.

The whole next week, when Father wasn't working, he and Momma were real quiet. They only spoke to each other when they had to, and that was in very short sentences.

"Want me to pick something up at the market, Merle?"

"No, Frank I don't."

"Want to take a drive to the river and watch the boats?"

"No."

Sometimes I'd catch Momma staring at Father like she didn't know who he was. When Father noticed, he'd look down at his food if he was eating, or at his paper if he was reading in the living room. The silence gave me the all-overs.

Chapter Seven

## FREED FROM DUTY

"Ten-shun." Father shouted as he strutted into the living room all decked out in his lucky plaid shirt. Sean called it a rumpled version of the American flag because it was bright red, white and blue. They weren't stars and stripes though. They were squares. The red in the shirt clashed with his red hair. He only wore it when he felt like everything was going good.

Sean, Brucie and me made our usual line up in front of the sofa, ready for the week's orders. A vase filled with flowers – roses intermixed with green ferns – was on the side table. That was another good sign. Sean elbowed me and nodded towards the flowers to make sure I didn't miss seeing them. As if I could.

"Yes, sir," we replied all at once – standing side by side.

"Tiz, twelve-oh-one, and thirty seconds...the MacLean Clan can retire from duty," he said popping off the lids of two beers. "And Fiona," he added, "don't scare me like you did last week – ever again."

I nodded, but I wasn't sure if I could do what he asked. I didn't want to run through the forest at night again. And I sure didn't want to scare him, or anybody, or get my brothers into trouble. But, no one, no how, was going to keep me away from Grandma, or from learning Indian Ceremonies. Since I was a mixture of so many things I figured I could pick and choose the parts I wanted.

Momma smiled for the first time all week. The black and blue marks on her wrists were gone. The whites of her eyes were clear again. She walked over to the radio. The skirt of her print dress flared out as she moved. *Graceful*, I thought. *Just like a movie star.* Momma fiddled with the dial until soft music came out. Father came up behind her and handed her one of the beers. She took a sip. He leaned in and kissed her on the neck.

The next thing I knew they were dancing across the floor. Each had a beer in one hand and each other in the other. "I wanna be loved by you, just you, nobody else but you," Father sang along with the radio. He dipped Momma way back and twirled her around, all without spilling anything. "Did I tell you you're beautiful?" Father cooed in Momma's ear.

"Not in a while." Momma's cheeks turned cherry red. Brown soft curls, held tight by a silver barrette, rested in the middle of her back. You could tell that the Lilt Home Permanent Ann Marie gave her was still new.

Sean gave me one of his "told you so" looks as he walked towards the door with Brucie — Goldy in tow. I walked backwards at first with my eyes on Mom and Dad. They looked so happy dancing across the living room floor. It was hard to believe that they barely spoke for over a week. Now they were acting all gushy.

Turned loose, I ran down the street and headed for Donna Tiger's house, a block and a half away. I stopped at the Jackson Street bridge and looked over the railing. The creek water had narrowed. Most of the earth around the gully was all dried up, and full of big gray cracks. A frog jumped in and out of the reeds. The polliwogs were all gone. Tiny fish, who had been no bigger than the tip of my thumb, now had four legs and croaking voices.

At first all I could see, as I headed towards her house, was a pair of feet sticking straight up from the grass. As I got closer I could see it was Donna. Her black pigtails flew from shoulder to shoulder over and over again as she turned.

"Lonestar!" Donna flashed me a big smile and ran out to meet me. "I missed you." Her dark skin and black hair made her green eyes leap out of her face. "I rang your door bell for a whole week, but your mother kept saying you couldn't come out." Donna's forehead wrinkled into a few thin lines. "Is your momma sick? She didn't look good."

I couldn't tell her I ran away or that my mom and dad had a fight. Her mom might not let us be friends anymore. I took a deep breath and reached out for her hands. "Missed you too," I squealed. We jumped up and down and laughed like we always did when we'd been away from each other.

Donna stood sideways, "ready to practice?" she asked. We'd been working out a routine of dance movements just for fun. I moved away to give her room and nodded. Donna lifted her arms up into the air and flung herself into a cartwheel. I followed right behind her. "Whoop," she yelled at the end of one turnover. "Whoop," I echoed. After five, we did a turn to the right, a turn to the left and a shuffle-hop. The turns and shuffle-hops were my idea.

After five sets of our routine, we were so dizzy we had to lay down. "Ahhhhh," we moaned laughing. I rolled my head back and forth against the soft grass. The tree branches hovered over our heads like a giant umbrella.

"You're so good at cartwheels you could be in a circus, Donna."

"Wow! That'd sure be fun," Donna chirped while still lying down next to me.

"When Momma took us to Barnum and Bailey last year there was a woman who swung from a rope by her teeth."

"Her teeth? No way. There must've been a trick of some kind."

"The rope was tied to a metal bar way up high at the top of the tent. She twirled one way, then the other. I kept thinking her teeth might come out and she'd fall."

"Scary stuff."

"Yeah, they probably take classes everyday to do tricks like that. Sean said people in the circus teach their kids to dance and do gymnastics from the time they're born."

"Oh! That reminds me. "Donna rolled onto her arm and sat half way up. "Didja hear about the new dance school?"

"Dance school?" I sat up in a flash. Nobody'd said anything to me about a dance school.

"It's just around the corner, on Telegraph Road, half a block up from Morrie's Bar."

"Jeez! Donna, why didn't you tell me that right away." I dug the heel of my shoe into the grass. Flashes of me traveling and dancing like Aunt Dawn prophesied exploded in my head like the Fourth of July fireworks. "A dance school? A real live dance school?"

"Um, humm." Donna's mouth pursed into a tight line. "Momma signed me up for classes."

"Man-o-man!" My stomach scrunched up into a tight ball. "You get everything you want." I slammed my hands down hard onto the ground. "How'm I gonna get my father to let me go?"

"Can't you ask your mom?" Donna pulled at the grass. The thin blades came out in bunches.

"Yeah! Sure! But, she's not the one who earns money. It's Father. So he's the one who gets to decide how we spend it."

"Just because my momma works is no reason to be mad, Lonestar."

"My father won't let my momma work, Donna. He says she's got enough to do around the house." I lowered my head over my bent knees and pulled my arms tighter around my legs. It made me feel smaller, like maybe I could crawl into an ant hole.

"Well, my dad is always working out of town, so he wants my mom to stay busy while he's gone." Donna scooted, crab like towards me. She pulled my left hand away from my knees, brought it down and tucked her fingers in-between mine.

Donna's hand felt warm. I raised my free hand up in front of me and tried to catch shadows from the Maple Tree. *When you want something, Lonestar, you have to figure out what work you need to do to get it.* Grandma's words echoed in my head. I reached inside my jeans pocket and rubbed my gray stone for luck.

The next Saturday morning I sat on one of the metal chairs behind the dancers, and watched my friend Donna and a few other girls glide across the wooden floor at Trixie's Dance Studio. I wasn't mad anymore.

Huge mirrors stretched from wall to wall across the front of the room. Miss Trixie, the teacher, stood in front of the dancers and called out French words like: *glissade* and *plié*." It looked like a glide that ended with bent knees. She struck the floor with a short red stick and called out "one, two, three," in a singsongy voice.

I prayed as hard as I could, day after day, for Father to think I was such a good girl that he'd let me have dance lessons. As soon as he came home from work I had a nice hot bath ready for him. While he was in the tub, I put on one of his Glen Miller records and fluffed up all the pillows on the living room furniture. As soon as he finished his before-supper-drink, all relaxed on the sofa, I stood ready to get him another.

"Fiona sure knows how to take care of a man," Father said to Momma. "Not like you."

"Sometimes you are just not funny." Momma threw the socks she was darning into her sewing basket, crossed her arms over her chest, and clenched her teeth.

"Come on, can't you take a joke?" Father replied in that voice that sounds all sugary.

I watered the lawn, took out the garbage, dried the dishes and helped Momma in every which way I could think of. I didn't want her to feel left out.

"You're a good girl, Lonestar," Momma said as we folded laundry together on the kitchen table, "and real helpful."

Towards the end of the week, when Father was relaxing on the sofa, I took a deep breath, crossed my fingers and asked "can I have dance lessons with Donna?"

"No," he said in his deepest voice. His eyes barely peering over the top of the newspaper.

I sat on the front porch and watched the guys play football in the street out front.

Watching their game was like watching a silent movie. All I could hear was Father's "no".

Sean ran to the imaginary line, fifty feet down the street with the ball.

"No," Father's words clanged inside my head.

A wet, sloppy tongue licked my hand. Soft fur brushed up against my arm. I looked down. It was Goldy. She let out some happy crying sounds, then ran to fetch her ball.

"No, Goldy," I said. I was in no mood to play.

I sat on one of the metal chairs in the dance studio and watched Donna and the other girls again. Sometimes, Donna wobbled a bit. When she did Miss Trixie always told her not to give up. "A good *arabesque* is worth the struggle," she'd say in a soft yet firm way. "Arching your back, lifting one leg high up behind you, turns you into a beautiful swan."

Miss Trixie didn't just stand at the front of the room and call out orders like some of my teachers at school. She demonstrated each step slowly and with such grace that it was beautiful to watch.

My ears drank in her words; my eyes pressed each movement into secret places inside of me that I didn't know existed.

When Sean, Brucie and some of the other kids went to the clubhouse after school, I stayed home and danced in the backyard. *"Glissade, plié*, one, two, three," I said to myself. The grass made it hard to glide as I bent one knee and scootched forward, but I did it anyway.

Chapter Eight

# DREAMS SHOULD NOT BE BROKEN

In the fall, when the leaves began to turn yellow, red, and burnt orange, after Father got home from work, I quickly fluffed up the pillows in the living room, put a cold beer on the living room table and waited. I hoped Father would change his mind as quickly as the leaves were changing colors.

Time was flying by and I just had to take dance lessons with Donna and not just practice on my own or it'd be too late for me to have the future Aunt Dawn saw in my *Talisman Stones*. Grandma would say, *Dreams should not be broken. Even if they don't come true it's important to have them. They are part of the mystery of life that helps your spirit grow strong. It's the steps you take along the way that help to build the person. The steps always teach you something.* I wasn't that interested in the steps along the way. I wanted what I wanted, and I wanted it now.

As soon as he sat down and took a sip of beer, I reached into my jeans pocket, rubbed my gray stone between my thumb and index fingers, took a deep breath and said, "Father..."

"No," he said setting his drink down. "America's appointed itself the guardian angel of the whole world again. We're at war with Korea." He raised one of his eyebrows like he did sometimes. "We have to work overtime, longer and harder for the same pay or we'll fall behind in our government contract. President Truman wouldn't like that."

I didn't think any of that had anything to do with me getting dance lessons. There had to be a way. I just didn't know what it was yet.

Father stretched full out on the sofa, covered his face with the news and drifted off to sleep.

I went out and sat on the porch again. Goldy tried to cheer me up again. It didn't work. *Maybe Aunt Dawn was wrong, maybe dancing wasn't going to be part of my Earthwalk. The lessons I'm supposed to learn on Earth. Maybe I was supposed to learn something else. Maybe I wasn't supposed to want anything. The "maybes" marched through my head like they were in their own war, not the one in Korea.*

Dolly Duffield walked Fi-Fi back and forth in front of her house, in that jittery way of hers, so Fi-Fi could get her exercise. "She sure takes good care of that dog," Momma would say. "She'd die if anything happened to Fi-Fi." I figured that'd mean she'd feel like I did, but I didn't say anything. It'd just make Momma feel bad.

Harriet Helmsly next door, watered her lawn like she does day after day. I looked away and studied the cracks in the front porch or the bark on the tree. I didn't want her to wave and say something happy. I couldn't wave back. No way could I look happy.

I wanted to go to Grandma's, but if I ran away again, I'd just get my brothers in trouble again. I didn't want everybody else to suffer because of me, so I just sat on the porch and stared out at the world.

Momma tapped me on the shoulder. I knew it was her without looking. Her soft finger touch was like a leaf falling from a tree. I didn't really want to talk, so I kept my head down and just looked up with my eyes. She put one finger over her mouth, then curled her hand into a waving motion while holding the screen door open for me to come in.

We tip-toed past Father asleep on the sofa. Short whistles blew out of his mouth.

I followed her down the hall like a shadow, then into her room. I didn't know what she was up to. She picked Father's trousers up off the bed, went through the pockets, took out his wallet, rummaged through some bills and handed me a twenty dollar bill.

As much as I wanted to take the money, I couldn't. It was too scary. I mean, Jeez, Father'd really have something to be angry about. For all I knew he memorized all the numbers on the bills in his wallet and could put a tracer on them. I shook my head *no*.

"Go on." Momma cooed in a soft voice. "Take it. It's part of my allowance and I want you to have it." Her long slender fingers waved the bill through the air. The diamonds on her wedding ring shone in the afternoon light. I looked up into her eyes. They were bright and cheery. She didn't look frightened.

I reached out and took it. The green was faded, like maybe it'd been washed in someone's pocket a few times ago. I wondered how many hands it had passed through. How many other wonderful things it had paid for. And, how many times it had been stolen. Guilt mixed with excitement as I pressed the bill into my jeans pocket. It was enough for two months of lessons

My heart fluttered like a nest of baby birds was about to break out of their shells as Donna and me walked in the front door of the dance studio. My hand shook as I handed Miss Trixie my twenty dollars. She smiled real big, and tucked the money into a small canvas bag she wore around her waist. "Glad to see you joining us, Fiona." I liked that she knew my name.

My reflection looked back at me as I stood all lined up with the other girls: blonde short hair, blue eyes, pointed nose, long neck, straight back. It didn't matter that the other girls had ballet slippers and I wore heavy socks. It didn't matter that they wore leotards and I wore pink shorts with a T-shirt. What mattered was that I, Fiona Lonestar MacLean, was on the dance floor and not sitting on the chair watching. "Thank you God, Jesus, Great Spirit, *Kokumthena*," I whispered so nobody could hear me.

"Two steps right, two steps left, turn; *balancé* right, rock to the right, *balancé* left, rock to the left; *detourné*, turn." Miss Trixie sang the words, as she demonstrated what she wanted us to do.

I kept my eyes glued on her feet, and repeated her words in my head as I did what she asked. "Two steps right, two steps left, turn; *balancé* right, *balancé* left; *detourné*." The piano melody on the record beat out the same waltz pulse.

Suddenly, the record stuck. Miss Trixie stomped on the floor. The record stayed stuck. She threw her hands up in the air, hurried over to the corner table, lifted the needle off the player and set it down again. "Stay," she demanded.

This time it did what she told it to do – just like we did. "Okay girls," she clapped her hands. "Once again." Miss Trixie smiled and looked in my direction. "Make it smooth, Fiona, like you're waltzing at a grand ball."

Happiness leaped out of every pour in my body. I was already at that grand ball.


Back in our street clothes Donna and me danced our way back down Telegraph Road. Puffy clouds laid out in dots like penny candy above us. A soft breeze made the ends of my straight hair tickle my neck.

"We're gonna be friends for ever and ever," I said.

Donna reached out for my arm and yanked me to a halt. A worried look flashed across her face. "Isn't that your father coming out of Morrie's Bar?"

I looked up the block. In the distance I could see Father's back. His short, buzzed hair poked out of his head like new mown grass. Two men stood in front of him. They were arguing about something.

"Guys," Father cried in that happy voice he used sometimes even when he wasn't happy. "It's all a misunderstanding. I told you before I'd catch up." He reached into his back pocket, took out his wallet and handed them what was probably the last of his paycheck. "I...I'll make up the rest next week." Father laughed.

I froze. My knees started to shake. *Father must have lost money gamblin' again. Now he was in trouble and it was all my fault. I took his last twenty dollars and gave to Miss Trixie.* Donna took my hand and pulled me back toward the dance studio.

## Chapter Nine

## BROKEN PROMISES

I opened my mouth to drink in the cold snap in the air. I liked the way it circled around my teeth, the top of my mouth, around my tongue then sprang like a cat deep into my stomach. I held it inside for as long as I could, then slowly released it back into the world to form little puffs of smoke.

"Hurry up Fiona. Kick the can then make a run for it," Sean yelled as he, Brucie, our neighbor Herbie and me played on the graveled road in front of our house.

I set the empty soup can down in front of me, pulled my foot back as far as it would go, which was pretty far considering how strong I was after taking dance lessons, and let 'er rip. It sailed into the air. Sean caught the can and started after me in a flash. I zigzagged one way, then the other trying to tag Herbie. Tagging Brucie would have been too easy.

Music from The Good Humor Ice Cream truck blasted out from the side road. We all knew it was headed our way so we stopped our game. "Time out," I cried.

"What'll ya have kiddos," Mr. Mack the driver sang out in that happy way of his as he pulled to a stop on the side of the road. He ran the tips of his fingers across the brim of his white cap as he sat in the open front of his truck, a square box with four wheels.

Herbie dug into his pockets and took out some change. "Eskimo Pie," he said to Mr. Mack. "Part of my allowance," he grinned.

When Momma had money she bought ice-cream for any of the neighbor kids on the road. Herbie just bought for himself.

Sean shot me one of his side ways looks. "Gotta go," he said to Herbie. "Almost time for dinner. I nodded. Brucie lowered his head and kicked at the gravel. Herbie bit into the chocolate crust of his Eskimo Pie, "right," he mumbled. We watched him eat as he headed for home, clueless about sharing.

"He always has everything," I said as we headed for our font stoop. Once there, I sat on my hands so my rear wouldn't get too cold.

"Yeah!" Sean replied as he sat down on the step above me. "If I had his money I'd buy some barbells like my friend Dickie has." He pulled up the collar of his blue wind-breaker and crossed his arms over his chest. "They help develop your muscles."

"I'd get more dance lessons," I said. I pointed my toes out to the side and brought my heels together.

"You out?" Sean asked stretching his long legs out beyond the step.

"Yeh! This week. It's been two months." I looked up at the sky. The last rays of the Sun made the edges of the clouds look firm, like a stage you could dance on.

Brucie shivered. "I don't know what I'd want." Brucie shrugged. "Maybe a Spider Man Comic Book." He looked up at me and smiled, the dimples in his cheeks deepened.

Sean tapped his foot on the cement in short dots like a secret signal of some kind. "Everybody I know gets an allowance." He bit down on his upper lip. "Dad promised if I took good care of Goldy, raked the leaves, kept the weeds cut, and emptied the garbage – he'd pay me."

"Maybe he forgot," I said.

Sean blinked. Lines formed across his forehead. "I'm tired of him forgetting."

After dinner, Brucie and I sat in the corner on the living room floor next to the bookcase. Father was on the sofa, adjacent to us, reading his paper and sipping his after dinner drink.

Our bookcase was dark wood, a little lighter than the color of the night sky. It had five shelves, three feet wide. A dim glow from the porch light shone through the window and onto the edges of the books. After what Aunt Dawn had said about my future – traveling and all – I imagined the books filled with places to see and people to meet – things I still hadn't experienced.

Brucie was making a book of his own for a school assignment and I was helping him. "I don't know what to write," Brucie said as he bit down on his shirt collar. I yanked the collar out like I always did.

I heard Sean come into the room and start talking to Father, but I didn't look up. "What about Spider Man?" I said. "Tell me why you wanted to have allowance money so you could buy that particular comic."

Brucie sighed. "Because...Spider Man can crawl up walls and over mountains." His eyes lit up with excitement. "He can go anywhere, escape anything."

"That's good," I said. "Write that down." I leaned forward so I could whisper in Brucie's ear. "Grandma says spiders can weave a web that circles the whole Earth." I ran the tips of my fingers over the designs in the carpet playfully spinning a web of my own.

"Give'em an inch. They want a mile," Father yelled. Brucie and I stared at each other. I swallowed hard. My heart thumped wildly in my chest. I turned slowly. Sean was standing in front of Father. *He must have asked for his ... allowance.*

"It's what you promised," Sean's voice trembled. "I've done everything you asked for...months."

Father's nostrils flared as he stared up at Sean from where he sat on the sofa. "There's a roof over yer head, food on the table and clothes on yer back. What else do you want from me?" He took a swig of beer and shook his head.

The tone of Father's voice sent sharp arrows into my heart. I sat stone-quiet on the floor next to Brucie, reached out for his hand and squeezed it tight.

Sean's eyes flinched like he'd been slapped across the face. He took a deep breath and walked out the door. Tears welled up in my eyes, I brushed them away with my free hand. *It's not fair*, I thought. *Promises should not be broken.*

Momma raced into the room. "What's going on?" she asked. Father grabbed the ends of his newspaper and gave them a quick shake. The crinkling noise hurt my head. "Nothing," he replied. Momma clamped down on her jaw, turned and left the room.

Cries echoed down the hall and woke me up. I sat up straight in bed and listened closely. "Where are you Lady Luck? You let me down." It was Father. Lady Luck was his gambling angel. He prayed to her like the rest of us pray to God, Jesus, *Kokomthena* and the Great Spirit.

Father's cries were followed by heavy thumping and grunts. The moonlight from our small window cast gray shadows over our bedroom walls. The howling of a dog shimmied through the trees behind our house.

"Listen," I called out to my brothers from my top bunk. "Father's crying. We should check on him." We were all light sleepers, so I figured if I heard something so did they.

Sean let out a low moan from the bunk below. "Leave him alone. He doesn't deserve any help," he mumbled.

"Goin' out there'd just get us into trouble," Brucie muttered.

"Well, I'm going." I pulled back my blanket, crawled to the end, and climbed down from my top bunk. "I'll hide at the edge of the hall," I whispered.

I tiptoed across the floor, opened the door and stepped out into the hall. The door to Momma and Father's room, across from our room, was closed. It was quiet. Momma was asleep.

"Huh, huh, huh." Father grunted.

My stomach tightened. Coming out of my room at night was against the rules. But, I wanted to make sure Father was okay. I hated that he broke his promise to Sean, but now he sounded like he needed help. I inched my way along the edge of the hall, about ten feet, and stopped at the edge of the living room. I crossed my fingers, stuck my head out and peeked around the corner.

Lucky for me, Father's head faced out the front window, leaving his back to me. He was dressed in his Scots outfit. The one I'd seen him in at Morrie's Bar when we went to fetch him for my birthday party last July. The floor lamp at the end of the sofa spilled light onto most of the living room, but not onto the hall where I stood.

I watched as Father jumped from side to side. One arm raised high in the air. The other cinched at his waist. The back of his kilts flapped as he moved. The pleats made a sort of wave, like when the wind blows hard on the Detroit River. Puffs of air exploded out of his chest.

I clung to the wall like a bug, hiding in the shadows, seeing but not being seen. As he jumped, the muscles in his shoulders rippled. Beads of sweat pooled under the back of his T-shirt. The puffs of air turned into "hums," followed by singing. *Oh! ye'll take the high road and I'll take the low road, and I'll be in Scotland afore ye; but me and my true love will never meet again on the bonnie, bonnie banks of Lock Lomond.*

Father turned. He jumped in my direction. Our eyes met straight on. My breath froze in my chest. My stomach tightened. I got ready for him to get mad at me like he did Sean. But he didn't. Tears popped into his eyes and rolled down his cheeks. He turned away. I hurried back to bed and hid under the covers.

The next morning, Father didn't say anything about dancing in the middle of the night, so I didn't say anything either. The night sounds went on all the next week, but I didn't sneak in to watch.

Chapter Ten

## BUTTERFLIES ARE FREE

Grandma and Momma sat at the kitchen table trying to figure out how to earn some extra money. "I know Frank's scared," Momma said. "Everybody at Ford is scramblin' to get their work done. The longer this Korean War goes on the more equipment's needed. He's drinking more...to ease the pain. And ... I know he's gamblin'. I hate it ... but I can't fix it." She glanced out the window and listened to my brothers playing in the back yard, then picked up her fork and fiddled with the cake that lay on a dish between her and Grandma.

"Why don't we do a tent show and charge admission?" Grandma asked. The smell of strong coffee and fresh Shawnee cake filled the room. "It'd be like a powwow, only instead of arts and crafts and watching dance competitions, it'd be a mish-mash."

"A show like a powwow?" I jumped up from the linoleum floor where I'd been doing my homework. "You think anybody'd pay to come?" I'd never thought about making money for a tent show. My stomach jittered. Hummingbird wings fluttered in my head.

"Um, Hmm," Grandma sang. Her thin lips pursed together into a fine line.

"Can Donna and me dance?" I asked breathlessly.

"Don't see why not." Grandma sipped her black coffee then stuck her fork into the shared cake. "You, Donna, Sean and Brucie can all share in the show, and the earnin's." She lifted the cake to her mouth and tilted her head from side to side. I loved it when she did that.

"Can't you go farther away, Brucie?" Sean pleaded. I glanced out the window. Sean held up a ball and motioned for Brucie to move back. "You keep creepin' in too close."

Momma sighed, "boys." Her jaw clenched as she bit down hard on her teeth. "It'll do 'em good to all work together as a family. And...God knows every nickle counts."

After a while Momma turned and looked me square in the eyes. "I'll have Harriet Helmsly, next door, make costumes for you."

"Regalia, Merle. Costumes are for Halloween, Regalia, is what ceremonial dancers wear." Grandma's shoulders lifted up as she took in a big breath and let it out like she was really onto something big.

Momma clapped her hands like a little kid and squirmed in her chair. "Ann Marie, Dolly and ... well everybody'll come." She sprang forward, wrapped her arms around my waist and hugged real tight.

"You tell all your friends, Merle," Grandma nodded to herself in a thinking kind of way then turned her head towards me. "Lonestar, you and Donna are gonna learn some new steps." The way she said "new steps" gave me allovers. I could hardly wait to see what was going to happen next.

Grandma drummed her fingers on the table. "We'll think of somethin' for the boys." She grinned, "and I'll come up with a few surprises of my own."


We crayoned invitations and put them up on all the telephone poles for blocks around. **Come one, come all to the MacLean backyard, 1779 Jackson Street, sensational powwow tent show this Saturday at 1:00. One dollar per ticket.**

We did some signs in red and several in blue. No one could walk or drive down Jackson, Ziegler, or Champaign Road without knowing that something grand was coming up.

I put one of our red invitations on the windshield of Father's car. That way he'd be sure to come straight home after he finished work on Saturday. Momma said he only had to work from six in the morning 'till noon on Saturday's, unless there was an emergency of some kind.  I crossed my fingers and prayed that he'd like my dancing and Grandma's surprises.

Brucie sold tickets door to door, up and down the road.  We put a sign on one of Momma's old Crisco cans so all he had to do was ring the bell, hold the can up and smile.

The morning of the show, Sean carefully clothes-pinned four bed-sheets together, folded two over Momma's clothesline and clipped the others to form a four walled tent. "If you want you can fold the front flap and pin it to one side," he said as he opened it to show me how it worked.

"This is great!" I squealed as I went in and out of the opening. It'd taken us a month from beginning to end to get everything together.

He laughed. "It's just something boys know how to do." It felt good that he was doing something nice for me.

Grandma came early. We sat on the living room sofa as she brushed my hair and pulled it back with pink barrettes. Her eyes sparkled as she fussed over me. Donna and me had been practicing the steps Grandma taught us every day after school.

"What's the surprise you said you'd have for me today Grandma?" I thought the surprise was hidden in one of the big pockets of her purple and white flowered apron.

"Well then, Lonestar, if I told you it wouldn't be a surprise now would it?"  She looked at me sideways and raised her eyebrows in an impish kind of look. Her hair was braided and twisted into a bun on top of her head like it usually was. But this time she had a silver comb stuck in the top, at the front of the bun. It looked real pretty.

"Your grandfather gave it to me," she said when she saw me looking at it.  "Silver hair-bobbles were one of the few things his mother, your great-grandmother, brought from Scotland." Grandma sighed. "She died a few years after he saved enough money to pay for her to join him in America." She shook her head. "People gave up everything they knew to risk that long voyage from Europe to America."

"There's so many people in our family I don't know."

"Maybe so," Grandma said. "But they all live in your bones."

Tingles went through my head just thinking about that. "In my bones, Grandma?"

Grandma laughed. "When you're dancing today, others who danced before you will be with you."

At twelve o'clock we chained Goldy up to the front tree so she wouldn't wag her tail and bark while everybody was here.

At twelve-fifteen, Grandma and me laid out some extra blankets a few feet in front of the tent for people to sit on, set the kitchen chairs up towards the back and pretty much checked to make sure everything looked good.

At twelve-thirty, I put my one-piece, blue bathing suit on, careful not to muss up my hair, and covered myself with one of Sean's big shirts.

At twelve-thirty-five I double checked the back yard while Grandma helped Momma make coffee in the kitchen.

At twelve-forty, I helped Sean set up the drums he made out of old oil cans and leather.

At twelve-forty-five, I did some of our dance steps in front of the tent to make sure we had enough room between us and the blankets we had laid out so I wouldn't trip.

At twelve-fifty, just when I decided nobody was gonna come, Harriet Helmsly came running over from next door carrying a big box followed by her daughter Geraldine carrying folding chairs. Mrs. Helmsly had on blue checkered tight pants with a blue sweater and a long feathery blue boa, wrapped around her neck. She looked like a big happy blue bird.

Geraldine had on long black trousers, a brown tweed jacket, a white shirt and a beige tie. She always dressed like a boy. Grandma says sometimes boy's spirits live in girl's bodies and girl spirits live in boy's bodies. I didn't care which spirit Geraldine was, she was our friend.

"I'll put this in the tent." Mrs. Helmsly grinned from ear to ear as she walked past. The ends of the bright orange ribbon on the box waved in the wind. I couldn't wait to see the wings she'd made for us. We'd been practicing with some of momma's old scarves.

I took a deep breath and let it out slowly as I helped Geraldine find a place to set up their chairs.

Momma and Grandma brought out a tray filled with coffee cups and set it by the back door.

"Sean, Brucie," Momma yelled, "come on out here. It's time." Momma was all dressed up in a mint green dress with a matching sweater and a new blue bib apron. She looked real pretty.

I looked up to see Dolly Duffield from across the street making her way slowly across the grass. She had on rhinestone trimmed high-heels. Since our lawn was soft, her heels sank into the sod with each step. I prayed she wouldn't fall.

"Girls, isn't this exciting?" Dolly ran her fingers through her white hair to fluff it up even more than it already was fluffed.

Momma gave Dolly a big hug then turned to wave at Ann Marie Thorsby.

"Do you like it, Merle?" Ann Marie purred as she pointed to her bright red head.

"You look like a move star," Momma said.

Geraldine, Harriet, Dolly and me all agreed. We knew she could go to Hollywood and star in movies if it weren't for the fact that her husband hated movies.

"Don't forget to smile a lot, kiddo. People like it when you smile," Ann Marie sang out as she gently brushed the hair out of my eyes. "Great," I muttered. *Now I have to not trip, not forget the dance steps and remember to smile.*

Donna came with her mom. I was really glad to see her...and relieved. I sure didn't want to do the show by myself.

"This is for you." Donna reached into the front pocket of the long coat she wore to cover her bathing suit and handed me a little yellow star.

"Momma said when things seem out of reach, to remember that it's the journey that counts." Donna's cat-eyes gleamed. "It's like your name don't ya think? A lone star."

I ran the tips of my fingers over the outside of the star as I cupped it in my opposite hand. The wood felt soft and smooth.

I brought it up to my face. It smelled fresh like the air in the forest.

"Wow!" I looked back up into Donna's eyes and opened mine real wide. "Thank you! It's really a great present." I was embarrassed that I hadn't thought to get Donna anything.

"Sold a lot of tickets," Mrs. Tiger said. "My friends at Hudson's Department Store couldn't come, but they wanted you to have this." She held up a big brown envelope full of money. I swallowed hard. Grandma was right, people were willing to pay for our show, even people who couldn't come.

Aunt Raven, momma's youngest sister; Uncle Howard, her husband; ten year old cousin Shiloh Blue and seven year old cousin Willow, waved as they stepped onto our lawn from the side-street. Willow looks like what she's named after, a tree with skinny branches. Shiloh was named after a famous Indian scout who could make himself invisible. We all think the scout has come back to live inside my cousin. He stands so still and straight it's hard to know he's there.

"Did I miss anything, Lonestar, uh Fiona," Aunt Raven said breathlessly? "That Howard's such a slow poke." Uncle Howard rolled his eyes up to the sky and hit his fist against his chest. "Why's everything always my fault? You're the one who got up late this morning?" Aunt Raven shot him a look to kill. "I couldn't get your motor runnin' for love nor money."

Relatives and neighbors kept filling in places in our small yard 'till it looked like a patchwork quilt Grandma might make. I searched through the crowd for Father's face. I couldn't find him. He didn't like some of the Indian things Grandma shared with me, but our show was different. At least I hoped it was. I wanted him to be proud of me.

"It's time, Lonestar," Momma whispered. She held her watch up for me to see.

My heart tightened. *What if nobody liked our show? What if I looked stupid?* More fearful stuff ran through my head. I took a deep breath and walked toward Donna. She was sitting on a blanket near the front with her mom.

"It's time," I said softly as I got down on all fours next to her. *Was she scared too?* I wondered. We scooted into Sean's amazing tent. Quick as a wink we stripped down to our bathing suits, pulled on our flowing white skirts and slipped on the bright orange leggings that Momma had laid out for us. Next we tightened the multi colored ribbons around our waists to make sure our skirts didn't fall down, then I tied Donna's headband around her forehead making sure that the attached spotted feather was right in the middle of her forehead. She did the same for me.

"We saved Harriet Helmsley's surprise for last. I untied the bright orange ribbon on the cardboard box, removed the lid and lifted the top shawl out of the box. Donna looked at me with eyes so wide open they looked like dots on the wings of a Monarch. Mine must have looked the same to her.

"It's huge," she said. I nodded. "A shawl is sure not a scarf. It's almost as big as we are." Happy tears welled up in my eyes.

Flashes of orange, black, white and yellow painted the inside of the once white tent as I carefully draped the shawl over Donna's shoulders. The material softly rippled with my every move. The colored fringe on the bottom of the shawl was over a foot long. A huge butterfly graced the back, surrounded by pink, red and purple flowers. I smiled thinking about butterflies and flowers and how they need each other to survive. Grandma says that everything is important, even worms and without all that there is we wouldn't be here. I wasn't sure about some things. I mean flies? Who needs them?

Donna lifted the other shawl out of the box and draped it over my shoulders. The fringe across the bottom of the shawl gently brushed my wrists and ankles. I blinked a few times to wash my happy tears away. As I looked into Donna's eyes I heard a whooshing sound in my ears, an eery sense that something was happening to us that I couldn't describe flew into my head. Maybe it was what Grandma said, I was connecting to an ancestor living in my bones. Donna smiled, then waved her hands just like I had done. Happy sparks flashed between us.

Grandma was going to give us a sign when it was time to begin. I wasn't sure what the sign would be. *The unknown keeps you in a state of wonder,* she had said. As I listened, every mumble, laugh, cough, moan, and chair creak had me ready for action.

*Bump, tada, bump, tada, bump, bump, bump,* several drums thumped in front of the tent. Donna and me both let out a silent scream. Along with the rumbly sounds of Sean's handmade drums there was a new deep booming flutter. A flutter that shook the Earth and soared through the air like a thunder storm. The hair on the back of my head stood up in full alert. I peeked out of the flap, careful not to let anybody see me.

A man with long gray hair tied back with a piece of black string sat facing the crowd next to Brucie on the far left. A long white feather dangled over one shoulder. Deep ridges of life cut into his face. His dark, agile fingers beat wildly over the stretched leather that covered the top of his wide drum. Shadows from the overhead Sun playing in and out of the trees fancied up the base.

"It's Johnny Whitefeather," I whispered breathlessly to Donna. "Grandma's friend who found me in the forest when I was lost."

Donna and me flew out of the tent. Johnny Whitefeather looked at me and smiled then softened the beats. Pulses of heat raced through my body.

Donna moved over to the right near Sean while I edged my way to the left where Brucie and Johnny were. I swallowed hard and tried to catch my breath. Grandma sure knew how to make a surprise.

*Bump, tada, bump, tada, bump, bump, bump,* the drums exploded loudly again. The sounds bounced against the back of the house, rolled over the green lawn and filled the sky and everyone in sight with their rhythms. "Oohs" and "aahs," spilled out of the audience as we both stood there for a minute caught in the web of excitement.

We lifted our arms as we arched our backs back and forth just like we did in ballet class. The breeze made the fringe look like fingers reaching out for something I couldn't see. The light material ballooned out one way, then the other like wind-sails.

I nodded to Donna that I was ready to start. Johnny Whitefeather softened his touch on the drum again. Sean and Brucie followed his lead. *Walk slowly and gracefully but boldly and proudly,* Grandma had said. I stepped forward. "Heel, toe, heel toe," I said to myself as Donna and me moved across the front of the tent in unison. "One, two, three; one, two...." We rocked to the right, left, then forward over and over again. The rocking part was the same as ballet only with different arm movements. *Balancé* right, rock to the right, *balancé* left, rock to the left. Once we crossed each other and ended on opposite ends, we stopped, reached our arms out and fluttered our wings again. It was just like we'd practiced, only having scarves like butterfly wings and drums made it seem bigger, more important.

I lifted my arms to get ready to circle the yard. But, before I could someone caught my attention. It was Grandma. My breath caught in my chest as I watched her clear a path down the center of the lawn. She'd taken her flowered apron off and slipped on a long, full, beige skirt that matched her blouse. Instead of the black leather shoes she was wearing earlier, she wore beige beaded moccasins. A deep maroon shawl covered her shoulders. People moved their blankets and chairs quickly out of the way as she headed toward us. I didn't know that Grandma was going to be part of the surprise too.

"Just follow the story," Grandma said to Donna and me as she gathered up the folds of her skirt and sat next to Johnny. I looked out at the crowd. All eyes were on the six of us. Everybody was sitting down, but Momma. She stood at the back porch near the kitchen. I still couldn't see Father. Maybe she was waiting for him.

"It happened long ago," Grandma said in a deep cavern like voice. "In ancient times, my sisters, the Butterflies, died." Grandma left pauses between each few words. "They did not die of old age. They died because Mountain wanted to hold beauty in his hand."

Johnny, Sean'n Brucie beat hard on their drums then softened the beats again. The strength of their movements made the sheets, that made up the front of the tent, ripple.

"He did not want to share," Grandma thundered She turned back toward us and nodded. Donna and me stepped forward, bent over, lowered our heads and peeked up at Grandma. My shawl caught the wind, fluttered, then fell softly over my arms. The long fringe flayed out onto the soft grass.

"When Mountain watched my sisters flitting from flower to flower on his land, he felt important." Grandma raised her fist and shook it at the sky. Donna and me stood up again. I took one step forward and slowly moved my arms to the right, then the left so my shawl could wave in the wind again. Donna did the same. Mountain wasn't the only one who felt important. I had to look down to make sure my feet were still on the ground.

We continued our movement, one step forward, arms to the right then the left, waved in the wind, then moved forward again until we stood on opposite ends of the tent. I'd always loved butterflies, but now, pretending to be one, made me love them even more.

"Focus on the steps," I said to myself as I made my way towards the outside of the circle. "Heel, toe, heel, toe, *balancé* right, rock to the right, *balancé* left, rock to the left, *detourné right,* turn right, *detourné* left, turn left." I said inside my head again. Midway around I looked across the crowd to catch Donna's eye, then nodded as we both reached our arms out and fluttered our wings again. I'm not sure if the drums followed us or we followed the drums as we circled the crowd.

"Keep it simple," Grandma had said. "It's repetition but with a flare."

We repeated the same moves as we made our way back across the front of the tent. Brucie looked up at me and grinned as I passed in front of him. Donna bent down to smell an imaginary flower. I stopped and did the same. Then we raised up, held our arms to our side, faced the audience and waited for the next part of Grandma's story.

"Then one day Mountain couldn't see my sisters, the Butterflies. He searched day after day through the trees, behind the heavy brush, and around the stones where his lower ridge met the Earth. But they had gone beyond his view. With them gone, he felt lonely," Grandma cried out in a sad shaky voice.

I lifted my arms above my head, raised up on my toes, and waved my wings in the wind. Since Grandma had cleared a path down the center of the audience, I decided to dance all the way back to where Momma stood. That way we could hide behind the audience. Donna followed. I didn't look at anybody, but I could feel the heat of their eyes on me.

Momma turned her back away from us real fast as we moved to within a few feet of where she was standing. She frowned and held her hands behind her, just under the bow of her blue apron. I couldn't tell if she was hiding something, or mad. I stumbled on the thick grass, but caught myself before I fell down.

"The next morning, Mountain put some flowers just inside a cave on his east side, facing the rising Sun," Grandma shouted. Momma side stepped around us. A sweet scent of perfume trailed behind her as she rushed up the center path. When she got to the front she held up a bunch of yellow lilies for everybody to see. Her eyes sparkled, her cheeks flushed red as she laid them near the tent opening, then stepped aside. *That's why she turned away. Momma wasn't mad, she was part of the show.*

"My sisters flew back from the land they had wandered to and went to feast on the sweetness of the lilies," Grandma called out.

I nodded at Donna. She moved past me, edged over to the center of the path and danced toward the lilies. I followed. The vibrations of the drums moved through us like an invisible current. Once there, we got on our knees next to Grandma and bent our heads down to breathe in the full sweetness of the lilies.

"When they did, Mountain blocked their way out." Grandma's words came out tight and crisp. Donna crawled through the tent opening, then pulled the flowers the rest of the way in. I followed behind her.

"Days went by. Mountain felt very important. He had Butterflies of his very own. Thinking they might be hungry, he rolled back the rocks to give them some fresh flowers. When Mountain looked inside the cave, he was horrified. Instead of his beautiful orange and black Butterflies, he saw thin, beaten wings. Instead of life, he found death," Grandma sighed and whimpered.

We crawled out towards Grandma, flapped our shawls like wings a few inches off the ground, let them fall, then put our foreheads down on the ground.

"Mountain's heart was broken. He cried so hard that it began to storm. The wind blew. Rain came pouring down." Out of the corners of my eyes I could see Momma flap a blue scarf over our backs, Johnny, Sean and Brucie hit the sides of their drums with stiff brushes that made it sound like rain.

"Sun took pity on Mountain. "'If you promise to never be selfish again, I'll give you back your Butterflies,' Sun said.'"

"'I promise,' Mountain cried. 'I promise.' Stones began to fall away from Mountain's side. Earth in the meadow began to shake. Sun made new flowers sprout out of the loosened damp soil. Their fragrance filled the air. Petals of white, lavender, yellow, and orange dotted the meadow."

Grandma's long skirt rustled as she stood up between Donna and me. "Get up Butterflies," she said. "Mountain is setting you free." Donna and me leaped to our feet. Grandma took our hands, lifted them into the sky, then brought them down in a bow. I could hardly believe all the whistling and shouting. Even cousin Violet looked happy. Grandma then turned to face Sean, Brucie, and Johnny Whitefeather and led an applause for them. She pointed to Momma and waved her forward. I was so excited my skin felt like it was on fire.

Grandma motioned for Violet to stand up. Violet pulled a basket out from under a cloth, reached inside and started throwing bags of jelly beans out. The jelly beans looked like tiny butterfly eggs. The kids all scrambled for a treat. *The*

*mystery of Violet's niceness and joy was solved. Grandma
made her part of the show.*

"And so it was, the following spring, when the flowers were
in bloom: my sister's eggs turned into caterpillars, cocoons
birthed new Butterflies and Mountain had more than enough to
share," Grandma's face beamed. "Like Butterflies, we each
hold the sacred memory of our ancestors in us. That's how the
Great Spirit turns death into life."

Standing up there with so much happiness around me sent
another bolt of energy crashing through my body. If I didn't
know better, I would've thought I was struck by lightening. I
wondered if I'd turn into black ashes with everybody clapping
and yelling.

I glanced at Momma. She was proud of us. It showed in
her eyes as she poured the coffee she'd made earlier.

Donna and me counted up the money we'd collected. It
added up to fifty dollars. We could hardly believe it. Donna
said she wanted to give me her share so we could both take
dance class. That left $20.00 for me $10.00 for Sean, Brucie
and Momma.

"Where've you been, Frank?" Momma called out later that
night. I'd heard the front door open, then shut. Momma
must've been sitting on the sofa waiting.

My brother's and I were in bed. Sean, on the bunk
underneath mine, Brucie in his army cot next to Sean. My
mind was revisiting glimpses of our powwow, so I was awake.

"Had a lot to do today Merle." Father said in a clipped way.
The door creaked and the metal hangers rattled as he put his
jacket away in the front closet. Voices and noises in the living
room didn't have far to go to get to our room. I laid real still,
just in case he came looking for me.

"The kids put on a great show today and you missed it."

Momma sounded sad. I was glad that she was telling
Father about our show. I wanted him to be proud of me.

"I hear they weren't the ONLY ones in this here show."

My stomach tightened. Father didn't sound happy.

"No! They weren't. And don't think by makin' them wrong you can get away with not bein' here," Momma barked. "They're half you too ya know."

I clenched my fists, drew myself into a tight ball and tried to disappear. They were fighting over me again.

"That's what's scary." Father's voice softened. "Everything that's part of me dies."

Something creaked followed by rustling noises. I think Father sat down next to Momma.

"I'm sorry about your mother." Momma cooed. "What happened then wouldn't happen today."

"What makes you so sure? Just a few years ago 25 blacks and 9 whites got their lives snuffed out within 10 miles of here fighten' over who should live on some stupid piece of earth; the fighten' Irish are at war with anyone who's tryin' to take their jobs away; and the Catholics and Jews haven't made peace since Jesus was crucified. Prejudice doesn't vanish just because we want it to."

"Well maybe not, but there's no war going on in Taylor Township right now."

Get real Merle. Everybody's out for themselves, anyone different gets thrown to the wolves. it's just a matter of time 'til there's another blood bath."

"What makes you so sure that anyone would want to target us?"

I could hear Father's deep sigh all the way back to my room. "People target anyone who's different. All I'm askin' is for you to teach our kids to blend in, that's all. Let's not blab our mixed bloodline to the rest of the world. Zip it up or there'll be trouble."

Listening to what they said set me wondering about what happened in Father's family such a long time ago. *Was there something about our bloodline that was dangerous? What was so terrible about Father that made people die?* As questions scampered through my head another part of me knew that in the morning whatever was going on would never be discussed openly. They were just more of the things that Father wanted to forget.

Chapter Eleven

## THE TWIRLING FLOWER

The first Saturday after our powwow I went to dance class again. This time I didn't sit in the back watching. I joined the rest of the girls on the dance floor. They'd been working on their routines and getting ready for the Christmas dance recital since October. It was now mid November, I was a little behind, but because I'd been practicing on my own, I could do most of the movements pretty well.

The recital is a big deal. All the girls get to be in the chorus, but some of the better ones get solos. As soon as Miss Trixie explained some of the routines, I knew I wanted to be the twirling red flower. Red was the color of Christmas. A day we doubly celebrated — it being Jesus birth and Momma's birthday.

"Hold your arms out to the side. Soften your legs. Step right. Bring your left arm across to meet the right. Push off with your left foot. Turn," Miss Trixie called out in class. "Good, Lonestar. Chaîné, chaîné, chaîné, step-turn, step-turn, step-turn."

I kept my arms rounded in front of me, head high, legs tight, as I spun across the wood floor as quickly as I could. The momentum stirred the air and whipped it around my body. I focused on one spot in the corner of the room as I turned so I wouldn't get dizzy

I felt strong, sure and steady. Something deep inside moved me forward, urging me on to be the best I could be. When I reached the far side, I stopped and looked around, suddenly everything seemed quiet.

When I told Momma about wanting to be the red flower, she asked Harriet Helmsly, our next door neighbor, to make a special tutu for me to wear to class. Since she made those beautiful butterfly wings, I figured she could make anything.

I stood on a wooden crate in Harriet's basement. That's where she kept her sewing supplies. My head buzzed with excitement.

"I'm throwing him out Merle." Harriet told Momma through a mouthful of pins as I got fitted for my red tutu.

I kept my chin up and stared straight ahead like I wasn't listening.

"What are you talking about?" Momma held the red netting up around my waist.

"Good for nothing! My husband's been carrying on with the woman in that red brick house on the next block," Harriet shook her head sideways. "Our bank account's whittling its way down to zilch. Our house payments are in arrears. And when I ask what's goin' on, he just shrugs his shoulders and shakes his head. It's all too much." Harriet gathered the netting into folds, took a few pins out of her mouth, and stuck them into the top of the waistline. "Your husband's a saint Merle. He's been doin' my husband's jobs for over a year. Painted the living room. Repaired the washer. Put a new light fixture on the front porch."

Momma was real quiet for a long time, then she finally asked, "didn't your husband say he was sorry?"

Harriet dabbed at the tears in her eyes then stuffed the hanky back into her waistband. "Sure. But I can't trust 'em. He's put everything we own into jeopardy." She unwrapped the red netting from my waist and walked over to her sewing machine. The machine was up against the long brick wall in front of me, in between two metal shelves filled with material, feathers, gold ribbons and jars full of antique buttons.

"How are you gonna keep your family together without a husband?" Momma walked over and stood next to Harriet.

"Been workin' at the factory for over a year. I don't make as much money as my husband, but I can pay the mortgage.

Geraldine is almost out of school. I'll get by on my own." Harriet pumped the pedal and pushed the material along.

I sat down on the box I'd been standing on and watched the pedal go up and down. It made a kind of whirring sound, like wind blowing through trees in the forest. Suddenly, I felt dizzy. I stood up, walked over to the old stuffed chair Harriet kept in the corner and sat down.

"It's never easy to give up, but sometimes it's harder to hang on," Harriet mumbled.

I leaned my head back over the soft arm of the chair and closed my eyes. I'm not sure how long I slept, but when I woke up Momma and Harriet were still talking. My red tutu hung from the top of the left shelf on a hanger.

I tried to lift my head, then my arms and legs, but I couldn't. The air burned it's way down my throat like I'd swallowed a hot poker when I opened my mouth to speak.

That night Momma had me gargle with salt water. Before I went to bed, she slathered my neck with Vick's, then wrapped some strips of old flannel p.j.'s over the yucky thick grease.

I felt much better in the morning. Not totally okay, but good enough to go to school.

"You stink," Sean said as we stood in front of Ann Marie's house waiting for the school bus.

I ran my fingers over my throat to make sure I'd taken the flannel off. "Do not," I snarled.

It was so hard to wait for Saturday. Even though I was going to bed earlier every day, on account of I was tired, it still seemed like each day was a week in itself. Momma'd kept up her Vick's treatment. No amount of moans and groans could make her stop.

"Do I smell like Vicks, Donna?" I asked as we walked to dance class.

"Yeah! Lonestar." Donna pulled the collar of her pink jacket up to cover her neck.

"Bad huh?" My stomach tightened.

"Just mediciny. That's all." We crossed at the light on Ecorse Road and Pelham.

"Good." That didn't sound as bad as Sean made it out to be. Sometimes brothers can be a pain.

I pulled my red tutu on over my shorts and T-shirt when we got there, put on my new ballet slippers and laced up the pink ribbons Momma sewed on. Donna's eyes got real big.

I stepped onto the dance floor and looked at myself in the mirror. Goosebumps jumped out on my arms. I looked like a *real* dancer. As I stared straight ahead, my image shifted, I became a red flower. The flower twirled in and out of six other girls on a stage with such grace that it took my breath away.

"Nice tutu." Miss Trixie's voice jarred me back to where I was.

I blinked my eyes. Donna was at the ballet bar doing warm ups with the other girls. I turned to join her. Some of the girls gave me a weird look, but I didn't mind.

"Focus on a point in the corner of the room," Miss Trixie shouted as she called us out one at a time to do our turns diagonally across the floor. "One, two, three." She pounded out the rhythm with her foot. "Step-turn, step-turn. Chaîné, chaîné, chaîné."

When it was my turn, I did everything Miss Trixie said. I focused and turned over and over again. Half way across the floor I started to get that dizzy feeling I got when Harriet was making my tutu. I tried to take in more air, but the dizziness just got worse.

The next thing I knew, I was lying flat on my back on the dance floor. I tried to get up, but I couldn't. My legs felt like Jell-O. I was so embarrassed.

Someone must have called Momma. She borrowed a car from one of our neighbors to fetch me. "Why didn't you tell me you were gettin' worse instead of better?" Momma put her arms around my waist and pulled me up.

"I didn't want to miss my chance to be the twirling red flower," I mumbled.

"I'll bring your stuff by your house tomorrow," Donna said. "You'll feel better then."

Momma put me to bed in Sean's lower bunk. It was too hard for me to climb the ladder up to my bed. She wrapped my neck in Vicks slathered on strips of old flannel p.j.'s again, pulled the blinds down and kissed me on the forehead. "Sleep's a good cure, Lonestar."

I didn't have a choice. As soon as Momma left I was out cold. *I felt like I was in a small boat drifting out to sea.*

When I woke up I heard Momma talking to Ann Marie, Sean and Brucie in the living room. The smell of Momma's coffee drifted down the hall and into my room. The blinds were still shut. Flashes of light peaked in through the cracks on the bottom and edges.

"Some kids never walk again," Ann Marie said. "I hear people talk when they come to the club to hear me sing. If she has Polio, she might even die. It's an epidemic you know."

"Die?" Sean said in a worried voice. "She's too tough to die. I've watched her dance when she doesn't know I'm looking. Goes up on her toes, spins, leaps in the air."

"Yeah!" Brucie added, "she's strong."

"Well she's been asleep for two days," Momma's voice dipped up and down. She sounded real worried. "I tried to wake her up to eat, but all she'd have was water and chicken broth."

*Asleep for two days? What happened to Saturday?* I wondered. *Polio? Never walk again? When did I have sips of water and broth?* I lifted my head up. I had to tell them I was just a little woozy.

My head fell back on my pillow. I reached my hands up towards the wood slats on the bottom of the top bunk to pull myself up. But, I couldn't. I fell back asleep. *In my dream, I ran with a kite, but instead of the kite catching the wind, I did. I flew high up into the sky. The Earth below was as small as the back of a turtle. It was scary. "Help," I cried. "Help."*

When I opened my eyes a strong smell of sage filled the room. The shades were open. Light streamed through the window near the dresser. Warm hands glided over the outside of my body, above the covers. "Grandma," I whispered.

*"E'ne,* I'm here."

"I have to get up," I said. "Momma's worried." The words stung my throat. I pulled the blanket back, rolled over onto my side and tried to throw my legs over the edge of the bunk-bed. But, my legs wouldn't move. Some elephant took over my body.

"Lonestar," Grandma's eyes fixed on mine, "don't go so far away."

"Okay," I rasped. But I couldn't help it. I snuggled back into the bed covers, closed my eyes and drifted off again.

*This time as I flew into the sky, white fluff started to whirl around me. Slowly, the fluff turned into a bear. Animals bring messages from the other side, Grandma said. I tried to talk to the bear, but I couldn't.*

I opened my eyes. Grandma was still on the floor beside me. Her fingers tapped out a rhythm on my arm. *Tat a tat.* "Where are you going in your sleep?" She asked.

"Into the sky." I swallowed hard. The pain was back.

"What are you doing there?"

"I don't know. Last time I saw a bear. I tried to find out what she wanted to tell me from the other world, but she didn't say anything."

"Bears hibernate. They go into the Earth for the winter to reenergize, dream, and remove themselves from ... life." Wrinkles raced across Grandma's forehead.

"Hibernate?" I said. "Do people hibernate?"

Grandma reached up and put her hand across my forehead. "You feel real hot," she said. My question got lost in the worried look on her face. She jumped up and ran to the doorway. "Call the doctor, Merle," she shouted.

Pots and pans clanked. Feet padded down the hall. "Frank hates doctors, you know that." Momma wiped her hands over the front of her blue apron as she looked at me over Grandma's shoulder.

"Do it anyway," Grandma answered. "Now! Before it's too late."

Chapter Twelve

## CONTAGIOUS

Dr. Young came for a house call. His office was up on Telegraph Road, two blocks away. We passed it whenever we took the bus, but we'd never actually seen him for anything. Any doctoring we needed usually came from our kitchen...or Grandma's.

"She's gonna be okay isn't she doctor?" Momma stood above Dr. Young while he bent down to check my heart, throat, ears, eyes, and knee joints. "We'll see," Dr. Young replied. His eyes looked bloodshot, like Father's did when he was up all night.

"Of course she is." Father stood in the doorway, just beyond the foot of the bunk bed. He wasn't wearing his lucky shirt.

When Dr. Young finished he looked up at Momma, bit down on his upper lip, then moved away from my bed and stood in the doorway with Father. "She has a bad infection; her throat's red and filled with pus. Looks like a strep infection. Her lymph nodes and joints are swollen. My guess is that she's had it for a while and now it's moved into something more serious."

"Oh! My God, it's Polio isn't it?" Momma cried. She slapped her head like she did sometimes when she thought she should have known something ahead of time.

"No. It's not Polio but it is serious ... and contagious. She has to be isolated." Doctor Young took off his heavy rimmed glasses and wiped his forehead with the sleeve of his white jacket.

My eyes felt heavy, but I forced myself to stay awake so I could listen. Momma sounded real nervous.

"If it's what I think it is we have to start her on antibiotics as soon as possible." Dr. Young whispered, but I paid close attention.

"The disease affects the body's connective tissues — primarily the heart and joints. Sometimes it lasts a lifetime. It can weaken her so much that she may never be able to walk again."

"May never walk again?" The doctor's words sounded like gravel shooting out from under tires on the road. Why do people keep saying that? I wanted to shout out that they were wrong about that part. I was gonna walk, for sure I was gonna walk, and dance.

"What're we gonna do? We only have two bedrooms?" Momma's voice sounded far away.

"No school. No stress. No moving around," Doctor Young said. "Give her a shot of Penicillin every four hours and I'll drop in to check on her in a few days."

"A shot? You want *me* to give her a shot?" Momma squirmed.

"It's a wonderful thing this new medicine. But, Rheumatic Fever is a very serious illness and it's going around right now."

"Rheumatic Fever?" Father questioned. "Come on Doc. She can't have anythin' that serious. She was runnin' around playin' just a week ago. Romantic Fever is more like it, hey Lassie?" Father called out to me. "You'll be fine."

*Yes, I'll be fine.* I thought. *Father's right. I'll be up and around in no time.*

"MacLean's know how to fight anything and anyone. They've made their way from one country to another with nothin' but pride in their hearts." Father came over to where I was, knelt down next to my bed and put his hand on mine. It felt good to have him next to me. *"Bas no beatha,* Lassie. Life or death." A flicker of worry flashed across his face. "You can beat this thing."

"For sure," I said. I liked that Father believed in me.

A week after the doctor visited, Momma told me that a man in a dark blue suit from Public Health nailed a quarantine sign to the front door. CONTAGIOUS DO NOT ENTER, was written in black letters on a piece of heavy cardboard about a foot wide and six inches long. Donna couldn't come and visit. None of the neighborhood kids could. We didn't need a sign to keep my friends away. I didn't want anybody to catch what I had.

Father carried me across the hall and tucked me into the double bed he and Momma had in their room. There was a big window that faced Jackson Street next to Momma's vanity and mirror. "You can watch the kids play in front of our house," Father said. "It's not like bein' out there, but it's better than nothin'." His eyes glassed over as he turned to close the door.

Momma slept on my top bunk in the room across the hall. Father slept on Sean's lower bunk, next to Brucie's old army cot.

Sean was sent to live with Aunt Raven, Uncle Howard and their two kids so that he wouldn't catch my disease. I'm not sure why Brucie wasn't sent away too. What with him hurting himself all the time, maybe they figured he wasn't safe no matter where he was.

Sometimes I heard Mother and Father talking about me through the crack in my door.

"It's been a month and I don't see her getting better," Momma said. "She sleeps mostly, Frank. My heart hurts so bad for her. I put the little wooden star Donna gave her in the tip of her new ballet shoes and hung them on the vanity mirror, just above her red tutu, but I don't think she's noticed. It's so sad that she didn't get to use them for the show she wanted to be in. She's just like one big stuffed doll."

I pulled myself up and leaned my head against the backboard. Sure enough, my ballet slippers were just where Momma said they were and just below – on top of the vanity – I could see the red netting that made up my tutu. The light from the front window made the pink satin look soft and warm. The red netting looked like a bird nest big enough for an eagle.

I wanted to get up – put my shoes and tutu on – feel the softness of my wooden star – but I was too weak. I wondered if my small gray stone was still safely tucked away in my cigar box in the chester drawers I shared with my brothers.

I put my head back down on the pillow. The cracks in the ceiling got fuzzy. My mouth felt dry.

"I gotta figure out how to pay for all the doctor's visits and those meds, Merle," Father's voice drifted down the hallway. "That Penicillin costs a fortune. It better work."

*It's gonna work,* I thought. *For sure, it's gonna work.*

Momma made fresh chicken soup every week. She added carrots one day, peas another and something like squiggly weeds on other days. She propped me up with a pillow so she could spoon feed me. Even though I slurped and spilled she still called me her "good little girl".

Whenever she had time, she grabbed a volume of the Book of Knowledge from the living room bookcase or another book on history, sat next to me in bed and read something she thought I should know.

"In the 18th and 19th centuries, thousands of Scots, like my father, your grandfather, brought their clan spirit to America." Momma wrapped her arm around my shoulders and hugged me close. "They were powerful craftsman and adventurous explorers."

Momma sighed. "My father knew how to fit pipes, so when homes and businesses added indoor plumbing, his trade was in demand. He was a hard worker, your grandfather. I was just fourteen when he died."

I nodded and snuggled deeper into Momma's shoulder. I thought about Grandma's quilt. It was made up of old clothes from people she loved. One blue piece was my grandfather's. It felt rough.

"Many of the Scots, separated from their families in the old country, intermarried with American Indians. The marriages often caused problems. Even though the Amerindians shared their expertise in hunting, fishing, and growing crops, the Europeans looked down on them. They saw them as uneducated, 'stupid'. Sometimes they took children away from their tribes to educate them in what they called the 'American Way'. They took away their language and everything that would have been familiar to them. So, this new mixture was forced to lie about who they were."

*Father didn't talk about his family, I thought. Maybe they'd learned to lie and hide a long time ago. But, a long time ago wasn't now. No reason to lie and hide now.*

Giving me shots every four hours made Momma nervous. She'd rub her hands together, say a quick prayer, then find a new spot to stick the needle into my rear end. "I never planned on bein' a nurse," she joked. But it was always with a quiver in her throat. Afterwards I could hear her in the hall crying.

Goldy snuck in when Momma forgot to close the door tight. She'd put her face up on the bed and lick my fingers. "Bad dog," Momma would say dragging Goldy out by the collar. "You wanna give Lonestar another disease." But, I didn't mind. Her mouth always felt soft and clean to me.

Father seemed to be working even longer hours than before. Sometimes the days turned into weeks. "Ford needs him to travel a bit and kind of trouble shoot," Momma said when I asked about him. "You know how good he is with fixin' broken machines. And...well...with the war on and all...he's got a lot to do." The way her eyes darted around the room, I figured she was only telling me part of the story, but I didn't say anything.

With father gone a lot, Grandma came over more often. She didn't listen to the quarantine signs. "Gets rid of all the bad stuff in the air," she said one evening as she waved burning sage like a wand around me, the bed, and the room. I breathed in its snappy smell. The overhead light cast its soft glow across Grandma's head and shoulders as she moved.

When she was done, she lit a white candle and placed it in a dish on top of Momma's vanity – away from my ballet shoes and red tutu. She reached into the deep pocket of her beige skirt, took a pinch of tobacco out of her small leather pouch and dropped it onto the top of the candle. The smoke turned a soft gray as its fingers flickered upwards. "Great Spirit, *Wakontah*," Grandma said as she lifted her arms toward the sky. "Bring your healing light – from the moon – stars, and sun, into this room." The long braid that she usually wore on top of her head hung down the middle of her back and stopped at her waist. She stayed motionless for about a minute, then turned and walked toward the bed, and me.

"Why do you use tobacco?" I asked as I looked up into her dark eyes. "You used it in the Stone Circle when you gave me my last birthday present. Aunt Dawn used it when she gave me the Talisman Reading. I know it's ceremonial – and you're not supposed to smoke it – but what does that mean?"

Grandma sat on the edge of the bed. The candle continued to flicker over her left shoulder. "Well...some folks do smoke it...but it's really meant to be used in a sacred way." Grandma wobbled her head from side to side like she did sometimes when she was thinking. "The fire helps me focus on my words and trust that my prayer will be heard." She reached out for my hand. "The smoke from the burning tobacco serves as a witness to my sincerity. It's called 'The Truth Bearer'. Prayer makes me feel like I'm not alone."

"Me too," I said.

Grandma took a deep breath and sighed. "It's hard to be alone." She waited a few seconds, then went on. "After two months in bed, I think you're getting better. You didn't fall asleep while I was talking."

"Two months?" I questioned. "Did I miss Christmas and Momma's birthday?"

Grandma bit down on her lower lip. "We didn't really celebrate this year. Too much other stuff got in the way."

Chapter Thirteen

## DON'T GIVE UP

"Red Rover, Red Rover send Brucie on over," voices called out in front of our house one afternoon in mid February. I pulled myself up, leaned against my pillow and looked out the window.

Five big kids stood in a circle on our front snow covered lawn holding hands. They were dressed in heavy coats and gloves. Brucie stood about twenty feet away. I could tell by the look on his face that he was scared. If he didn't break through the line, his team would lose.

I took a deep breath and watched as Brucie dug one foot after the other deep into the snow – moving forward as fast as he could. His nose and cheeks pink from the cold air. His green scarf flapping in the wind. Little wisps of warm air puffed out of his mouth like smoke from a pop gun. They shot out, then disappeared into thin air like the days, weeks, and months I'd spent lying in bed. In a second, it was all over. Brucie went flying backwards into the snow. His teammates threw their hands up into the air and cried out in frustration.

I had to get up and walk. Not just to help Brucie, but to start my life over again. I was missing school, playing in the snow, missing dance class and mostly missing Donna. Later that night when everyone was asleep I made my first move.

My pink dancing slippers hung on the far left corner of Momma's vanity mirror. My red tutu was laid out just below that – on the vanity shelf. I did notice them there – every single time I opened my eyes. When I heard Momma talking in the hall with Father about me not seeing them, I didn't say anything. What could I say that they would understand? Instead, I turned aside and stared at the cracks in the wall.

The porch light gave my pink shoes and tutu a fairy like sparkle. I knew I was supposed to stay in bed, rest my heart, let my body heal. But something in me didn't want to do that anymore.

I leaned my back against the wall, turned sideways, put one leg over the side of the bed, then the other. My heart pounded hard against my chest. I really, really wanted to get up, but doing it was something else. I hadn't tried to walk since last November, four months ago.

I eased myself up and leaned one leg against the side of the bed to balance. A whirring sound pulsed through my ears as blood rushed out of my head. Fire screamed through my body. It was burning through the dry rot – making room for something new to be reborn. I reached out for the wall next to the bed – steadied myself – and looked straight ahead at Momma's vanity. It was about ten feet away. Ten feet that seemed like a hundred miles.

*She's just like a big stuffed doll,* Momma had said. Tears welled up in my eyes. Momma was right. My old strong body was gone – lost somewhere in the dark past.

I took a deep breath – straightened up – let go of the wall – and stared hard at the dangling pink shoes. "You can do it," I whispered. The whirring noise in my head got louder. It sounded like Momma's washing machine doing a final spin. I lifted my head higher – pulled my shoulders back – inched one foot forward – then the other. My knees buckled. Hot flames from the fire burned the inside of my chest. I forced myself to breathe through the heat. The sizzling pain of new life made me dizzy.

"You can do it," I said again. "Remember how hard it was to learn to do those darned *chaîné* turns. You practiced – and practiced – 'till you got it right."

I stared at the red tutu this time – took another deep breath through the heat – and shuffled forward another inch. The whirring noise got louder. "Focus on the tutu," I said. "Focus on one part." My eyes stung as I willed them to do what I needed. My vision blurred. The vanity – shoes – tutu – and walls turned into one big gray cloud. I blinked my eyes over and over.

*Bring your healing light -- from the moon -- stars, and sun, into this room,* Grandma had said in a prayer. "Do it now," I pleaded. "Now."

My vision cleared. This time I stared at my pink shoes. I was going to walk again. Nothing was going to stop me. Aunt Dawn gave me my future. She read it in the talisman stones. *You're gonna move and have lots of adventures,* she said. I shuffled forward another inch – stopped – took another painful breath and again steadied myself.

*She may never walk again,* Dr. Young had said. "I will walk," I whispered. My lungs burned again. I felt shaky again. But I didn't stop. I stepped into the fire again, forced myself to breathe through the heat again, and shuffled forward again.

*Bas no beatha,* Father had said. *Life or death. You can beat this thing.* I focused on the pink shoes and shuffled forward. "Yes, I can. I can. I can," I whispered.

*You'll look so cute in your red tutu that Miss Trixie will let you be the dancing flower,* Momma had said. I focused on my red tutu and shuffled forward again, and again, and again.

Finally – head spinning – gasping for breath – I was there. I reached out. My hand shook as I unhooked the long ribbon that held my shoes. I put the ribbon around my neck so my shoes would hang over my shoulders. The sweet smell of wood, satin, and resin drifted into my nose. My chest quivered as I breathed it in.

I ran the tips of my fingers over the red netting of my tutu. It felt stiff – and still new – like it was waiting in the shadows – to be used. I wanted to put it on, spin across the room, go back in time, be a part of the show. But, I knew I couldn't. I left the tutu where it was and slowly turned around. It took all my strength to make it to the vanity. Now I had to make it back to bed before anybody came in.

"God don't let me fall," I pleaded as I turned around to head back. A car headlight flared through the edges of the blinds.

*Was it Father? If it was he'd for sure come into my room and I'd get into trouble.* I shuffled forward a little bit faster. Fireballs seared my insides. Explosions of life went off inside my heart.

*Did someone walk up the front steps?* I stopped and listened. No, it was quiet outside. The only sounds were of my heart beating like a wild drum and my breath forcing its way through the fire in my lungs.

I moved forward again. Fear mixed with joy. Pain mixed with excitement. My ballet shoes swung one way then the other as I made my way across the bedroom floor. I was in the midst of an adventure. Maybe not the kind Aunt Dawn meant, but certainly an adventure. Grandma's prayer had worked. The healing light – from the moon – stars, and sun was in this room. I could feel it. *You can beat this thing,* Father had said. "Yes," I whispered. "I know I can."

I eased myself onto the edge of the bed. It was still quiet in the house. I was safe. One leg jiggled, then the other, followed by a loud thump, in my chest as I slid under the covers. The thumping felt good, like something happy and alive was trying to get out. I reached across the front of my shoulder and brought one of my slippers up to my face. The leather felt smooth and soft as I rubbed it against my cheek. The rich scent filled my lungs and eased the searing pain in my lungs.

Then, something fell out of the slipper. A small object landed on my pillow, next to my head. I put the shoe back on my shoulder and fumbled for the object. It was the wooden star Donna and her mom gave me. *To remember that it's the journey that counts,* she had said. *Kind of like your name don't ya think? A lone star.* I'd forgotten that Momma said she put it there.

I missed my friend. Just thinking about her made my heart ache in a different way, one that felt good. I wanted to run down to the Jackson Street Creek and catch tadpoles, turn cartwheels on the grass, share stories, dance and go to school, with her.

I closed my eyes, put the star in the middle of my chest, took a deep breath and tried to find Donna's face in the dark.

At first all I could see was a shadow, then her feet, legs, arms, and face slowly came into view. "Donna!" I cried. "I miss you so much."

*"I'm here Lonestar. Right here!" Donna's ponytail bobbed up and down as she reached out for my hand, pulled me through a doorway and right into Miss Trixie's Dance Studio. We lined up against the far wall with about five other girls.*

*"No time to dawdle," Miss Trixie clapped her hands. "You go first Lonestar."*

*"Me?" I hadn't been in class for a very long time. Not only that, I'd been in bed, doing nothing. Nothing. I looked over at Donna. She just smiled and waved me on. I took a deep breath, found a spot diagonally across the room, pointed my toe, rounded my arms and began.*

*"Bravo," Miss Trixie called out. "Bravo."*

*"Don't we just have the best life in the whole world?" Donna said.*

*"Mmmmm. You betcha we do. The best life ever. Mmmmm."*

Someone shook my shoulders and jiggled the bed. I opened my eyes. Donna was gone. It was morning. Sun was coming through the window lighting up the whole room. I reached around for my slippers. They were still there hidden under the blanket.

"You were talking in your sleep," Momma said. Worry lines popped out on her forehead. She pulled her faded robe up around her neck. "Did you have a bad dream?"

I looked up at Momma and smiled. "I was dreaming about Donna. She came to play with me."

"Oh! Lonestar," Momma's eyes teared up. "I should have...told you before." Momma's shoulders started to shake, "but I didn't want to ... you've been so weak and frail ... and ... Donna can't come and play with you any more."

"It's because I'm contagious. Right?" My stomach tensed.

"Contagious ... yes ... no ... it's ..." Momma's chin quivered. She sat down on the bed next to me.

"She'll come back when I'm better." I squeezed my fingers around the star under my blanket.

Momma brushed my hair back behind my ears. "I didn't tell you before because you've been so sick, but...Donna...well, she's been sick too." Momma swallowed hard. "And, she's getting better like I am, right?" I stared at Momma waiting for her to tell me what I wanted to hear.

Momma shook her head. "No, she's not."

"She just needs more time," I said. "Yeh! Some people take longer to get better than others." Momma shook her head from side to side. "No, Fiona...the Penicillin...well it didn't work for her." I hadn't thought about Donna being sick. I hadn't thought about anybody else being sick. Most of the time I'd drifted from one dream to the other.

I looked hard into Momma's face. "She's still...getting better like me," I said. A dull ache in my heart told me I was wrong. Momma shook her head. "No, she's not." Tears rolled down her cheeks.

A flaming arrow shot into my chest. It started a wildfire that ripped through the hills and canyons buried deep inside of me. Sweaty beads rolled across my forehead and dripped into my eyes. Heat sucked all the air out of my body.

"Why didn't you tell me?" I cried. The vanity, windows, door, Momma's face all spun out into one big blur. I wanted to hit something. Make something else hurt like I did. I clenched my weak hands into fists and raised them into the air ready to strike out...but they fell limply down by my side.

Momma laid down on top of the covers and pulled my head into her shoulder. My body started to quiver so hard the bed shook.

"No. No. No." I yelled. The screams broke through a wall of numbness. Four months worth of pain tumbled through. I'd been getting better so I could dance with Donna. Now she was gone. "It's not fair!" I cried. "I want her back. Jesus brought people back, why can't we?"

"I wish we could, Lonestar." Momma sobbed alongside me. "Oh, how I wish we could."

Night after night, with my memory of Donna, when everyone was asleep, I dragged myself across the room, put my pink slippers over my shoulders and danced. I was getting stronger with her help. From then on I would dance for us both. *As long as I was alive I was never...never going to let her die.*

A few weeks later, when I was still half asleep, I felt warm, angel hands smooth out the wrinkles above my body again. Magic fingers moved a layer of light from the tips of my toes up to the top of my head. It made me feel tingly, like one of those sparklers we used to hold up on the fourth of July.

"Mmm." I opened my eyes. "Grandma?"

*"E'ne, yes."* Grandma leaned over the bed. She helped me sit up as she fluffed my pillow, then put it behind my head. When I was comfortable, she sat on the edge of the bed, reached towards the side table and handed me a small glass of juice. "Drink this." Her dark eyes flashed. Wrinkles sprang up around the edges of her mouth and at the tops of her round cheeks.

I took the glass and drank the green grass drink. "I've been dreamin', Grandma."

"Tell me." She nodded. "Dreams are good."

"What if what I think is real, isn't, and what I think isn't, really is real?"

"Everyone has to figure that out for themselves, Lonestar, that's part of the choices in your destiny."

"My head is such a jumble, Grandma. I don't know how I'll ever sort my way through things."

"You will, Lonestar. Be patient. But your way might not be like anybody else's. Your way will be just what makes sense to you. We're not all supposed to be alike you know."

"Uh huh."

Grandma got that certain look in her eye, like when she had a secret, reached into the top pocket of her yellow apron, pulled out my small gray stone, and laid it in the palm of my hand.

"Where did you find this, Grandma?" The stone felt warm and smooth.

"Oh! I didn't find it." Grandma got a mischievous look in her eyes. "It found me." She clasped her hands and brought them up to her mouth. "You're not contagious anymore. Doctor Young said you can start to learn to walk again."

"Not contagious?" Tears welled up in my eyes and rolled down my cheeks. I squeezed my fingers around my stone. *"Bas no beatha,* life or death. Warriors stick together," I whispered. It was hard to believe my siege was over. I didn't say anything about dancing in my visions with Donna. I didn't want her and Momma to worry that I was getting out of bed ahead of time.

"And there's a few people waiting at the door to see you." Grandma handed me a hanky. "Come on in," she yelled. I blew my nose. There was a loud bark and some scratching at the door. I wiped my cheeks with the sleeve of my pink pajamas. The door swung open. Goldy rushed in, followed by Sean and Brucie.

"They let me come back, Lonestar," Sean said in a deep crackly voice I didn't recognize. He must have forgotten to call me Fiona.

I looked up into his dark eyes. He looked taller than I remembered. "I'm glad you're home again."

"I'm sorry about Donna." He added in a sad voice. I nodded. Just hearing Donna's name made me feel like I'd fallen off a mountain.

"Wanna come down to the creek to ice skate, Lonestar?" Brucie said all excited.

"Soon as I get stronger," I said. Every move I made was still an effort.

Momma stood by the door away from everybody. Tears welled up in her eyes. She wiped them away with the hem of her faded blue apron. The one that was new a few dreams ago. The smell of Indian corn bread drifted down the hall and into my room. Father hated it. Momma never baked it when he was around. I wasn't sure how long he'd been gone and I was afraid to ask. *Maybe it was my fault he wasn't here,* I thought. *My fever might've scared him away.*

Chapter Fourteen

## THOU SHALT NOT

We got a postcard from Father a few weeks ago. "I'm sorry," it said. There wasn't a signature, just a postmark from Las Vegas. Harriet Helmsly gave it to Momma. She's been forwarding our mail. Momma threw it in the trash, but I dug it out and stuck it in my cigar box along with my small gray stone, the star Donna gave me and other special things.

With Father gone and no rent money coming in we had to move in with relatives. We've stayed with three of Momma's sisters, one at a time, for almost three months. Only a couple more relatives left to go. Not that we only have a few more, we have tons, but only a few more are moving-in possibilities. I wanted to stay with Grandma, but Momma said there wasn't room for all of us to stay there at the same time. I didn't think there was room for all of us anywhere. Momma was real upset. Big bald patches the size of dimes dotted the back of her head like she had a bad haircut.

"Thou shalt, honor thy mother and father." Preacher MacNeal said as he stood behind the altar. His gold and white satin alb hung over his small shoulders and floated down the front of his long robe. When he waved his arms in the air, and his full sleeves flapped back and forth. He looked like a giant bird ready to take off.

Momma, Sean, Brucie and me sat ten rows back on wooden benches. My mind wandered off and on, but I heard that honor part. Honor meant to obey. It was hard to honor Father since he wasn't around. Momma never did say why he left, but I figured it was my fault.

After the shalts, came the shalt nots. "Thou shalt not honor any graven images." Strange words. Thou shalt not run

102

away, wasn't on the list. Father went on a war path when I ran away last year, now he's done the same thing. *Bas no beatha. Life or death. Ye haf ta stick tagether,* he'd say. *But, now we're all unstuck.*

I clicked the heels of my patent leather shoes together as I sat listening to the sermon. It felt good to push in and out with the new muscles in my legs. It was hard to remember when I couldn't walk. It seemed like a far away bad dream. Donna dying seemed unreal too. Sometimes I think about running over to her house to dance and play. Then I remember ... I can't. She's gone. We're gone. And nothing is the same.

Grandma took me to Donna's house to say "goodbye" before we moved out of our Jackson Street house. The front yard where we used to practice our dance steps looked smaller than I remembered. The big tree in front of her house was still there, but since it was winter at that time, the leaves were all gone. The heavy branches looked like giant arms reaching into the sky for something I couldn't see.

*You were a good friend to my little girl,* Mrs. Tiger said as we all stood in her dark living room. All the curtains were closed. Her dark face was gray. *We were like sisters,* I replied.

I looked past Mrs. Tiger to the picture of Donna and me on the end table next to the sofa. Our bright smiles looked out into the darkened room. *We're gonna be friends forever,* Donna had said a lifetime ago. I bit down on my lower lip to hold back my tears. Losing her left a big hole that nothing can ever fill.

*I didn't know what to say,* I said to Grandma as we walked down Mrs. Tiger's front steps.

*Sometimes, it's best not to say too much.* Grandma squeezed my hand. *Showin' your love is enough.*

The memory gave me a lump in my throat. Momma reached over and put her left hand on my knee. Her touch felt warm, comforting. Sometimes she knows just what to do to make me feel better.

I looked down at her chewed up nails. Some of the fingers had band-aids on them. The inside of her wedding rings had band-aids too. They weren't broken, they just didn't fit anymore. Sean told her to take them off and sell them the other day. Momma pretended she didn't hear and kept right on whipping up the mashed potatoes she was making for dinner.

It was almost my birthday, just a few weeks away, June 16th. Thirteen would mean I'm not a kid anymore. Aunt Dawn gave me one of her prayer feathers on our last visit to her house. *This here's a really special one,* Aunt Dawn had said as she handed me a six inch white feather. *For special prayers.* Her dangling earrings made a ringing sound as she picked up a cardboard box with colored string and handed it to me. *Wrap the pointed end with colored string as you say your prayer,* she said. *It'll help you focus.*

Every time I could be alone, I took out the box with my supplies. "Bring Father home," I prayed as I twisted and re-twisted the yellow, blue and green string around the quill.

We shook hands with everybody near us like we always did when the sermon was over. Then Momma, Sean, Brucie and me headed down the corridor to Fellowship Hall.

Momma's relatives dotted the room like periods at the end of sentences in a book. I counted up nine aunts, five uncles and ten cousins. Grandma wasn't here, she was away on a trip. Uncle Bud never came. Momma says he lives on the streets so they won't let him come in. If you don't have an address you can't be a member of the church. We haven't had an address for at least three months, so I wondered when they'd throw us out.

Sean and Brucie took some sandwiches from the refreshment table next to where we were all standing and headed for the kids table in the back of the room. I stayed with Momma.

"So-ah," Aunt Raven said. "It's settled." Her head bobbed up and down making her big red hat shift across her forehead. *Still* and *silence* were foreign words to her. "You'll come and stay with *us* until you get a job, Merle." Aunt Raven's words came out like an order. She handed Momma a cup of coffee, then took a sip of her own. Steam circled above the cups like words we couldn't hear.

"Us" meant Aunt Raven, Uncle Howard, and their two kids, Shiloh Blue and Willow. The Gray's. That's where Sean lived while I was contagious. Their house was ten miles from Jackson Street in a town called Allen Park.

"You sure there's enough room, Raven?" Momma drew her small shoulders forward and looked down into her purse. Asking for help was part of Momma's "shalt nots."

"We'll make room," Aunt Raven said, dipping a cookie into her coffee. "It's not a palace, but it's warm, and there's always food in the ice-box." Aunt Raven took some waxed paper and brown bags with her wherever she went. That way, when people were finished eating, she could wrap up the extras and take them home. Of course, she didn't do that with strangers, just family.

Crowded or not, that night, with Goldy at our feet, Sean, Brucie and me made our beds on Aunt Raven's living room floor and Momma made hers on the sofa. I took Father's postcard out of my cigar box and put it under my pillow. It helped me feel like he was close by.

Sometime in the dark of the night, I started to smell Father right in front of me. Whiffs of beer, orange juice, and Old Spice after shave drifted around my head. *"Hi!" I said softly. "I've been waiting for you to come."*

*Father looked down at me and smiled a smile that made his eyes sparkle. Music began to play. Without saying a word he pulled me up from my sleeping position, held me close, twirled me into the air and set me down on a dance floor suspended somewhere in space.*

*With me standing beside him, Father reached his hand out into nothingness and came back with a tam just like the one he had on. He placed it on my head. I stood up, rolled my shoulders back and raised my chin like a proud warrioress.*

*Father held one arm up in the air, bent the other at his waist, pointed one foot out, then pulled it up against the side of* the opposite leg. The hem of his red plaid kilt swayed as he hopped from side to side, changing legs with each move.

Happiness raced up my spine and exploded all through me. I felt tingly from the tips of my fingers down to the ends of my toes. I looked up into Father's smiling face, took a deep breath and followed his moves.

When Father switched arms and legs, I was right there with him. Our arms and feet turned and twisted as we circled our way across the floor. The movements seemed familiar. Something buried deep inside helped me to move more gracefully than I'd ever moved before.

When the music stopped and it was over, my whole body felt like it had been stretched to the limit. Father reached out for my hand. He bowed. I curtsied. My heart was beating so hard against my chest that I felt like I could lift it out and hold it in my hands.

Loud clapping and shouts of "terrific, way to go, Lassie," and words I couldn't understand in my dream flew through the air. I squinted my eyes and looked out beyond the dance floor. I thought Father and I were alone. A giant man with bright red hair sat next to a dark woman wearing a long checkered dress. They smiled and waved real friendly like. I didn't know who they were, but they seemed to know me.

Father opened the palm of my hand and kissed it right in the middle, where the lines crisscrossed. It made my skin tingle. "I'll be back soon," he said.

I sat up and looked around the room. It was dark, but I could see the outline of Momma on the couch and Sean, Brucie and Goldy on the floor. I laid back down and cupped my hands together so I could hold the warmth of Father's kiss.

My prayer worked. The dream was a good omen.

Chapter Fifteen

## THE TRICKSTER CAN COME OUT OF NOWHERE

A week later, after school, Momma and Aunt Raven shooed us outside so they could have some quiet time together. Having five kids running around the house was putting everybody on edge. Brucie and Shiloh Blue went up the block to the school yard to play while Sean, Willow and I laid on the grass, heads together, in the front yard trying to see shapes in the clouds.

I loved the sky when it was dotted with puffy clouds. I imagined that I was leaping from one shape to the next and that the sky was endless.

"I see a rabbit," I said pointing up to two puffy clouds.

"Where?" Willow asked. I reached over, took her small hand, and pointed up towards the two clouds. The head was a smaller puff than the body. "Yeah! I see it now," she said. "It even has a tail." She let go of my hand.

I looked, but I couldn't see the tail. "Grandma says that rabbits are 'tricksters.'"

"Tricksters?" Willow asked.

"An animal that can come out of nowhere and disappear like magic." It felt good that I remembered Grandma's words. Going to the Stone Circle had been special. "Sometimes you see 'em and sometimes you don't." My back felt cool against the soft grass. "Grandma says that when you see a rabbit for real, or in a dream she's calling on you to reverse your thinking."

"How do you do that?" Willow asked still looking up into the sky.

I took a deep breath, tilted my head to one side, then the other trying to remember the rest of the story and how to explain it to Willow. I had been angry that Father had forgotten my birthday. It made me think I wasn't important to him. Grandma said that maybe rabbit would want me to see that Father forgetting had nothing to do with me.

"I think it means to not take things others say or do personally," I said. "Other's words are about them, not about you."

Willow rolled onto her side and sat up leaning on one arm. The pink and yellow flowers in her sun dress made her look like a small flower garden. "So, when Momma calls me 'big butt' I should see that I'm not too fat – that it's something about her?"

I smiled. "You are anything but fat, Willow. You're a rail." *I wondered if Aunt Raven thought she herself was fat.* Momma called her 'solid'.

Sean suddenly exploded with excitement. "Look," he said pointing up to the sky. "It's a gigantic dragon and he's swooping down on the ... rabbit." He stood up, grabbed my feet and dragged me forward across the grass. I held tight to my T-shirt to stop it from rumpling up. We all three ended up in fits of laughter, but I wasn't so sure that Sean's teasing was funny.

Our looking for more animals came to an end when Brucie came running up the front sidewalk huffing and puffing so loudly that we turned to see what was going on.

"He said I was a 'bastard'," Brucie cried, blood dripping down his nose and onto his chin. "So I told him he was a stupid jerk. Then he pushed me against the wall." His words spurted out. The front of his checkered shirt was ripped near the elbow.

"Yeah, big guy on the school playground up the street," Shiloh Blue added breathlessly as he caught up. His dark eyes opened as wide as saucers.

"Brucie, you'd find trouble if it was hiding six feet under the ground." Sean made a fist with his right hand and struck the air. "Don't you know better than to pay attention to some kid who's looking to prove how big and strong he is?"

I wondered what Sean was talking about. A few days ago he came home from the school playground with a chipped tooth and blood on the back of his hand. I glared at Sean, put my hands on my hips and rolled my eyes.

"Better get used to bein' called names, little brother," Sean continued to egg Brucie on. "Father's not comin' back, he's ..."

"What, he's what?" I snapped at Sean. "Who made you the great seer of the family?"

Sean puffed out his chest. "At least I see the truth. Which is more than I can say for everybody else in this family." I didn't say anything back in words, but my eyes sent arrows in Sean's direction.

Brucie brushed his torn sleeve over his chin. "What's a bastard anyways?" He looked at the blood on his shirt sleeve and shrugged.

"Shh," I looked around to see who was listening. "Don't say that word. It's nasty – means you don't have a father."

"Isn't that the truth!" Sean growled. Shiloh Blue looked down and dug his foot into the soft grass. Willow shrugged. A look of puzzlement crossed her face.

I took Brucie to the back of the house, turned on the garden hose and washed his face with an old rag I found on the clothesline. I didn't want Momma to see him hurt.

After dinner that night, in the middle of playing Chinese Checkers, Brucie announced that he was not gonna go back to school. I knew it was because of the fight he had on the playground, but I couldn't say anything.

"Not going back to school isn't a choice, Brucie, it's something you've gotta do." Momma piled up the dishes on the sink while we played our game at the table behind her. Her brown hair was fastened with a rubber band in the back in a way that hid most of the bald patches.

"You didn't go back to school." Brucie looked down at the board and jumped his yellow marble over my blue one.

"Brucie, that was not because I didn't want to. I didn't have a choice." Momma turned her face in our direction. A tiny flicker of sadness washed across her eyes.

"Why?" Brucie questioned, still looking down.

I moved my blue marble over one of Sean's red ones then looked up at Momma again.

"Well, I was pregnant with Sean only I didn't know it was Sean then."

"They don't let you go to school when you're pregnant?"

"Not then. The principal called me into the office and said that if he let me go to school I might start an epidemic of some kind."

"An epidemic?" Sean scoffed examining the Chinese Checker Board. "That's stupid. There's no such thing as a pregnancy epidemic."

"Well, I guess I should have had you there to tell him that." Momma pursed her lips.

"Yeah. You should've told him how many of your great-grandmother's relatives died during the European smallpox epidemic in 1837," Sean said angrily as he jumped his marble over mine, killing my men – one after the other. "That was when all of those foreign settlers claimed Indian land and killed them off with their diseases. Now, that was an epidemic." Sean looked at Mom and raised one of his eyebrows like Father did sometimes. "It wiped out entire villages – the Cherokee called it 'rotting face.'"

"Hmm ... well I never was much good at talking back." Momma's eyes narrowed as she studied Sean's face. "I just walked out of Northwestern High School and gave up." Frown lines sprang up on her forehead.

I felt bad that Momma didn't finish school. She was smart. She would have made straight A's, probably would have been the head of the class. Thinking about what happened to the Indians made me sick to my stomach. Too bad they didn't have penicillin way back then. What saved me, might have saved them. But, then maybe not. It didn't save Donna.

Nothing I did or said could take back what happened to Momma or the Indians. But, as I sat there listening something shifted in me. I knew that I was never gonna give up. Not when anybody tried to stop me from doing what I wanted to do. Not when anybody hurt my brothers. Not for anything.

The next day, late afternoon, Brucie and me went back to the playground at the school where the guy had called him a bastard and pushed him against the wall so hard it made his nose bleed. It was just around the corner, but I'd've walked much further if I had to. Fair was fair. *Bas no beatha,* Father would've said. *Life or Death. Ye haf ta stick tagether.*

"That's him." Brucie pointed to a kid leaning against the fence watching a basketball game. His cap was turned backwards. Stains dotted the number 12 on his yellow jersey.

From the size of the guy I figured he was at least three years older than Brucie. He was a good four inches taller and fifty pounds heavier than me. His neck looked like a big tree stump. My heart raced, sweat rolled down the side of my face as I strode towards number 12. I took a deep breath and rolled my shoulders back, Tecumseh style. *Tecumseh was one of the greatest Shawnee warriors,* Grandma had said.

"God, *Wakontah*, Great Spirit, help me to walk tall and be strong," I whispered. The boy jerked his head back a bit and lowered his eyes to meet mine. My stomach tightened into a knot. I took another deep breath and pulled myself up as tall as I could. "You the one who hit my brother and called him a bastard?" I said.

"That twerp next to you?" Number 12 hissed.

My jaw clenched as I held my warrior stance. "Don't you ever pick on Brucie or anybody in my family again." The words flew out loud and strong from some newly carved passageway inside. I felt shaky, but for the first time I knew what it was like to stand up for somebody you loved. I looked over at Brucie. *"Bas no beatha,"* I said. He smiled and nodded.

Number 12 glanced at the boys playing basketball then back at us. He opened and closed his fist. The muscles on his arms expanded. Everyone on the basketball court stopped playing and watched to see what was going to happen next.

"Just shoved 'em outa my way's all," Number 12 mumbled. "And hit him and called him names," I snapped. "Now, leave him alone."

Number 12 shrugged his shoulders, turned around and walked away. I wasn't sure if I scared him or if he just didn't want to be seen hitting a girl.

The next day, Sean, Brucie, Willow, Shiloh Blue and me went back to finding animals in the clouds again. This time, we put our heads together, in the center, forming a circle. That way we could see more easily what the other discovered in the clouds.

Sean found another dragon. This time he found a bow and arrow to go with it. The bow and arrow were strapped across the dinosaur's back. I didn't see it and I didn't think Sean did either.

Willow found a coyote and after studying it for a while announced that it had a collar with a red leash. Shiloh Blue saw two eyes, a nose and a mouth, but not really anything that looked like an animal. Brucie found a tiger, with big sharp teeth.

I found another rabbit. As I laid there thinking about what it was trying to tell me, I heard two voices inside my head. "Father's not coming back," the first voice said. "Yes, he is," the second voice replied. The first voice sounded like Sean. The second voice was soft and gentle – a new one I hadn't heard before. I liked that voice the best.

Momma, Aunt Raven and Uncle Howard came outside for a breath of fresh air. When Momma saw us all laid out, head to head, feet straight out, she ran back in to get her Brownie Camera.

"Don't move,'" Momma yelled as she stood on the porch. "Lyin' like that makes you look like a big star that's fallen from the sky." She smiled as she aimed the camera at us. "Say, 'cheese'."

"Cheese," everyone yelled, but Sean. He said, "twinkle, twinkle" just to be clever. Momma looked into the lens and clicked the gray button. "Oh, my God!" Momma gasped. She lowered the camera and stared over our heads. Something was wrong.

We all sat up and turned to follow Momma's eyes. They stared out at the street. A white car inched past. Momma kept staring at the car – her eyes glassed over.

Momma had been eyeing people in cars, buses and stores for months. Once she went up to a stranger at the market. The man sauntered like Father. She took a deep breath, went up to the man and tapped him on the back. When he turned around – she nearly fainted. It wasn't Father.

"Frank," Momma cried. The car sped up and disappeared around the corner.

"It's *not* Father." Sean glared at the road. "He's not coming back." He turned and stared hard at Momma.

I shot Sean one of my mean looks. The one where I squint my eyes and tighten my lips into a knot. "Sean's just speaking for himself, like the Trickster says," I told Willow. "Father is coming back. He's what I prayed to have for my birthday."

Momma turned away and rushed back into the house.

Chapter Sixteen

## CHOICES

After dinner, as we all sat in the living room listening to Bing Crosby singing "Blue Skies" on the Gray's record player, somebody walked up the front steps and slid a letter into the mail-chute in the door. It made a loud thud as the chute snapped shut. We all jumped up and ran to the window. It was the white car. And, for sure, it was Father. He didn't look back, just slid behind the wheel and closed the door. A web of stillness fell over the room

Aunt Raven put down her beer, picked up the letter and handed it to Momma.

"Throw it away!" Sean hissed. "It's just full of lies." I hated it when Sean was nasty.

Momma held the envelope in her shaky hands. Her chin trembled.

I crossed my fingers behind my back and threw some eye-daggers at Sean. We couldn't keep moving from house to house. We needed help. We needed Father.

Momma stood in the middle of the room, opened the envelope and pulled out the letter. "Dearest Merle," she read aloud. Mist flashed over her eyes. "Each day, without you, is like a rose trying to grow without the Sun." Momma swallowed hard, then cleared her throat. "I miss you so much. Can we try to begin again?" She pressed her lips together and took a deep breath. Her chest quivered. "I've changed a lot. I'll come back for your answer this Saturday evenin' at five." Tears rolled down her cheeks; she brushed them away with the back of her hand. "Your adoring husband, Frank." Deep sighs leaped out of her mouth as she crunched up the letter and held it like a small cloud in the palm of her hand.

She looked at the door, shook her head, looked down and started to pace.  We all moved out of the way to give her room. She walked back and forth, over and over again. After five or ten minutes she looked up. "I'm doin' fine without him, aren't I?" Her voice sounded little. Not like a thirty-one year old mother of three. "Who needs a husband anyway?" Her thin body slumped forward into a question mark. "Especially one who's only home when he wants to be. My friend Harriet Helmsly is makin' ends meet – raisin' Geraldine on her own – I can do it too."

I looked into her watery eyes not knowing what to say. Father had been gone a long time. He shouldn't have run away. But, now we need him back.

"He must think I'm crazy," Momma said.  The evening light cast soft shadows on her hollowed cheeks. Her once fresh blue Easter dress hung loosely around her waist and hips.

"Next thing is he's gonna send you flowers," Sean clenched his jaw. "He probably copied all that sugary stuff he wrote from a book."

Momma stopped pacing, looked at Sean, then moved her eyes slowly around the room, taking in the scratched furniture, chips in the walls, rips in the arms of the big checkered chair in the corner and our sleeping bags and pillows stashed under the side table.  She looked at Brucie then again at Sean, heaved a big sigh and handed me the letter.

I smoothed out the wrinkles as best I could.  The note had purple violets with a green vine all around the edge of the writing.  Momma's name, at the top of the letter, was surrounded with red roses.

On the Friday before Father was supposed to come back, Momma, Aunt Raven and Aunt Dawn sat side by side on the green sofa in the living room.  Their voices made a humming sound as they chitchatted back and forth. Momma was having a hard time deciding if she should let Father come back into our lives. *Her pacing has carved out a deep ridge in the living room rug,* Sean had said earlier. *Yeah!* I replied. *If we're not careful she"ll fall in there and never come out.*

My brothers and cousins were outside playing Hide and Seek. I stayed in the kitchen and leaned against the doorway so I could watch what was going on.

A bright red cloth lay in the center of the coffee table. Aunt Dawn's special beaded bag and a candle were set up on top of the cloth.

*You're gonna travel*, Aunt Dawn had said when she read my stones a year ago. *And dance.* I pushed my toes against the floor, rolled onto the balls of my feet, then rolled back. It felt good to be strong again. I'd been practicing the exercises I remembered from Miss Trixie's class whenever I could.

The wind blew hard against the window behind Momma and her sisters. The buzzing stopped. Silence fell over the house like a net. All I could hear was my breath as it moved in and out.

Aunt Raven shifted her position on the floor after a while. "I just don't see how tossin' stones can have any meanin'?"

"You've been saying that for years, Raven, since we were little kids." Aunt Dawn spoke slowly and evenly. "And I keep telling you it's not just the stones. It's the voices I hear on the inside of me. The stones help me listen to the inner mystery."

"If I heard voices they'd probably lock me up," Aunt Raven laughed.

"You have to be quiet. Inner voices come from the depth of silence." Aunt Dawn lit the candle with one of the wooden matches on the table. The beads on her bracelet jangled like they always do.

Once the flame was strong, she took a pinch of sacred tobacco out of her small leather pouch and dropped it into the light. "Fuzzzzz." The candle flickered. Thin fingers of fire reached out for the broken leaves and transformed them into a sweet, pungent smell.

"Grandmother Earth give me balance," she said softly. "Great Spirit speak to me. You who hold the answers to questions large and small. Let me see through your eyes, and hear through your ears. Let me voice your words through my tongue. Ho!"

The candle cast flickers of light across Momma's face and those of her sisters. I sunk deeper into the wood of the doorway, quiet and still, like a part of the tree that had been cut and formed into this passageway. The only movement was the thumping of my heart as I waited breathlessly to hear what Aunt Dawn was going to say. Her words were my future. Momma would listen to her big sister like a child listens to a teacher. My life flickered in the air as surely as the candle. One strong wind from the wrong direction could put it out.

"Say your name seven times Merle," Aunt Dawn said as she shook the bag.

"Merle MacLean, Merle MacLean."

"Say your Indian name too, Merle," Dawn said. "The one Momma gave you."

"Merle Blue-sky MacLean, Merle Blue-Sky MacLean..."

"Yes, the color of your eyes, different than the rest of the tribe." Aunt Dawn spilled the stones out onto the red cloth. I'd never heard Momma called Blue-sky before. *Why didn't she use it?* I wondered, but I knew the answer.

Aunt Dawn's dark eyes got soft as she examined the formations. "These stones are joined into a long line," she said in that buzzy voice that makes her sound distant. "It looks like a snake." She shook her head up and down and back and forth like she was listening to her inner mystery. "Next to the snake is a mouse ... snakes eat mice ... snakes scare some people," Aunt Dawn said still using that distant voice. "They can be dangerous ... even poisonous," she paused.

Momma took a deep breath. Her shoulders quivered. It didn't sound good.

"B-u-t. A little poison can be a healing medicine. Too much, you die." Aunt Dawn said with a note of fear.

The hair on the back of my head stood on end. It sounded like someone had to die.

"Merle Blue-sky MacLean," Aunt Dawn said. "The stones tell me that if you stay you must not back away from doin' the right thing for you and the kids." She nodded. "You see, you're the mouse ... and he's the snake. He can be healing or dangerous. You have to learn to speak up."

"What do you mean, Dawn?" Momma questioned.

"They say he's got two sides. One is kind. The other is . . . demanding or harsh."

"Yeah," Momma replied. She took another sip of beer.

"Is he ... dangerous?" Aunt Dawn questioned. "Does he ever hurt you? Or the kids?"

"No ... he doesn't really hurt us. You know I have a bad temper and sometimes when he's been out late ... and I want him home with me, and the kids ... I get angry. Sometimes I go through his pockets looking for anything that looks like ... gamblin'."

"Well, it's your call." Aunt Dawn clapped her hands like she did when she finished my reading. "But if I were you, I'd finish school or learn a trade. Gives you more choices." She looked deep into Momma's eyes. "Having an education will also teach you to speak up. I'm sorry you didn't get to finish school. You were a good student – smart as a whip."

"Merle," Aunt Raven said. "You can stay as long as you like; do what Dawn said, finish school."

Later that night we all settled into our regular sleeping places. Momma on the sofa, Sean, Brucie, Goldy, and me in the middle of the living room floor. Sometime in the middle of the night I had one of those dreams that seem real

*I walked down a school corridor on my way to class. Suddenly, I couldn't remember where I was supposed to go. I quickly ruffled through my notebook. I'd written it down somewhere.*

*The room number wasn't there. Fear flooded my body. Fear that I was going to flunk out of school and never learn everything I wanted to. There was a giant hole in my head and memory was leaking out like water through a sieve.*

"No, no, no," a voice called out. I opened my eyes and turned to look one way then the other. No one was there.

Shadows danced on the ceiling above me. Night noises filled the air. It took me a few minutes to come back from my dream life to Aunt Raven's floor. I turned to search through the dim light. A small body twisted and turned nearby. It was Brucie.

"It's okay." I reached out and put my arm around Brucie's shoulders. The tension of not knowing what was happening next was getting to all of us.

Father's letter was tucked underneath my pillow – in the pillow case. *He's close,* I thought. *Real close.*

Chapter Seventeen

## HAPPY 13TH BIRTHDAY

Father knocked on Aunt Raven and Uncle Howard's door at exactly five on Saturday.   Sean, Brucie and me were all dressed up in our best church clothes ready and waiting. Cousin Violet gave me a pink sun-dress that she'd outgrown. It had ribbons that tied around my shoulders and a full skirt that went down past my knees. When I walked it flared out and made a rustling sound. It made me feel like a princess.  It was one of those times when having Violet as a cousin was a good thing.

Momma'd tried on everything she owned.  I hadn't seen her care about what she was wearing since Father'd been gone.

"The blue dress," I said when she finally put on what she'd worn to church last.   Blue always made her eyes look like pieces of sky.  Blue-sky, like her middle name. The dress was too big now, but so was everything else and when she cinched it at the waist – it didn't look too baggy.

Aunt Raven took Shiloh Blue and Willow into the bedroom. Uncle Howard went for a long walk.  Goldy wagged her tail so hard that it nearly knocked the lamp over.  Sean made a lunge that saved it.

"Come in," Momma said as she opened the door and stepped aside to let Father in.  We stood in a row, a few feet behind her.  Father wiped his feet on the small rug just inside and hung his checkered jacket on the coat rack next to the door. I wondered if he'd notice how much I'd grown. I wanted to run forward, give him a hug, tell him how much I missed him, but Momma stopped me with her words.

"Don't get too comfortable," she said looking at Father, her hands on her hips.  "We've got a lot to talk about."

I ran my fingers down the folds of my skirt. My stomach tightened. My birthday was a week away. I just knew that having Father back was going to be my present.

Father pressed his lips together, bit down on the inside of his cheek, and nodded. "I know, Merle."

"Well, will you look at these three *big* kids," Father said walking over to us. "Now let me see," he rubbed his chin, "don't tell me." He brought his fists back and playfully hit Sean in the arm. "Ouch", Father cried as he rubbed one wrist, then the other. "Strong boy!" Father laughed.

Sean crossed his arms over his chest and patted his arms. A flicker of a smile crossed his face.

"And the small fry here," Father twisted his mouth from side to side as he stared at Brucie. One of his eyebrows shot up higher than the other as he swooped Brucie up and threw him over his shoulder. "Weighs about, what two hundred pounds?" Brucie laughed so hard it made him cough. "At least I'm still bigger than *one* of my kids." Father set him down and turned to me.

"Pretty face. Nice eyes. Looks a lot like Merle." Father put his big hand under my chin and lifted my head up. "And maybe a teensy-weensy bit like her old man." I liked that he thought I was pretty like Momma. It made me feel warm inside.

I heard Momma say, "so where in tarnation have you been?" as my brothers and I went to join Aunt Raven in her bedroom. It was agreed ahead of time that we'd leave them alone to work things out.

"What'll we do if she doesn't take him back?" I asked Aunt Raven as Sean, Brucie and me sat on the edge of her bed. Sean stared out the back window. Brucie jiggled his knees.

"She'll take him back, Aunt Raven said. "For sure, she'll take him back. After he agrees to sign the list of commandments she put together."

"Commandments?" I asked. I hadn't heard anything about that.

"Well, a list of 'thou shalts', and 'thou shalt nots," Aunt Raven said. "You know, like in the Bible, only different.

Sean took a deep breath then let the air out with a sigh. "What makes her think signing a list is gonna do anything?"

Aunt Raven puffed out her chest. Her dark eyes flashed. "If it doesn't, it doesn't, and then she'll figure out somethin' else. But right now, she thinks she has to give him the chance to prove that he means to make good by signin' the list of changes she put together."

"Next weekend's my birthday," I said. "I hope he signs the list by then." Aunt Raven smiled and put her arm around my shoulders. "That'd be a real nice present," she said. "And I'll bake you a cake with thirteen candles."

An hour later Momma knocked on the bedroom door. "You kids come out and say 'good bye' to your father," she said.

When we walked into the living room – he was gone. We went to the window and watched his white car pull away from the curb. Momma shook her head one way, then the other. "Stubborn," she said.

"Is he coming back?" I asked. Momma crossed her arms over her chest and tapped her foot on the floor. "We'll see," she said. A piece of paper with his name on it lay open on the side table next to the sofa. Momma walked over, refolded it and put it in her skirt pocket. I knew it was the list.

Sunday night when the doorbell rang, Sean, Brucie and me ran to the front door. Momma was already there. Father stepped in, wiped his feet on the small rug like last time, smiled at us and handed Momma a bouquet of red roses. "For you," he said.

"Did you think about what I asked?" Momma said as she took the flowers. Their sweet perfume filled the air. Father clenched his jaw. The muscles in his face twitched. "Merle, you know how I am," he said in a light hearted way.

Momma sank deeper into herself, turned and walked away. "Just go," she said as she looked down at the worn carpet. The floor lamp behind the green sofa gave the room a yellowish cast. Father shook his head and stomped out the door.

My heart sank. "You sent him away just like that," I said. "He ... brought you flowers ... he means well ... and you didn't even ... talk." My breath caught in my throat. "At least you could *say* something." Drums beat in my head. "Give him a chance."

Momma let out a deep sigh. She looked so frail that I thought she might fold in two. "I've talked and talked 'till I'm blue in the face," Momma said. "He's got to sign the commandments I've put down on paper. If he doesn't ... it won't work." Momma pursed her lips and handed me the roses.

"We can make it on our own," Sean said as he moved forward out of the doorway. "Yeh!" Brucie added, "we're okay." Momma slumped onto the sofa. A distant sliver of the moon hung over her shoulder.

I glared at Sean. "Make it on our own? Are you crazy?" My whole body started to shake with anger. "We've moved from house to house. Gone to one school after the other. We're sleeping on the Gray's living room floor. And it doesn't look like we have a way out." I stomped away, took the roses into the kitchen and put them in a vase. There were thirteen all together. Thirteen, like I was going to be on Saturday.

Wednesday night when Father rang the bell he barged in as soon as she opened the door. "You can't do this to me," he said. "I told you I've changed. I've gotten my old job back, paid off everybody I owed money to, and searched the area for a house for us to live in." Sean, Brucie and me stayed back this time, near the hall doorway. "Then sign the paper," Momma took the list out of her pocket and extended it towards Father.

"Let me see that again," Father said. He glanced at the list then looked up. "What if I sign all but two?" he pleaded. "That's four out of six."

Momma's pony tail bobbed from one shoulder to the other as she shook her head 'no'. Father let out a deep sigh and flicked his fingers against the paper. The noise made my ears hurt. "You drive a hard bargain Merle MacLean." Father folded the paper and put it in his jacket pocket.

"Saturday's Fiona's birthday," Momma said. "You can come to celebrate with us, but that's all, until you sign that list."

"I promise I'll be here," he said in a soft voice.

"Happy birthday to you, happy birthday to you, happy birthday dear Fiona, happy birthday to you," everybody sang as we all gathered around the Gray's kitchen table. I stood at the far end, in front of the strawberry cake Aunt Raven baked for me. Everybody meant: Aunt Raven, Uncle Howard, Cousin Willow, Cousin Shiloh Blue, Sean, Brucie, Momma and ... Father. I had to pinch myself to make sure I wasn't just dreaming.

"Make a wish sweetie," Momma called out from across the table. She looked so happy her face beamed. I looked into the flames of the 13 candles surrounded by pink flowers encircling the cake, "*God, Great Spirit, Kokumthena,* please let Father sign that list," I whispered real low – so nobody could hear.

"Now blow 'em all out," Brucie cried. His eyes opened wide. A big grin spread across his face.

"Looks like a bonfire," Father beamed. He reached out for Momma's hand – she stiffened – then let go. The dimples in his cheeks deepened. My stomach tightened. They looked happy together. *Did that mean he signed the list?*

The hum of music from the radio and buzzing sounds of familiar voices filled the room. I took a deep breath and blew as hard as I could – but they didn't all go out. Brucie leaned in and blew out the two I'd missed. He looked real handsome in one of Shiloh Blue's plaid shirts.

Momma moved forward to help me cut the cake. "Did you make a wish?" she whispered as I handed her a plate. I gave her a sheepish grin.

Momma cut the cake, put it on a plate and handed it back to me.

I gave Brucie the first piece. He stuck his finger in the frosting and licked his lips. "Now, everybody move into the living room," Momma said, "and," she looked over at Sean, tilted her head down and raised her eyebrows.

"And ... I'll help," Sean moved closer. As I passed a plate, Momma put cake on it and Sean whisked it away.

When we were alone I turned to Momma and asked, "is he gonna sign that list you made up?"

"Look in my skirt pocket," Momma whispered. I pulled out a folded piece of paper and opened it. It was the list. I read it to myself. One — Thou shalt not run away again. Two — Thou shalt not disappear for even one night. Three — Thou shalt not hit the kids with a belt. Four — Thou shalt not yell. Five — Thou shalt not hang out at Morrie's Bar. Six — Thou shalt not gamble.

Father's initials were signed next to one, two, three and four. On five, father added — *more than once a week.* On six he added — *more than $1.00 at a time.*

"Is this okay, Momma?" I questioned. "He's signed all of them, but changed two." I swallowed hard.

Momma smiled. "Now, look at the bottom of the page. She cut into another piece of cake and put it on a plate. "Oh!" I cried. My hands started to shake. "Our own house?" I couldn't believe my eyes. "Can I have a room of my own?" Momma nodded. "A pink room, just for me?" It was hard to imagine. Tears welled up in my eyes. I brushed them away and looked up at Momma. "Happy thirteenth birthday," she said.

Sean came back in, reached for another plate and stopped. He looked at me — then Momma. I handed him the list of commandments. "You've gotta be kidding," he snarled after he read them. "This seems too good to be true."

"It's gonna work out," I said. "For sure, it's gonna work out." I rushed into the living room. Father was sitting next to Uncle Howard on one of the kitchen chairs we'd moved earlier. He winked at me as I came in. I nodded. For sure, everything was gonna be okay.

"You know if this war with Korea keeps up, our boys'll soon be drafted." Father said as he turned back toward Uncle Howard. "Sean's not quite fifteen. Shiloh Blue's just ten. You think it'll last that long?" Uncle Howard replied. "Time has a way of speedin' up just when you wanna have it slow down," Father said.

I went behind him, put my arms over his shoulders, bent close to his ear and whispered, "Thank you." He patted my hand and went back to talking to Uncle Howard. *Time does have a way of speeding up,* I thought. *A year used to seem like forever.*

Chapter Eighteen

## MY LUCKY DAY

By September, we moved into our new house. 1305 Rose Street, the address rolled off my tongue like honey. It was such a relief to have a place of our own that I kept wandering around room to room touching the walls to make sure they wouldn't fall away. There was even a room for Grandma since she moved in with us. "I need the company," she said. It had two stories, four bedrooms, a dining room, living room, kitchen and a huge back yard. Father said it needed a paint job, but it looked like a palace to me.

Sean and I were going to go to the same school. Even though we'd missed a lot the principal said we were too old to leave behind.

"This'll bring you good luck," Grandma said as she gave Sean and me small brown leather bags filled with *Kin.ni.kin.nick*. "It has some special herbs in it, mixed with the tobacco, that I found in the forest," she said. Grandma tied the bag around my neck with a long leather string and did the same for Sean. "Tuck it under your shirts," she said as my brother and I stood in the living room ready to go to our new school, Lafayette.

"Thanks Grandma." I held the pouch up to my nose, then tucked it under my shirt like Grandma said. The mixture smelled like fairies dancing on damp crushed leaves. Both Grandma and Aunt Dawn used ceremonial tobacco on different occasions, but this was the first time I'd ever worn it. I pulled on my yellow wool coat and grabbed a scarf. It was chilly outside, and windy. The coat was a left over from last year. It felt good that some of the buttons at the top wouldn't close. A sign I was growing. Not as much as Sean, but some.

Sean had gone to bed one night and woke up a foot taller. His thin arms and legs turned into solid muscle. His voice sounded almost as deep as Father's.

"Don't talk about the *Kin.ni.kin.nick* to anybody. Okay?" Grandma warned as she took one of her hairpins and tucked a strand of gray hair into the bun on top of her head. "And remember, tobacco is never to be smoked. That's ..." Grandma stumbled a bit, then caught herself.

"Bad luck," I said quickly. We'd been warned before. I wondered what made her stumble, but I didn't say anything. I figured she was just a bit worn out helping Momma organize stuff in the house.

"Thanks, Grandma." Sean put on his blue coat and pulled a cap over his head.

"Don't let anybody see'em either," Grandma cautioned as she wiggled her nose like a rabbit, "and don't tell Brucie. He's too young to carry *Kin.ni.kin.nick*."

Sean and I laughed. Having Grandma with us was fun. It was better for Momma too. Her hair seemed fuller. She stopped biting her nails. And the circles under her eyes were less puffy. Best of all, she was gonna go back to school and get her high school diploma.

"Are you talkin' about me out there," Momma called from the kitchen at the back of the house.

"Nooo." We yelled. Sometimes I wondered if Momma could read my mind. She was real smart. Not in the same way Father was. He could fix motors and do math on up to the wazoo. But Momma knew what wasn't put on paper or talked about.

Lafayette was a three mile walk down lower Fort Street. Sean walked a half block ahead of me and only glanced back every block or so to make sure I was still alive. Sometimes I thought he hoped I wasn't. Even though we were only a grade apart, he liked to act like he was much older.

Last night's rain left big puddles along the sidewalk. I took a running jump and leaped across one after the other. It felt good to fly through the air. Most of the houses along the road were red brick with inset porches. I waved at an old woman sitting on her porch in her rocking chair. She didn't wave back.

I'd curled my hair in tiny pin curls last night so it would be fluffy and full, but the more I walked the more I could feel it going back to its natural state, lifeless and droopy. By the time I got to school it was stringing down the sides of my face. So much for wanting to make a good impression my first day of school. I ran to the girls room to brush my hair and fluff it up as best I could.

The room was long and narrow. Six sinks hung on the wall to my left. Each had a mirror just big enough to see a reflection from the neck up.

The smell of heavy perfume filled my lungs as I passed two girls and headed towards the last sink. I took my brush out of my book bag and tried to refluff my hair.

"That Skipper Roulette's soooo cute," the dark haired girl at the first sink, said. "What a *dream-boat*." She pinched her cheeks till they turned pink.

I wondered who Skipper Roulette was. It was hard not to know anybody. I was glad that we had a new house, but I wished I could've brought some of my friends from Jackson Street with me.

"Yeah. He's a dish all right," a second girl in scarlet lipstick agreed as she stood next to her friend. "Wanna try some of my Sweet Lips? It'll make your mouth look big and luscious." She giggled and held out the tube.

"My father'd kill me if he saw me doing this." Pink Cheeks took the lipstick from her friend and carefully applied the scarlet color.

A cool breeze blew across my face from the open window to my right. It made my shiver. My father would kill me too. I stared into the mirror. My blue eyes, long face, and half straight hair stared back. I turned my chin one way, then the other. *One day I'll wear scarlet lipstick whether Father likes it or not,* I thought. I walked toward the other girls.

"Didja see that new kid in the blue coat in the hall just now?" Scarlet Lips asked her friend.

"The cute guy with the chipped tooth?" Pink Cheeks answered. "Yeah. I even introduced myself. His name's Sean something."

Shivers went up my spine. They were talking about my brother. After the last school I should've been used to girls thinking he was cute, but I wasn't. It made me feel like something I thought was mine was being taken away from me. I stopped and looked at them for a second, but then went on out the door. I didn't know what to say.

I liked all my classes. The teachers seemed nice, especially my homeroom teacher, Mr. Jesue. He taught history.

"Twentieth-century America," he said pulling on the tips of his thin black mustache, "seemed to be a woman's country."

I sat in the third seat back, in the middle of five parallel rows. The boys snickered when he said "woman's country." The girls perked up and sat straighter.

"Women run schools and churches. Women spend most of the money. Women build, furnish and direct activities in the home." Mr. Jesue walked around to the front of his desk so he could be closer to all of us. It felt strange to have a man talking about women being so important.

"Most American children know more of their mother's than of their father's family." His eyes fixed on mine like an arrow hitting the target. I thought about Father's family. *That photograph of the Indian woman I found in his drawer and those letters from someone named Dancing Feet were still a mystery. Momma's family was different.*

"Lester Ward, propounded the theory of the natural superiority of the female sex which he called gynecocracy." Mr. Jesue pulled himself up onto his desk. I thought about *Kokumthena.* The Shawnee deity was a *she.* Grandma said her Indian ancestors always felt women had a *double* intelligence. One from the head and one from the heart.

"Ah! sure." "That'll be the day." "My ole man'd never stand for that kind of talk." Kids mumbled as they headed out for their next class. I didn't think Father would agree with gynecocracy either. *Funny word,* I thought. *Kind of like democracy with a gyne in front of it. And propounded?* I'd have to look that up in the dictionary.

It was hard moving through the halls alone. Kids gathered together around the lockers in the hallway and waved at each other as they passed outside the classrooms. The hum of their voices filled the air. I wanted someone to talk to. I wondered how Sean and Brucie were doing as I headed toward my next class.

"I hope you enjoyed your summer vacation," Miss Baker, my English teacher said with a sideways tilt of her head. Even standing up, Miss Baker looked like she was sitting down. I smiled as I watched her move about the room calling out names, checking them off.

"Writing and reading are two of the most important ways we learn. Sooo." She elongated the "o's" as she began to pace up and down the aisles looking from one student to another. "Your first assignment is to write a paragraph or two describing something unusual or memorable that happened to you during the summer and bring it in on Monday." She stopped pacing near my desk, sniffed the air, then went on. "It can be about your holiday, family, or anything that strikes you."

"What if I didn't do nothin' all summer?" A boy on my right, wearing a white T-shirt and Levis asked.

Miss Baker looked down at her seating chart. "Ike," she said. "It is Ike, isn't it?" The boy nodded. "What are you doing right now?"

"Nothin'," Ike said. "Just sittin'." He fiddled with his pencil then tucked it over his ear.

"And what are you thinking as you sit?" Miss Baker asked.

"I'm thinkin' I'm gonna flunk English cuz I can't think of nothin' to write."

Nervous laughter filled the room. "Wait, class. This is important." Miss Baker looked around the room. The laughter came to a sudden halt. She turned to face Ike again. "That's a perfect start," she said. "Write down your thoughts about not being able to think about *anything* to write."

The bell rang. The kids filed out of the room, some of them arm in arm, others on their own. "We went to Florida." "Uncle

John took us to Lake Michigan." "Dad taught me to fish." "Mom took us to Aunt Jean's farm." Shared journeys. Family adventures. I jotted down some notes on a piece of paper first, so I was the last to leave.

"See me after school, Fiona," Miss Baker said as I passed by in front of her desk.

"You wanted to see me," I said to Miss Baker as I walked into her classroom after school. I figured it had to do with me being new.

"Oh! Fiona," she said pursing her lips, "we don't allow our children to smoke. It's such a dangerous habit."

I stared at her in disbelief. "Pardon me?" My voice dropped in and out of some invisible crack in the floor.

"Tobacco," she said sternly. "It's a definite scent."

My stomach pinched into a tight ball. *Tobacco scent?* I thought. *She thinks I smoke.* I took a deep breath. Miss Baker was right. A slight scent of bark, dried leaves and tobacco filled my lungs. Grandma said not to talk about the pouch she gave me – so I didn't.

"Write, *I will not smoke* one hundred times on the blackboard," she said quickly. Another girl was already writing on one of the squares of the blackboard at the front of the room, so I moved to her left. She was scrawling *I will not tell lies,* over and over. I picked up a fresh piece of white chalk, lifted my arm as high as I could and started.

Miss Baker went to a teacher's meeting but promised to be back within the hour. I'd written about twenty-five lines when the girl next to me spoke up.

"My name's Margaret Vatroba," she said in a sweet voice. "You're new aren't you?"

"Yeah. We just moved into the neighborhood. My folks, Grandma, two brothers and me." I glanced in her direction but kept writing. Even at a distance I could tell that Margaret was taller than I was by at least three inches. Taller and thinner. "My name's Fiona Lonestar MacLean. Friends call me Lonestar, unless my father's around. He doesn't like the name Lonestar."

132

"I bet it's hard to move, Lonestar. We've lived in the same house since I was born."

"Yeah. It's hard. Everybody here knows everybody else, but me." I stopped writing and looked at her side of the board.

She caught my eye and shrugged her bony shoulders. "Some folks call not telling the truth – lies. I call it self protection." She held the chalk up like a dueling sword, swirled it over her head and lunged forward. "On guard!" she cried.

"On guard!" I laughed as I quickly mimicked her movements.

"I think one of your brothers is in my math class." Margaret's hand stopped mid air as she turned towards me.

"Sean?" I asked.

Margaret smiled, "he's cute."

My stomach clenched.

"You upset?" Margaret asked still writing.

"About my brother?"

"No, because I'm older than you?" She laughed. "Of course about your brother."

"A little," I took a deep breath. "How old are you?"

"Fifteen. By a week. I had to start school late so I'm the oldest in my class."

"Oh! Well, I'm thirteen," I said.

"You seem older."

"Maybe it's from all the moving around we've done." I liked that she thought I looked older.


"Grandma," I yelled as soon as I made it up the porch stairs and through the front door. "Guess what?" I put my books down on the coffee table next to Father's *Detroit News*. "I found a new friend," I said jumping up and down. "Her name's Margaret. Margaret Vatroba and she lives just two blocks away. She's two years older than me, but that doesn't seem to matter. We get along great."

"Whoeee," Grandma cried clapping her hands in excitement over my good news. She wiggled her hips, put one foot forward, one back and called out "gobble, gobble, gobble."

"The turkey trot," I laughed as I stepped behind her. We danced from the living room to the dining room then stopped. We danced slower than we had last time, but it was still fun. I didn't tell her where I met my new friend. Then she'd have to know about the teacher making me write about not smoking on the blackboard. I kept that to myself.

I heard some muffled sounds coming from the back of the house. "Is that Momma?" I asked looking up. I unbuttoned the few buttons that did up on the front of my coat. I wanted to give her my good news and hear about hers. I took a step towards her room.

"Leave her...alone." Grandma blocked my way. "Your momma's not feelin' up to par ... she didn't get to enroll in adult school today like she wanted to."

My stomach sank. It'd been such a lucky day for me – but not for Momma. She had her heart set on getting her high school diploma.

## Chapter Nineteen

### THE *CIIPAA*

"I'm not goin' back to school," Brucie announced at dinner, Friday night. It was the end of our second week in our new schools. Momma and Father sat on opposite ends of our dining room table. Brucie sat to my right, Sean and Grandma sat opposite us in front of the side table with glass doors.

Momma smoothed out the edge of the lace table cloth. The area around her eyes looked puffy. "We went through that before, Brucie." She sighed. "School's important."

"You're not goin' to school – why should I?" Brucie, pushed the carrots and potatoes onto the side of his plate. Sean looked at me and shook his head. I pursed my lips. I hated that Momma didn't go back to school.

"Your mother doesn't need to go back to school, Brucie," Father said in a firm tone. "She's got her hands full takin' care of our new house and you kids." He took a bite out of his chicken leg,

A heavy veil of silence fell over the room.

Momma glanced at Father and clenched her jaw.

"School's fun, Brucie." I tried to ease the tension. "You just have to try harder to make friends."

"Brucie, eat your vegetables," Father ordered. "You'll not leave the table 'till you do."

"Yeah!" Sean taunted. "Eat your vegetables."

Brucie lowered his chin. "Somethin' is after me," he said.

Sean shook his head, "I told you just to walk away when somebody picks on you."

"It's not a body," Brucie whispered. "It's...a...thing."

"A thing?" I questioned. "Like the monsters Sean makes up to scare us?"

"I didn't make this one up." Brucie slowly turned his head from side to side. "It's real – I feel it."

Sean looked at me and rolled his eyes. I hunched my shoulders.

Grandma stiffened. Lines sprang up across her forehead.

The next morning, after breakfast, Grandma came into my room. I was sitting up in bed, looking out the window, thinking about what to write for English class. "Get your coat, Lonestar," she said. It's our turn to walk Goldy.

"I didn't know we were takin' turns," I said.

"Well, we are now." Grandma's hand shook a bit as she struggled to button her coat.

I went to my closet and grabbed a jacket. It felt good to have space of my very own. Sean and Brucie shared a bedroom down the hall. The unfinished room Grandma had moved into was right next to mine. One wall was still bare boards, no plaster, but she didn't mind. *It's what's inside of you that's important, Lonestar*, she said in defense of the bare wall.

We went down the stairs and called for Goldy. She was there in a flash.

"Good girl," I said as I picked up Goldy's leash and hooked it onto her collar. Goldy sighed like I'd given her the best present in her whole life. Grandma and I went out the front door with Goldy in the lead.

"We're gonna leave our scent in the neighborhood," Grandma said as we walked. "Of course we can't spray things like dogs do, but we can touch bushes, fences, buildings and even...fire hydrants with our eyes."

I laughed. It was a good thing nobody else was within earshot. Sometimes Grandma acted like a mischievous little kid. We stopped and waited at the empty lot on the corner while Goldy left her scent.

I glanced back at our house. The morning Sun painted the front porch with a yellowish cast. Some fallen leaves nestled in the arms of the Maple Tree out front. It looked like a home in one of the *Good Housekeeping* magazines Aunt Raven subscribes to.

"Brucie wants me to look in on somethin' at his school, Lonestar," Grandma said as we waited for Goldy to finish. "Want to come with me?"

"Sure." I gave Goldy a little tug to get her moving again.

"He said a *ciipaa*, a ghost, followed him down the school hall outside to the playground."

"A ghost?" *Another one of his cockamamie excuses not to go to school,* I thought.

"He didn't want to say exactly what was going on in front of ... everybody," Grandma said. "He knew you wouldn't believe him."

"Yeah! Sometimes it's hard to know what's true and what isn't with him."

"From his description ... I think it's true." Grandma stopped, took a deep breath and then moved forward again.

"You okay?" I asked.

"Just gettin' old, Lonestar," Grandma replied.

"Me too," I joked.

"Yep! Thirteen is gettin' up there," Grandma laughed.

Brucie's school was just a few blocks away. The building hunched down like an ugly spider. Metal bars hung thick and heavy over dingy windows. With or without a *ciipaa*, it was a creepy place.

Grandma walked forward slowly. We headed for the far side of the spider. She reached her hands out to feel the air ... turned her head one way ... then the other, listening for something I couldn't hear.

Goldy growled and pulled hard on her leash. "It's okay," I said. Grandma waved us forward. We crept along behind her ... she stopped again. This time Grandma turned around in a circle like whatever she was sensing was real close.

"Is it one?" I whispered coming up behind her. Just thinking about it made me breathless.

"Nope," Grandma said taking a big breath. "But it's here."

I swallowed hard. "How do you know?"

"Well, I feel a tingling in my ears ... sort of like soft bells. Thoughts ... worries about tomorrow ... the future ... all disappear. Then ... a different kind of energy surrounds me ... like an invisible cocoon." Grandma spoke in a monotone, like she was half here and half in that place she was describing. "Then I know ... deep inside my gut ... that someone from the other side is near by."

I shivered in excitement. I wanted to sense that different energy.

We slowly rounded the end of the school and headed for the playground. About a dozen kids played on the swings, slide, monkey bars, and seesaw.

Nothing looked unusual to me. Just regular kids like Brucie, some younger, some older, doing what kids do. "How do you know when you've found one, Grandma?"

"It's always different," Grandma said softly, still in that half here and half there place. She scanned the area. "Sometimes you hear their words like whispers in your mind. Other times ... maybe a light flickers ... a tree rustles ... or a book flips to a certain page."

"I heard a voice call my name once," I said. "It was when I was ... runnin' through the forest to your house." My stomach clenched just thinking about that terrible night. *Momma and Father were fighting and we didn't get to celebrate my birthday.*

"That too," Grandma said. "Sometimes people from the other side call out to let us know we're not alone," Grandma said. "Other times, like this one who's scarin' Brucie, they want to tell us somethin'. Maybe they left the Earth-plain feelin' unfinished."

"How do you know what they want, Grandma?" The more she talked the more I wanted to know.

Grandma fixed her eyes on a little girl in a pink outfit by the slide. "I just have to be open and listen." The girl went down the slide and landed on the blacktop below. Then she ran over to the swings, put a stone on the seat and gave it a light push. The little boy next to her, pulled his red cap down, shook his head and pumped his legs so he could go higher. Grandma took a deep breath and quivered.

"Anything else?"

"Usually I send out thoughts that tell 'em I'm here and ready to help with whatever they need. Then I stay inside that cocoon and wait." Grandma put her finger up to her mouth, "shh." She tilted her head slowly one way, then the other ... reached her hands out to touch the air ... and turned in a wide circle like she had before.

"Is someone there?" I whispered, as I held tight to Goldy's leash.

"Listen, Lonestar. Not with your ears. Listen with your whole body. Don't think about anythin' other than bein' right here ... right now." Grandma's eyes got glassy.

"The great Shawnee warrior Tecumseh's twin brother, Tenskwatawa, spoke to ghosts," Grandma mused. "He tried to be a medicine man, but kept failin'." The wind picked up pieces of dust and swirled them around Grandma's feet like it was protecting her from something. "He failed at everything, except drinkin' and fightin' with his wife."

Tenskwatawa sounded a little like my father. Or, at least the way he used to be.

Grandma watched the little boy as he continued to swing. The tail of his red plaid jacket flapped out behind him as he pumped higher.

"Then one night he fell into such a deep trance that everybody thought he was dead." Grandma went on, "they washed his body and got ready for the two day wait to bury him. But, he didn't die. He came back to life. From then on, he saw things that others didn't."

I took a deep breath and held tight to Goldy. "What did he see?"

"Tenskwatawa saw paradise. It was filled with lots of fish, hunting grounds, and fine corn fields." Grandma pulled on the sleeves of her coat to make them longer.

"Paradise has fish, Grandma?"

Grandma smiled. "Paradise is filled with whatever anyone needs, Lonestar. Food. School. Old friends. That's why it's called paradise."

"Sounds like a good place," I said.

"Tenskwatawa also saw hell. The spirits who had hurt others in their lives were punished until they were really sorry for all the bad things they'd done. Once Tenskwatawa knew he had to be responsible for his actions and that there would be consequences for the harm he had caused others, he got scared. He stopped drinking. He said warriors must treat each other as brothers, stop fighting with their wives and stop a whole lot of other things. He changed the entire Shawnee Nation." Grandma's shoulders softened. "Seeing consequences does that. Our actions always affect others."

Grandma moved her attention to an empty blacktop area. She nodded her head up and down like she was talking to somebody. "It's too bad ... but sometimes people have to experience a deep loss before they take responsibility for their actions."

A strong wind came out of nowhere. It blew hard and pushed us toward the swings. My heart beat loudly in my ears. I knew it was a *ciipaa*. It was just like Grandma said. A different feeling deep inside signaled that something I couldn't see was there.

*"Ni-neem-e*, I see it." Her voice dropped. "This is a man, Lonestar."

*A man?* I thought. *Why would a man would want to scare Brucie?*

*"E'ne,* yes." He ... has light brown hair...a stomach that hangs over his trousers ... and, he ... pushed himself and his son very hard."

Flickers of sounds and visions pulsed through me as I tried to hear and see what Grandma did. It was hard to tell if they came from Grandma's words or from a place deep inside of me.

Grandma rubbed her chest, and shivered. "He had a weak heart, but no one knew it."

I felt a little tug on my heart. *Is that what the ciipaa was feeling*? I wondered.

"George Ikebouer," Grandma smiled and nodded again. "That's his name, Lonestar." She reached out for my hand, squeezed it real tight, then loosened her grip. "George had a fight with his son the morning before he died because the boy didn't clean up his room. The son thinks the death was his fault ... if he didn't fight with his father he wouldn't have had a heart attack." The wrinkles in Grandma's face deepened. "The father's been coming to him in dreams to tell him it wasn't his fault. After tryin' for three months, with no results, he turned to Brucie."

"Why Brucie?" *I was amazed Grandma knew all of this.*

"The father knows that Brucie is sensitive. It's part of our family bloodline."

A stillness swept over me as I listened to Grandma's words. *Do I have this?*

We walked to the swing where the little boy was. The boy was Brucie's age, but heavier.

Grandma motioned for me to sit on the swing next to him, to his right. The little girl in the pink outfit was still on his left. Grandma pushed me in silence. My insides felt like they were filled with electrical sparks.

After a few minutes he stopped swinging and dangled his feet in the air.

"George Junior," Grandma said gently.

The little boy looked over at Grandma then at me. "You know my name?"

Grandma nodded, "this may sound strange, but your father, George Senior, wants you to know you're a good boy." She moved closer to where he sat. "*It* wasn't your fault."

The little boy gasped. His hands tightened around the chain. "Yes, it was."

"Your father wasn't well ... it was his time to leave. He wants you to be happy. You're not the reason he died."

Little George got real still. Tears sprang out of the corners of his eyes. He wiped them away with his hand ... and smiled.

I looked up at Grandma, then down at the little boy. It was a good feeling to be able to be a part of bringing such an important message from the other world to this one.

When we got home Father was there. "Where've you been?" he yelled. "You should'a been home helpin' your mom with chores?" My back stiffened. "I ... went for a walk ... with Grandma." I unhooked Goldy and put her leash back on the side table. She lowered her tail and raced up the stairs headed for Sean and Brucie's room.

"You," Father said pointing at Grandma. "I let you come and stay with us, but that doesn't mean you can brainwash my daughter with crazy nonsense."

"What are you talking about Frank?" Grandma said. "Brainwash? We've been through this before. Just because I see things differently than you doesn't mean my thoughts are crazy." Grandma turned away and defiantly climbed the stairs to her room.

I didn't know what Father was talking about either. Everything Grandma and I did together was private. I never told anybody. My stomach clenched. *He must've driven by the school yard when Grandma was standing out in the open using her hands like divining rods.*

My ears rang with the sounds of their voices. I hated fighting. We'd had such an amazing adventure and now Father was making it wrong. I took a deep breath and followed Grandma up the stairs.

I knocked on my brothers' bedroom door.

"I heard." Sean said as he opened the door. "Another stupid fight." He flopped down on his bed and leaned against the headboard. A sketchbook lay open near his feet. "Seems like Dad's the only one who can have a private life."

Brucie looked up from the floor. He was petting Goldy. "Did you find the ghost," he asked.

"He won't scare you anymore," I whispered. "But I can't talk about it."

Sean shook his head. "This house is built on secrets," he said in a nasty tone.

Later that night I sat on my bed with the overhead light on trying to think about what to write for English class. "Write a paragraph describing something unusual," Miss Baker had said. I brought the brown leather bag filled with *Kin.ni.kin.nick* up to my nose and took a deep whiff. The sweet scent raced through my head, down my throat and into my chest.

Everything about my life was unusual. It was a matter of which part was okay to share. We weren't allowed to talk about bad stuff, and anyway I didn't want to write about what Father said. Most of what I did with Grandma was secret, not just to Father, but to everyone.

I got up from my bed and opened my French windows. A cool breeze brushed over my cheeks. When I leaned out, and looked up, I could see that our house was blanketed in stars. *If you look closely you can see animals in rock formations, clouds, and the sky,* Grandma said. *They bring messages of all kinds.*

As I stared into the stars twinkling lights, a figure started to take shape. Legs ... a long body ... then antlers formed.

It was an elk. A whole one, not just the head like I'd seen at Morrie's Bar. I closed the windows, went back to bed and wrote.

*You never know where you're going to end up from one day to the next. Once I was roaming the forest far away from humans. I ate grass that grew wild in the fields near my home. Birds sang to me during the day and crickets chirped me to sleep at night.*

*Then one day a two legged cousin came to my forest. He shot me in the chest. I couldn't hear the birds after that. The crickets stopped chirping me to sleep. I felt myself rising above the Earth.*

*I don't wake up in the forest anymore. Part of me is nailed to a wall. People party in the bar below where my head is kept. They think I don't see them. But I do. I see them from another place now. One day they will know me as their four legged cousin. Until then, they won't know how to respect my part of their Earth connection.*

Chapter Twenty

## SECRETS

November was a cold month. Last night's melting snow left small pools of ice on the sidewalk. I adjusted my ice skates, so they wouldn't bang against my shoulders.

"Glad you're going skatin' with me," Margaret said as we made our way up Lower Fort to school.

"Me too." I zipped across one of the icy patches. "Momma balled up newspaper in the toes so they'd fit. It's good to have cousins who outgrow things."

Margaret laughed as she zipped across the next patch. "Did'ya get that blue coat from your cousin too?"

"Yeh!" I pulled up on the collar. "How'd you know?"

"It still smells like moth balls." Margaret raised her eyebrows and pinched her nose.

I sniffed at the collar. "Yuck!" I grimaced. "Maybe it'll air out before we get to school."

"Race ya the last three blocks." Margaret kicked a small mound of snow. Flakes flew into the sky.

We flew up the school stairs like a strong wind ... neck and neck ... tied. My heart pounded like a drum as blood coursed through my veins. I pushed my shoulder against the heavy door ... rushed in ... and ... slipped on a wet patch. I dropped my book bag ... reached out for balance ... and hit the floor like a smashed snowball.

"What a fumble." "Slow down." "Should'a looked." And other remarks filled the air. I was so embarrassed.

"Can I help you up?" A deep voice asked. I struggled to my knees, and looked up. It was Skipper Roulette ... the boy the girls giggle and exchange secrets about. The patch on his leather jacket read FOOTBALL. "I ... should've ... been more careful," I stammered.

"Accidents happen." Skipper squatted down, picked everything up and pulled me back into standing position. "It's a good thing your skates didn't cut you." He adjusted them over my shoulder, then handed me my book bag. "Thank you," I mumbled. I wanted to say more, but I couldn't.

"You sure you're okay?" He asked towering over me. He must have been six feet tall.

I swallowed hard. "Yes ... I'm fine." The way he looked at me gave me the all-overs. My stomach tensed. Heat raced up my spine. Drums beat in my head. His eyes were an unreal color of green, like a river on a stormy day. His hair was short, cut into a burr. That's where the hair, half an inch thick, sticks straight up. His high cheek bones and olive skin made me think he was a mixed breed, like me.

"I'm Skipper Roulette," he said extending his hand. "You're that new girl aren't you?"

"Umm, yes, I am," I mumbled. I shook his hand as well as I could considering my arms were loaded. He didn't need to tell me who he was.

I looked down at my shoes, then up into his stormy river green eyes and quickly down at my shoes again. My shoes really were ugly. Every other girl in school got to wear delicate black and white oxfords. Mine were clumpy brown ones.

"See ya." Skipper made two quick clicking noises with his tongue as he turned to go down the hall. His broad shoulders moved straight ahead like he was still wearing football armor.

Questions danced in my head. *Does he like me? How did he know I was new? Did he think I was a clumsy oaf?* I took a deep breath to quiet my racing thoughts then started down the hall towards my homeroom.

"He likes you," Margaret whispered as she stepped in beside me. Her white figure skates dangled over one shoulder. A canvas book bag draped over the other.

My face flushed with heat. "Bite your tongue." The thought of Skipper liking me was exciting and scary at the same time.

Margaret cocked her head, pressed her lips together and nodded. "Consider it bitten."

All through my classes all I could think about were those river green eyes and his gentle voice. *Skipper Roulette,* he said. *My name's Skipper Roulette.* It just came tumbling out of his mouth like there was nothing to it. On the other hand, I stood there staring at my shoes and smelling up the hallway with mothballs.

"Rehearse," I said to myself. We rehearsed for other things, why not rehearse what to say next time you meet? That is if you meet. If he ever wants to say anything to you again. *Hi! I'm Fiona, Fiona Lonestar MacLean. I'm in Mr. Jesue's home room. Hi! I'm Fiona,* I practiced over and over again in my head.

I don't know how I made it through the day, but somehow I did. In history class when Mr. Jesue asked us to write what we thought about so many women being in the work force, I drew figure eights around *Skipper* and *Lonestar*. When Miss Baker asked me why proper grammar was important, I went blank. The girl, on my right answered: *Without good grammar ya can't get a good job.* I knew Father would be really mad at me if I didn't pay attention and get good grades, but I was stuck in a deep place and suddenly I didn't want to find my way out.

"Do you really think he likes me?" I asked Margaret as we walked towards the ice rink, after school, she in her long brown coat, me in my smelly blue coat.

Margaret stopped, turned towards me and gave me a funny look. "You've never had a boyfriend! That's it isn't it?" She banged her head like it was a Coca-Cola machine that didn't deliver. "I bet you've never even been kissed."

"Well, no." I swallowed hard.

"You want to practice?"

My stomach did a somersault. *Kissing a girl is not okay,* I thought. I wasn't even sure if kissing anybody full on the mouth was okay. Before I could think the whole thing out, Margaret stood in front of me. Closed her eyes. And leaned in.

Margaret's lips felt rose petal soft. And warm. Steamy breath brushed over my cheeks. Whooshing sounds pulsed in my ears. I wanted to move away, but I didn't want to at the same time. "Thou shalt not," Preacher MacNeal's words echoed in my head.

A flick of wet broke through the rose petal softness and forced its way between my teeth. It searched out places I never knew lived inside of me before. Fourth of July fireworks exploded inside of me.

My knees buckled as Margaret pulled away. It was cold outside, but my breath felt fiery hot. Margaret was standing close, yet she seemed far away. I knew I was small, but suddenly I felt as big as the moon.

Everything was jangled. Wrong. Not good. I looked around to see if the whole of Lincoln Park was staring at me. I had sinned and just like Tenskwatawa — I was headed for hell. Beads of sweat broke out on my forehead. I quickly brushed them away. *What was Father going to say?*

Neither one of us said anything as we picked up our stuff and headed for the ice-rink, six blocks away. If kissing Skipper was anything like kissing Margaret I didn't think I could survive.

When we finally got to the ice-rink my hands were so shaky it took me twice as long as usual to put my skates on. Margaret was fast. I watched as she skated out to meet a group of girls I'd seen at school, but didn't really know. They were a few years older than I was, about Margaret's age, fifteen or so.

Strange feelings from the kiss still lurked inside of me. *You don't have to tell everybody what you do in private, Lonestar,* Grandma always said. *Some things you can keep separate just for special friends, or for yourself. Self protection,* I thought. I took a deep breath, stepped onto the ice, and headed in Margaret's direction. Our kiss was gonna stay locked inside of me for the rest of my life.

When I skated up to Margaret, the girls she was with put their hands over their faces, turned, and skated in different directions. A red coat, yellow coat, and gray coat whizzed past me. The sound of their blades slicing through the ice made me feel numb all over again.

Even though our kissing was locked inside of me, I figured it wasn't locked inside of Margaret. *She must've told her friends and now they didn't want anything to do with me,* I thought. *She probably told them about Skipper Roulette while she was at it.*

"Don't look, Fiona, uh, Lonestar," Margaret said quickly.

"What?"

"Nobody's supposed to know who they are."

"Who, what?" I stammered trying to bring myself back out of my numbness.

"It's a secret club, The Big Mommas. You can't know who they are unless you're a member. I was just talkin' to them about bringing you in. I told them you were old for your age, but there's still a probation period of a few weeks."

"Me? A part of The Big Mommas?" I asked slowly starting to wake up. I'd never been a part of a secret club before. A heaviness fell over me like a dark cloud. Something felt dangerous. I brushed the feeling away. *Being in a secret club would be fun. It made me feel important.* "They didn't care that I was younger?"

Margaret screwed up her mouth like a prune and shook her head *no*. "They didn't care that you were younger."

I stared into her eyes to see if there was anything hidden. But there wasn't. She hadn't spilled the beans about our kiss or about Skipper.

We practiced our figure eights and *arabesques* over and over again. When nobody was close by, Margaret told me about her special club. They went on adventures together. They even took the bus across the bridge to Canada and back once. Nobody knew but The Big Mommas. It all sounded really amazing.

Grandma met me at the door when I got home. A new beaded belt hung over the shoulder of the patchwork apron Aunt Raven made for her. Grandma was always working on one thing or another. "How was school today?" She asked cheerily.

I wanted to tell her about the club, but I couldn't. It was a secret. I didn't want to talk about Margaret. *Kissing a girl was a sin. If I didn't talk about it maybe the fact that it happened would just go away,* I thought.

It was too early to say anything about Skipper Roulette. If my brothers got wind of me liking a boy I'd be teased 'till I was blue in the face.

I swallowed hard, "Fine." I put my books on the table, hung my coat on the rack just inside the door, and stuffed my gloves in the pocket.

"Just *fine*?" Grandma sat down in the big stuffed chair across from the sofa. A bottle of beer sat on top of a white doily on the small round table next to the chair. She laid the belt across her lap, reached into the basket on the floor near her feet, and took out a tray of beads. Christmas was a month away, so Grandma was getting a jump on new presents.

"Do I look old for my age, Grandma?" I looked at myself in the mirror, ran my fingers through my shoulder length blonde hair and turned one way, then the other. My face was changing. It was more oval now, less round. I spun around and waited for her answer.

"That depends." Grandma put some thread between her teeth and pulled hard. The thread broke. She held up a needle to the light and poked the thread through the eye. "Depends on how old you want to look."

"How about fifteen?" That's how old I thought Skipper was.

"You plannin' on skippin' a few years?" Grandma laughed so hard it made her cough. She leaned forward and patted her chest.

"You okay?" I didn't like the deep rumble of her cough.

"Right as rain, Lonestar." Grandma took a deep breath and smiled. She rolled the thread into a ball, stuck the needle through to knot it, then pushed the needle through a hole in the belt making it ready to receive one of the beads from the tray.

I nodded and turned toward the mirror on the opposite wall. "Hi! I'm Fiona, Fiona Lonestar MacLean. I'm in Mr. Jesue's home room," I mumbled.

"You say something Lonestar?" Grandma looked up from her sewing.

"No. Just talkin' to myself." I picked up my stuff, walked through the dining room and ran up the stairs to my bedroom.

Chapter Twenty-One

## PLANTING SEEDS

Grandma and Momma were in a happy mood when I came down to help with dinner. Grandma met me in the doorway with a song. *Fly like an eagle,* she sang grinning from ear to ear. She'd been doing that more lately.

Momma turned away from the vegetables on the stove and sang back, *Fly like an eagle. Fly way up high.* Her eyes were glassy. Six empty bottles of beer stood on the kitchen table.

*Fly like an eagle. Into the sky.* Grandma sang a little louder as she reached out for Momma's hand. Momma set her spoon down, *Fly like an eagle. Over the moon.* Momma stumbled as she reached out for my hand. I held her tight so she wouldn't fall.

Soon, Grandma had us all in a line. She was in front dancing her way around the kitchen with Momma behind her and me behind Momma. It was so fun. There I was trying to be older, when everybody older was acting younger.

Momma grabbed some plates while I picked up the silverware and napkins. We danced our way through the doorway to the dining room table. We kept singing and dancing until the table was all set.

I thought I heard someone come in the front door, but my breath was so loud, I wasn't sure. I listened for someone to say *hello*, but when no one did I went back to dancing.

*Flying up high,* Grandma sang, motioning for Momma to keep playing with us. She quickly checked the oven, looked over at us and fell into line again giggling like a kid.

"Honey, I'm home," a deep voice called from the living room. We froze on the spot. Momma dug into her apron pocket and pulled out some mints. She quickly popped one into her mouth and handed one to Grandma. Grandma grabbed the empty bottles of beer, three in each hand and made her way out the back door to the garbage can.

I heard the toilet flush outside the hallway. Then the water run. "I'm gonna change clothes," Father yelled. The sound of his leather shoes made a light tapping sound as he crossed from the bathroom to the bedroom.

Momma wiped her face with her apron, got out the orange juice and vodka, poured some in a glass and motioned for me to take the drink into the living room and wait for Father. I held the cold drink up to one cheek, then the other to help me cool down, then headed for the living room.

I set Father's drink down on the table next to the sofa, turned on the floor lamp, straightened out the new flowered slip covers, and organized the magazines and newspapers on the table in front of the sofa.

"Hi! I'm Fiona, Fiona Lonestar MacLean. I'm in Mr. Jesue's home room." I mumbled to the mirror next to the sofa again while I waited for Father to change.

"What's that Fiona?" Father asked as he came in wearing his one piece checkered jumper. Besides his lucky shirt, jumpers were his favorite thing to wear.

"Oh!" I turned around quickly. "You were fast."

"Yeah, guess I was." Father looked around the tidied up room. "You bring this in?" Father reached for his glass of vodka and orange juice and brought it up to his lips.

"Well, Momma made it. But, yeah, I brought it."

"Sweet nectar from the Gods." Father took a sip. "Good for what ails ya." He raised one eyebrow and nodded. "You're gonna make somebody a fine wife one day, Fiona."

Pictures of me walking down the church aisle, hand in hand with Skipper Roulette, popped into my head.

After dinner, while Grandma and I were doing the dishes, I asked her about love.

"It's like everything else, Lonestar. It starts out as a seed. The seed holds possibility. But it has to be fed, watered, given light, and cared for, in order to grow."

"Can't it happen, like in a second?"

Grandma laughed, "that's not love," she said. "But it could be a beginning."

It was hard to sleep that night. *Visions of Skipper pushed against my resting mind like groundhogs determined to tunnel through the darkness where they couldn't be captured. Skipper hung, like a low branch, from a tall tree. Leaves swirled over his head, arms, legs and body, intertwining like wild Ivy. I held a watering jug over the top of his head. As the water flowed out, the rest of him started to turn green too. The more I watered, the deeper the green became.*

*He got bigger and bigger. Vines shot out from his legs and arms. One of the vines reached out and wrapped around my throat. It was hard to breath. I pulled at the vine. Tried to loosen its grip. But I couldn't.*

When I ran into Skipper at school the next day, he knew who I was. "Hi, Fiona Lonestar MacLean," he said as we passed in the hall. My name came out easy, no hesitation, like he'd known it forever. All the practicing I'd done was for nothing. I couldn't speak. I gave him a half hearted smile and looked away.

Margaret dug her elbow into my ribs and gave me one of those looks of hers. The one where she cocked her head, pressed her lips together and nodded knowingly.

It was already hard enough to look Skipper in the eye without her prompting. I needed some of that Shawnee paint Grandma says makes you disappear.

Chapter Twenty-Two

## GOOD NEWS

The next Monday, as I came out of English class, I noticed Skipper leaning against one of the lockers in the hall. The piercing noise of the lunch bell mingled with the happy sounds of kids hurrying past. Some of the girls flashed him a friendly smile; a few of the guys nodded and one boy punched him in the arm. Skipper cried out in pain, bent over, then laughed.

I didn't want him to think I was staring at him, so I pretended I was waiting for someone. My stomach fluttered as he pushed away from the lockers and walked towards me. "Goin' to the cafeteria?" he asked.

I swallowed hard. "Sure." I tightened the grip on my books as we walked side by side. I didn't know what to say. *Should I ask him about football? Or track? Sean runs track. Does he know Sean?* The words stayed captive in my throat. Just when I thought I might explode into a zillion pieces, Skipper spoke.

"So ... uh ... what da you think of Miss Baker?" he asked.

"Umm ... she's a good teacher." I looked up and managed a half smile. "Different kind of, she gives us writing assignments."

Kids passed us at the doorway of the cafeteria. "I heard you wrote about an Elk once," Skipper said.

His words took my breath away. *How did he know what I wrote?* I wondered. I took a deep breath and nodded. My face felt hot. I glanced at the kids sitting or circling around the picnic style tables. Their lips moved, but I couldn't hear anything. Suddenly, I felt like everybody was staring at us. *I'd be the gossip of the day.*

Someone came up behind us and slapped Skipper on the back. He turned around and laughed. It was Sean. "Gotta go," I said. *Sean was gonna tease me for sure.*

Margaret waved me towards her table. She was sitting towards the back with some of the girls I saw her with at the ice rink, The Big Mommas. After I got my food, I headed in their direction. Flashes of a plaid shirt, a yellow dress, and a navy blue skirt whisked away as I approached. I figured they were part of the secret club so I didn't focus on their faces. I wasn't supposed to know who they were until I was accepted.

"So?" Margaret smiled. Her green neck scarf was tied into a perfect knot. "Did Skipper ask you to meet him at the sock-hop next week?" She raised her eyebrows and pursed her lips. "I saw you talkin' in the doorway."

My heart beat in that loud drum way it does sometimes. I looked around to see if anyone was listening in. Margaret's words, *Ask you to meet him at the sock-hop?* swirled in my head. They were exciting and scary at the same time. Lafayette had dances in the gymnasium on special occasions. Usually kids went in groups, then paired up once they got there. I'd heard about them, but never gone before.

"Uh, uh." I played with the turkey on my plate and took tiny bites. My insides were so scrambled that opening my mouth, and chewing, was hard. Each swallow became filled with the hope that Skipper would say something about the dance.

The next day, Margaret dragged me to the open field behind school to watch football practice. Mounds of dried leaves dotted the edges of the field like markers announcing the end of fall. We sat on some of the metal chairs behind the markers. Skipper threw the ball to a boy wearing a yellow jersey about twenty feet in front of him. The boy caught it and ran toward the goal post. Some of the other players, dressed in brown, chased after him.

"I don't know how they can throw a ball when my fingers feel like ice," Margaret said. She clapped her hands together, pulled her hat down to cover her ears and tightened her scarf. "Brrrr." Her nose, and I guess mine as well, was bright red.

Skipper ran forward, as did other members of the yellow team, and tried to protect the boy with the ball. It was getting colder by the minute. I rubbed my hands together, then brought them up to my face. The little heat I created helped. Skipper tackled one of the guys in brown and they both went down on the icy grass. It looked painful, but, they both got up, brushed themselves off and went on to the next play. *You had to be tough to play football,* I thought. Margaret and I watched as the boys went through various skirmishes.

After practice, Skipper walked over to us. The shoulder pads underneath his shirt made him look even bigger than he already was. "You guys cold? he unfastened the chin strap of his helmet.

I glanced sideways at Margaret. "Not really." My hot breath hung in the cold air.

"Eskimos like to freeze," Margaret joked.

On the way home, Margaret and I ran and slid across the icy sidewalks. "I feel so awkward with Skipper," I said. "I never know what to say."

"Just pretend." The tail of her scarf flapped in the wind. "Act like he doesn't matter."

"Isn't that like a lie?" I slid backwards so I could see her face as she answered.

She rolled her eyes, "It's like I said before, sometimes lies are self protection."


Two weeks later, on the Wednesday before the sock-hop, a friend of Skipper's ran up to me in the hall at school, handed me a note with his name on it, looked around, then disappeared. My stomach tensed. I shoved the note into my history book and headed for class. I wanted to read it after school, when no one was watching.

"What does history tell us?" Mr. Jesue asked pressing his fingers along the top of his mustache.

"Stories about time," I answered feeling the note burning through the top of my book.

"Exactly! And what is your favorite time?"

"After school," I said without thinking. The words just popped out of my mouth.

Everybody laughed. They were probably thinking I didn't like school, but I did. I just wanted this one day to be over so Margaret could stand next to me while I opened the note from Skipper.

After school, I asked Margaret to go to the girls room with me. Once we were locked into a stall, I opened the top of my book and carefully pulled out the piece of paper I'd hidden inside. "It's from Skipper," I said.

She patted her chest and let out a deep sigh. "He's askin' you. I just know it."

"Shh" I stayed real still and listened for footsteps. "Somebody'll hear you." I unfolded the note. "Will you meet me at the sock-hop ... this Saturday?" My eyes blurred. Flames burned through my chest. "It's signed ... Your friend Skipper."

We both let out a squeal at the same time and jumped up and down trying not to bang ourselves against the sides of the stall. When we stopped I looked at the note again to make sure I was reading it right. My ears buzzed with excitement. "That's what it says all right."

Margaret beamed. "Got more good news for ya," she said. "Your trial's over. You're gonna be sworn into The Big Mommas Friday night."

"Oh, oh, oh!" Hearing two good things at the same time made me dizzy.

On Thursday, I was still so puffed up it was hard to keep my feet on the ground. *Fly like an eagle. Flying up high.* I sang and clicked my heels together while working at the kitchen counter. My hand sliced through one peeled carrot after the other in rhythm to my singing.

"You sound chipper." Momma grinned as she stood on the other side of the sink cutting the celery and onions.

"Yep." I danced some of my sliced carrots over to the big pot Grandma was stirring on the stove behind us. I bent forward, held the carrots in my right hand, lifted them over my head, then slowly brought my arm down and dropped the carrots into the boiling water.

"Very nice," Grandma nodded. "I think the delivery adds to the flavor. "Instead of the *Nutcracker Suite* we could call this the *Dance of the Vegetables*." She dipped her wooden spoon into the soup, brought it up to her nose and smiled. The smell of onions, celery and carrots wafted through the air like perfume.

Momma glanced up at the clock on the wall. "Humm, five-thirty. She edged toward the sink, washed her hands and dried them on her apron. "It's time."

*Fly like an eagle. Flying up high.* I sang again as I picked up another handful of carrots, twirled across the linoleum and dropped them in the pot. I hadn't forgotten what I'd learned in dance class.

Momma mixed Father's pre-dinner drink and asked me to take it to him. I wiped my hands on the towel, picked up the drink and headed out the kitchen door. *Fly like an eagle,* I hummed as I sashayed across the dining room and into the living room. I set the drink down on the coffee table in front of Father and waited for him to look up.

"What were you singing, Fiona?" Father peered at me over the top of the Detroit News. His voice edgy.

"Umm. Just a song." I swallowed hard. I hadn't been thinking. The song just slipped out – riding the waves of happiness stirring inside of me.

"Go back into the kitchen and send your grandmother in here. I need to have a little 'heart to heart' with that woman."

I went into the kitchen and did what he asked. I didn't like it, but I did it. Grandma rolled her eyes upwards and headed towards the living room.

Momma and I stood by the sink and stared out the window. Grandma stuck a potato in a glass of water when we first moved to Rose Street and put it on the window sill. Tiny pieces of green poked their heads through the tough brown skin. *Life has a way of multiplying itself,* she said. There were so many parts of life that Grandma had brought into our house, and now Father was mad at her.

"I've told ya a thousand times to stay away from all that Indian stuff," Father growled.

Even with the kitchen door closed we could hear every word. I could tell by the tone of his voice Father was trying not to yell.

"Isn't it time you told your kids the truth, Frank?" Grandma sighed.

What truth? I wondered. I turned and looked at Momma for an answer. She stared through the window at the back garden gate like she was waiting for someone to walk in and make everything okay, smooth things out.

"What truth?" Father's voice shook. He was right on the edge of yelling again.

"The truth about your past. The more you hide it the more it festers," Grandma hissed.

"You're here, living in *my* house because of *my* invitation. That means you follow *my* rules." Father lost it. His words exploded through the air and bounced against every wall in the house.

That promise he made about not yelling anymore was good and broken. Tears rolled down my cheeks. I wiped them away with the back of my sleeve. If Father sent Grandma away, I was going with her.

"My husband scared me into silence for years," Grandma said. "I followed his rules. I wasn't allowed to have a job, or get a good education, or even vote. That's what's wrong with Merle. I didn't speak up, now she doesn't speak up. My husband's dead, Frank. I'm not gonna be here forever and ... I'm not scared anymore."

I looked over at Momma. Her back stiffened. Even if Momma didn't speak up, I knew, some day I was going to.

As usual, Father didn't say anything about being mad at Grandma at dinner. Instead, he talked about the price of cars going up to over a thousand dollars. Sean looked impressed. Momma nodded and Grandma just looked away. Brucie played with the carrots and peas on his plate. Goldy waited under the table for food to drop on the floor.

Chapter Twenty-Three

## THE BIG MOMMAS

Friday night, I waited 'till it was quiet downstairs, crawled out my French window, slid down the roof of the back porch, and dropped onto a small mound of new snow, ten feet down. Lucky for me Goldy was in Sean and Brucie's room, otherwise she'd of barked and blown my meeting with The Big Mommas.

I crept across the backyard, through the gate, and nipped up the alley to the next block. Snow was falling. The flakes glimmered in the moonlight as they blanketed everything around. I pulled my hat down and raised the collar of my coat to warm my ears.

As soon as I got to Fort Street, I saw Margaret. She was standing under the street lamp in front of Ernie's Everything Store, a block away. Behind her, a string of red, green, yellow, blue and white Christmas lights blinked on and off around the front windows. It looked festive.

Margaret paced back and forth and stomped the sidewalk to keep warm. Several girls gathered close by. Two huddled together under the blinking lights, and one swung playfully around the lamp post near Margaret.

Everything inside of me felt jangly, on edge. I crossed at the light, then hurried to where they were standing. "Heh," I said to Margaret, trying to act nonchalant.

"Heh," she said back. "You ready for the initiation?"

I nodded. I didn't know what the initiation would be, but whatever it was, I was more than ready. The idea of being in a secret club made me feel that I belonged somehow.

We went behind the store and stood between cases of empty Coca-Cola bottles and a garbage bin. It was quieter there, away from cars whizzing by and people going in and out of Ernie's. Margaret wrapped a bandana over my eyes.

*The Big Mommas, The Big Mommas, The Big Mommas,* she chanted along with the other girls. She turned me around clockwise three times.

"Are you, Fiona Lonestar MacLean ready to pledge your heart and soul to The Big Mommas? To treat each of us as sisters, for the rest of your life?" Margaret's voice sounded low and serious.

"I am." My heart raced like a train going full steam ahead. I always wanted sisters.

The girls started to sing out my name, "Fiona Lonestar MacLean, Fiona Lonestar MacLean," over and over again. The rhythms of their voices washed over the inside of me like rain trickling over pebble stones. Yellow candlelight flickered through the edges of my blindfold. The sweet smell of some kind of incense drifted across my face.

Someone turned me counter clockwise three times, then took off my blindfold.

"Wamagee, wamagee, wamagee, kaboom!" Everybody shouted as I stood there trying to steady myself.

"I'm Cheryl," the red headed girl with freckles lisped. "I'm Diane," added a tall skinny girl with heavy rimmed glasses. "And I'm Lorraine," clipped out the third in a British accent, "pleased to meet you."

Margaret pulled a Zippo lighter out of her gray coat pocket and lit a cigarette. I'd never seen her smoke before so I figured it was a part of the ceremony. Her dark eyes softened as the smoke went into her chest. When she was finished she handed the cigarette to me.

I held the cigarette between my first two fingers, brought it up to my mouth and drew in as hard as I could. Heat soared down my throat and chest like a flaming arrow. Sparks danced wildly behind my eyes. I wanted to reach out and hang onto something, or someone, but I was afraid if I did, I wouldn't pass whatever test the smoking part was. After what seemed like an eternity – the pain and dizziness lessened. I didn't know how anybody could do this and survive.

"Well then," redheaded Cheryl said. "Let's get on with it."

British Lorraine looked at me. "Lonestar, we all take turns giving orders and since this is my week, I get to choose."

I hoped Lorraine's choice would be something exciting like a river trip on a steamboat, a hike to the sand quarry, or a long bus ride to Canada like Margaret told me they'd taken before. I was open to pretty much anything, except more smoking.

"I think I'd like to go back to Woolworth's and see what we can lift. We can choose partners, just like we did before and take different aisles."

"What're we gonna do there?" I didn't understand what she was talking about. Woolworth's wasn't anywhere in my expectations.

"Well to steal of course," Lorraine answered.

*Steal? How did we get from river trips, hikes, and bus rides to stealin'?* I wondered. My hair stood up on the back of my neck. This was scary. *The last thing I'd stolen was a doll's dress from my friend Connie when I was eight years old. I felt so guilty I took it back.* This time when "Thou shalt not steal," echoed in my head, I pushed the thoughts away. *I have to do what the group says in order to fit in,* I reasoned.

"Put one hand out and examine an item, then quickly snitch what you want with the other," she said moving the fingers of one hand out like a spider, then jerking them back. "Wear something with big pockets and for God's sake don't wear red."

"Right," I said. "Big pockets, no red."

So that was it. I was in the group. *"Bas no beatha,"* I whispered. We were going to meet Saturday morning to go *shopping. I wondered what Father would say now.*

That night I had nightmare. *A man was chasing me down a dirt path somewhere. I couldn't see his face. I ran and ran until I couldn't run anymore. I was so thirsty and tired that I stopped to get a drink of water at a pond. The man came up behind me and handcuffed my wrists. I ended up in jail.*

I woke with a start, sat straight up in bed and shakily pulled back the covers. I put on my pink robe, grabbed my pillow and went into Grandma's room next door. I slept the rest of the night on the floor, under her bed.

When I woke up I could hear her hum-singing to herself as she sat at the vanity table. I watched Grandma pull her hair brush from the top of her head, across her chest and down to her waist as she sat facing the mirror. Her once strong back was beginning to curve above her shoulders. Momma said that happens when people get older. Gravity pulls them down. It doesn't stretch them up.

"You ever cut your hair Grandma?"

"Wha...?" She turned around quickly and patted her chest. "Lonestar what in tarnation are you doing here?" Her dark cheeks flushed pink and blended in with her flannel nightgown.

"I couldn't sleep so I tiptoed into your room and crawled under the bed." I rubbed hard on the back of my neck. I felt stiff.

"Well you sure gave me a fright." Grandma patted her chest.
"Sorry."

"You hear anything strange last night ... after dinner?" Grandma squinted as she look me in the eyes.

My breath caught in my chest. *Did she hear me crawl out my window and drop into the back yard?* I wondered. *Does she know what I'm doing?* "No, Grandma I didn't hear anything," I lied as I got up and stretched.

"Is there somethin' you wanted to talk about?" Grandma turned back to the mirror, divided her hair in half, then separated the half into three pieces. She slowly intertwined the three pieces of hair into one.

"You ever ... steal anything besides that tobacco you told me about, Grandma?" I asked real nonchalant like, as I sat down on the bench next to her.

"You thinking of stealin' somethin'?" Grandma looked straight ahead at my reflection in the mirror.

My stomach wrapped itself into one big knot. I'd never lied to Grandma before. At least not when she came out and asked me directly. Now I'd done it — twice. "Just askin'," I said quickly. I ran my fingers over the curves around the edges of the table and glanced sideways at Grandma.

"Well, besides that tobacco that made me sick, I stole my neighbor's dog once." She pursed her lips and raised her eyebrows. "But he ran home after I fed him." Grandma laughed so hard it made her cough.

"Stole some make-up at the drugstore too. Only we didn't call it a drugstore then." Grandma finished braiding her hair, wrapped it in a bun, and pinned it in place. *"E'ne.* It was a chemist."

I waited for a few minutes, then asked, "Did you ... get ... caught?"

Grandma stopped what she was doing, looked me in the eye, and frowned. "Not right away."

"I was fourteen." The corners of her mouth splashed with those wrinkles that formed when she pursed her lips. "Just six months older than you are right now. Girls didn't wear make-up much then."

"Some of the girls in my school wear lipstick." I didn't tell her I wanted to, but I did.

Grandma gently ran the tips of her fingers across my cheeks and over my forehead like she was trying to see inside my head.

"I went to a small country school," Grandma nodded. "It was kind of mixed, Indian-Scots, Indian-French, and some all white. One little white boy teased me because I was darker than he was." Grandma sighed. "I had a big crush on him. So big that I couldn't even think straight."

"Yeh, I know how that goes," I said. *I thought about how self conscious I felt with Skipper. Meeting him at the sock-hop was going to be scary.*

Grandma nodded, shook her head and continued. "Anyway, I stole some make-up to make my skin look whiter."

"Did it?" I blinked a few times. I'd never thought about Grandma wanting to be anything other than what she was, a nice cream color.

"Yeah! Made me look like a clown." She picked up her brush, motioned for me to turn around, and ran the bristles through my hair. "When my father saw the light color I used to hide my dark skin, he sent me out back to wash the *war paint* off." Grandma divided my hair and started to braid it just like she'd done her own. "We didn't have indoor plumbing, just a water pump in the back yard. After I washed my face I had to wash all the mirrors in the house ... every day for two weeks."

"What did the mirrors have to do with wearing make-up?" I sat still as she tightened my braid and secured it with a rubber band. I turned to the side to look in the mirror. My braid was much shorter than Grandma's, but I liked it anyway. I smiled at my reflection.

Grandma nodded. "I never asked." She shrugged. "Looking back, I think he wanted me to see who I really was, a mixture of a lot of things."

"I wish Father accepted all the mixtures in us – like my Great-Grandfather," I said.

"Me too." Grandma pinched her lips together and frowned. She looked like she wanted to say something else, but she didn't.

Chapter Twenty-Four

## TOGETHERNESS IS GOOD

I put on some Levis and the old brown sweater Sean outgrew. The faded color wouldn't draw any attention in my direction. The only toilet was downstairs in the hall off the dining room, next to the kitchen. As I stepped off the landing at the bottom of the stairs I could hear Sean, Brucie, Mom and Dad in the kitchen.

"Before you know it the whole of America will be run over by *commie's*," Father's voice boomed out through the closed door.

I went into the bathroom, cleaned up in a flash, then stepped back into the hallway.

"I thought it had something to do with community." I heard Sean say.

"Yeah. Everything's owned by the community, not the individual. So this house wouldn't be ours," Father went on, "it'd belong to whoever the bigwigs in the community thought should have it."

"Keep talkin'," I whispered. It gave me a chance to sneak into the master bedroom, and rummage through the closet. I grabbed an old black coat I hadn't seen Momma wear in a long time and put it on. Even though it was a little big it looked pretty good on me. I stuck my hands in the pockets. They weren't too deep, but then I wasn't going to steal anything that wouldn't fit in the palm of my hand.

"God, *Wakontah*, Great Spirit, don't let anybody come out 'till I'm gone, okay?" I tiptoed down the hallway, across the dining room, out the front door and down the steps.

Margaret, British Lorraine, red headed Cheryl, and tall skinny Diane were waiting for me on the corner in front of Ernie's Everything Store. Margaret picked up an old cigarette butt from a dry patch on the sidewalk, lit it, took a puff and passed it to me. I quickly handed it to Lorraine. No way was I gonna smoke again. Inhaling that cigarette at my initiation ceremony burned my throat something fierce.

"One, two, three," we yelled out as we headed towards Woolworth's. Our cries mixed with the roar of cars along the road. *Five girls on a secret mission,* I thought.

"Remember, pick something up with one hand, look at it carefully, then pick up what you want to steal with the other hand and put it in your pocket, or under your coat." Margaret's eyes darted one way then the other as we neared Woolworth's. A man in a long coat hurried past. Two women argued about who was going to buy what as they looked at a display in the window.

Nobody seemed to take notice of us. I waited for the other girls to go in, took a deep breath and walked through Woolworth's front door. I wasn't sure what I was gonna steal, but I knew it wouldn't be make-up. That was what got Grandma into trouble.

Red, green and gold streamers wrapped around the counters made everything look festive. Each aisle had a motif of some kind. Cheryl and Diane went down the aisle decorated with candy canes. Margaret and I went down the one with elves. Lorraine wandered back and forth between all of us so she could let us know if any cops came in. I crossed my fingers and prayed my dream about going to jail wouldn't come true.

I slowly ran my hand over some flowered boxes of stationery as Margaret examined notebooks and diary's. One of the cardboard elves on the edge of the counter stared at me, I looked away. It gave me the creeps.

"Look calm," I mumbled. When the salesgirl turned her back – I quickly moved my hand over to a row of fountain pens. They were the smallest items on the counter. I picked up a box of stationery in my right hand and quickly slipped a silver pen into Momma's pocket with my left.

"Blam-blam-blam," my heart screamed as it tried to break through my chest. "Errrrrrr," blasted in my head. My own dizzying alarm system. I glanced at the clerk. She was busy cleaning up supplies at the end of the aisle. *Did she see me?* I wondered.

It wasn't far to the front door, maybe one hundred steps at the most. But, it seemed like a mile. A long mile. Shakily I made my way to the front door and out into the fresh air. The cold wind bit into my face as I turned right and headed away from the five-and-ten-cent store. "Walk normal," I said to myself. "Don't look suspicious." A man hurried past. I jumped back, out of his way. A car honked. I stopped. *Was he honking at me?*

"Nice goin'." Margaret came up beside me. Her cheeks flushed. She brushed her dark hair away from her eyes as we increased our pace. After another block she opened her coat and took out a large diary from an inside pocket. A perfect size to keep records of our stealing adventures. "And, I got some Old Spice, for Ralph." Margaret giggled. She was proud of herself.

"That guy in Ms. Baker's class that keeps making eyes at you?" I looked around as we moved forward.

"Yep!" She smacked her lips together. "He's my date for the sock-hop."

"Wow!" I looked back to make sure we weren't being followed. Police did that in movies. They followed suspects for a block or two, then arrested them.

The only people I saw behind us were Cheryl and Diane. No police. We all went into the ladies room at the *Conoco Gas Station* two blocks up. The attendant gave us a funny look as we crowded in. Maybe it was because we didn't get out of a car.

The oil smell mixed with urine was pretty bad. I hoped it wouldn't sink into Momma's coat or she'd wonder what happened. I cracked the door open a bit.

"Lonestar got a silver fountain pen. I got a diary, Old Spice after shave for Ralphy and Sweet Lips scarlet lipstick," Margaret squealed.

*Sweet Lips,* I thought. The same as the girl I saw in the lavatory my first day of school.

"I got a compact with a mirror, eyelash curler – plus mascara, and Diane got a spangly bracelet with a necklace to match," Cheryl lisped.

*They got a lot more stuff than I did,* I thought. *Too much.*

Before I knew it, I was drawn into a circle of excitement. We jumped up and down holding onto each other, over and over again. Electricity leaped out of my whole body in every direction. Nothing mattered, but being with my new friends. I'd never experienced such togetherness with other girls. *"Bas no beatha,"* I whispered.

We separated under oath that no one would talk about what we did or who we were. Even Margaret and I took different routes home. She promised to zigzag while I went straight back down Fort Street. I walked backwards part of the way, just to make sure the cop in my head wasn't a real one tracking me back to Rose Street.

Chapter Twenty-Five

## PAINFUL PROTECTION

The phone was ringing when I stepped in the front door. *Oh my God,* I thought. *One of The Big Mommas must have been caught by the police and now they're coming after me.* I raced to the phone. I had to get it before Father did. "Hello." I drew into myself and held tight to the receiver.

"Lonestar?" the deep raspy voice said, "or Fiona, I'm not sure which to call you."

It was Skipper. A wave of relief swept over me. My fingers dug into the pocket of Momma's coat where I'd pushed the silver pen. It was a good thing Momma wasn't in the living room or she'd wonder why I had *her* coat on instead of mine.

"I just wanted to make sure you haven't forgotten about the dance tonight."

*Forgotten?* I felt a quick rush of adrenaline run up my spine. *How could I forget something that was more important than Harry S. Truman being the president of the United States?* Skipper's note was taped to the inside of my top drawer so I could read it everyday when I got my socks out. "No, I didn't forget." I held tight to the phone cord.

"Who's on the phone?" Father called out from the dining room.

"It's for me," I cried out proudly, holding my hand over the receiver. "Skipper Roulette's meeting me at the dance."

Father came up behind me. He jerked the phone out of my hand and slammed it down harshly. I looked down at the silent receiver, then up at Father. I saw him struggle to keep himself calm. He was raging inside, but his jaw was clenched tight in the effort of holding himself in.

I blinked my eyes, shook my head and glanced down again. The phone was still disconnected. It looked like a dead thing sitting on top of Mom's delicate doily. Father shook. He didn't say anything. I knew he was furious, but I didn't know why.

I put my hands up over my ears to stop the ringing. It was so loud I thought I was gonna explode. Then I went numb. My hands and feet disappeared. *I wondered if I was breaking up into little pieces and crumbling onto the living room carpet.*

Momma must've heard what was going on because she rushed into the room screaming, "how could you hang up the phone on a friend of hers?" Her face was beat red; eyes on fire. "What're you crazy." Momma clenched her fists and swung at the air.

I backed up against the wall to get out of the way. Momma was speaking up for me, but it was too late. Father had just ripped my heart apart.

"She's too young to go out on a date," Father's voice was flat. "It's a dangerous world out there." He waved his hands in the air. "Besides ... what kind of cockamamie name is ... Skipper Roulette." He choked. "It's ... not ... a Scot's name that's for sure."

"There are more people in the world than ... just the Scot's you know." Momma shook her head. "For God's sake Frank, your daughter's growin' up," she squawked, still not backing down. That familiar smell of beer was strong on her breath. "It's time you did too."

"I'm protecting her damn it," Father snorted.

"Controllin' her's more like it," Momma shot back.

I peeled myself off the wall like a strip of old wallpaper. "Stop it!" I cried. "I hate it when you fight. And I hate it even more when you fight about me. What happened to the rule of 'no more yelling?'"

They both stood stock still and stared at me as if they'd never really seen me before. *Oh, God! If he only knew.* I thought. *The only danger in the world wasn't outside, it was inside of me. I was a thief. I'd stolen something just to be a part of a group. Stealing was a sin. Skipper was a safe haven.* My thoughts scattered in all directions. The winds of the east, south, west and north lifted them out of my head and flew them on unseen wings to far away places. I stumbled across the floor, grabbed onto the banister and pulled myself up the stairs. My fist fell numbly on Grandma's door.

"I heard. I know. I'm so sorry," Grandma said as she opened her door to let me in.

But she couldn't know. Nobody could. I hated him. I was never gonna be the same.

She helped me take off Momma's coat without even asking why I was wearing it. Something I was worried about turned out to be the least of my problems.

We sat on the edge of her bed. It was the only place we could sit close together in her room. "My life's over, Grandma." Tears swelled out of my eyes.

Grandma pulled her quilt up over both of us. "Ah-e-ah-e-ah-e," she sang. "Sometimes it's hard to see. Ah-e-ah-e-ah-e. The path that's meant to be." Her arm held tight to my shoulders.

"I'm never gonna be able to face Skipper ever again." Sobs choked out of me. "He'll think I hung up on him ... and ... that I didn't want to meet him at the sock-hop."

"Never is a very long time, Lonestar. Just be with one minute at a time. It's easier."

I gripped the edge of the multicolored bird that Grandma'd so carefully sewed into the top of her quilt and held on real tight. I wanted it to fly me away, take me some place where I could have a Father who'd be happy that some nice boy asked me on a date.

"Sometimes," Grandma said slowly, "when what we *want* doesn't happen, then what we *need* drops in. It's part of a Divine Plan to teach us life lessons."

"I ... don't like ... these lessons," I sobbed.

Grandma sighed. "I know. They're not easy."

"Fiona, you okay?" Momma called from the hall.

I didn't answer.

"You know how he is sweetie ... gets carried away sometimes ... thinks he's ... protecting you."

172

"I know Momma, I know," I called back trying to hold back the sobs.  There was no need for her to feel terrible just because I did.  The truth was I didn't know.  I didn't know why Father wanted me to be a wife in training, but didn't want me to have a date.  I didn't know why he was so mad all the time.  If it was what Grandma said ... something about his past ... I wished he'd just blurt it out. His protection is painful.

For most of the rest of December, I avoided Skipper as best I could.  Instead of eating in the cafeteria, I took my lunch and ate away from the other kids.  When we passed in the hall I kept my eyes down and hurried past.  I was afraid if he asked me out again, and I said yes, Father'd figure out a way to embarrass me. The sound of the telephone being slammed shut still rang in my head. When Margaret asked me why I hadn't gone to the dance, I lied. "Got, sick," I said.  She just rolled her eyes and shook her head.  I think she thought I was too nervous to go. It was better for her to think that than to know what really happened.

Christmas day, the doorbell rang. When I opened it, I found Margaret standing on the front stoop. Her nose and cheeks pink from the cold morning air. Flurries of snowflakes danced over the front yard and as far as the eye could see.  Clumps of snow cradled in the branch forks of our tree.
"Got a present for you, Lonestar." Margaret smiled as she reached into the pocket of her coat and took out a box wrapped in red paper.
I nearly fell over when I opened it. "Oh!" I cried. It was the Sweet Lips scarlet lipstick. I peeked over my shoulder to make sure Father wasn't looking and slipped it into my Levi front pocket.
"It'll look great on you," Margaret said.   "I gave the Old Spice shaving lotion to Ralphy, and he gave me his ring." Margaret pulled out a silver ring tied to a string around her neck. "Means we're engaged to be engaged." Her dark eyes brightened.

I held the ring between my fingers – looked at Margaret – and nodded. "Wow! Engaged to be engaged.   That's somethin'."

After she left I ran upstairs to try my new lipstick.  I carefully outlined my lips in my bedroom mirror, smacked my lips together, then blotted the extra on some tissue.   "Older," I whispered.   "Definitely older and not Scot's." I opened my bedroom door to make sure nobody was in the hall. Since it was clear, I knocked on Grandma's door.

"What da ya think? I asked when she answered. I lifted my chin and turned one way, then the other.

Grandma pulled me inside and closed the door. "Mmmmm." She nodded, her eyes knitted together. "I think ... it ... makes you look ... older." She smiled.

"That's what *I* thought, Grandma."   I gave her a big hug around the neck.   "Now, I'm gonna wipe it off before Father sees me."

Chapter Twenty-Six

## SEARCHING FOR A WEDDING GOWN

The end of March, Margaret wanted to stop in at White's Bridal Shop, after school, to try on wedding gowns. The big glass windows were always filled with mannequins wearing long white dresses. I'd never thought about going in and looking around before.

"Don't tell anyone, Lonestar, or my folks'll have a conniption fit." Margaret said as we walked along. "I just know he's my soul-mate." She reached out and squeezed my hand. "I can feel it in my bones." Cars whizzed by on the busy road next to the sidewalk. Their tires made that familiar whirring sound as they sped over the damp cement. The heavy snow had given way to sporadic drizzle.

The block before the store, we both brushed our hair and put on some Sweet Lips scarlet lipstick. We didn't want the saleslady to think we were just kids.

Once we were inside White's, Margaret and I looked at one dress after the other until she found a long satin gown she oohed and ahed over.

"Do you think Ralphy'll like this one?" Margaret rolled her shoulders back and fluffed up her dark curly hair. Her deep brown eyes stared at the vision in white reflected in the mirror. She looked like a delicate lady bug in the midst of a giant white rose.

*Dum dum de dum, dum dum de dum,* I sang as I stood next to her. My head came up to her nose. She was about six inches taller than I was. "You will be the bride of the century," I said. We made a double reflection. Margaret in her satin gown decorated with tiny pearls, me in my Levis, plaid shirt, and saddle oxfords.

"It's soooo hard to wait 'till I graduate from twelfth grade to get married," Margaret said after we left White's.  "When Ralph holds my hand, I never want him to let go."

I thought about Skipper Roulette.  *I wondered if I would have felt the same way about him as Margaret did about Ralph if Father hadn't hung up the phone on us.* The memory of that moment still stung like a swarm of bees. Not that I would've wanted to get married, or even engaged.  I still have dancing and traveling in my future if Aunt Dawn's prophesy is right. But, still it would be nice to have someone hold my hand.

"Yeah," I said.  "It must feel great."

"By the way Lonestar who does that black Lincoln belong to that I see driving by your house in the afternoon?" Margaret asked as we walked back down Fort headed for home.

"What black Lincoln?" Someone honked at us as we started to step off the curb at Euclid.  We jumped back.

"You know, the one with two guys in suits and fedora's. Tough looking...like James Cagney, that movie star in gangster films."

I shook my head like I was trying to find something in it that wasn't there.  "I don't know.  Maybe they're just out lookin' over the neighborhood."

"Maybe, but someone who looks a lot like your dad talks to them sometimes."

My stomach clenched into a knot. *Was father in trouble again?*  "Probably Mr. Elkins, next-door," I said quickly. "He...uh...talks to everybody about everything.  Says he has a...bad...back so my dad'll shovel his snow in the winter, or...mow his lawn in the summer."  It wasn't a total lie, Father did do good stuff for neighbors.

Margaret wanted to stop in at Woolworth's and make a few notes on stuff she might need to set up house with Ralph. Stuff that was too big to steal.

"You go," I said.  "I've got to run to the market and pick up stuff Momma needs."

That was a total lie, the self protection kind that Margaret taught me about. I didn't want to go to Woolworth's. Even walking across the sidewalk in front of that store made me uneasy. I took that fountain pen back a few days after I stole it. When the clerk wasn't looking, I reached into my pocket, pulled the pen out with one hand, examined something in front of me with the other, and as quickly as I could, put the darned thing back where I found it.

I walked away whistling inside, trying to act like nothing had happened. But Jeeze, it was hard. Sirens screamed in my ears, "Eeee Eeee Eeee." Warning signs bleeped behind my eyes, "Wanted dead or alive, Fiona Lonestar MacLean for returning stolen merchandise." It was just as hard to take something back as it was to steal it.

Just past the bowling alley on Fort, about a half mile from home, I started to look up and down the side streets for that black Lincoln. Right when I hit the open field in front of our house I saw it. A big black Lincoln. It was going slowly down the alley. My stomach tightened again. I followed the car with my eyes. It turned left and disappeared behind Brucie's school near Garfield. It had two men in it all right. Two men in hats.

Goldy met me at the back gate as soon as I stepped into the yard. She pressed her wet nose up against my fingers, turned around in circles and sang out little happy noises. I patted her on the head and rubbed her ears. "Good girl," I cooed. She ambled over to the back gate, looked up at me with sad eyes, and made little noises again. They weren't happy this time, more like pleading cries. She wanted to go for a walk. Sean left her leash hanging on the side of the garage. I slipped it off the nail and clipped it to her collar. She started to turn around in circles again, but this time her back legs froze. Sean said she had rheumatism. He said sometimes joints got sore from old age. I bent down and rubbed my hands up and down both legs. It helped.

We crossed the street and headed into the field. This time the alley next to it was clear. No Lincoln. Just piles of dirty snow and gravel.  Goldy pulled hard on her leash, zigzagging one way, then another.

I used to be able to let her wander off the leash when she was younger, not anymore.  It was impossible to stop her from eating anything and everything she could find on the ground – smelly bits of old hamburger, green chicken, moldy pumpkin.  It didn't matter.  Being sick and throwing up didn't matter either.

Goldy headed for her dog house next to the garage when we got back.  All that sniffing and leaving her scent tired her out.  I could hear the rumble of the washer as I walked up the back steps.  Momma was doing laundry.  Some of it was already hanging on the back clothesline.  The bottom of one of Father's white shirts was stiff from the cold air; the top of the shoulders was fastened to the line with wooden clothespins.

"Yum," I called out to Grandma as I stepped into the kitchen.  "You boilin' bones for soup?"

"Just helpin' your mom's all.  Makin' stock." Grandma stood at the stove in another one of those hand made aprons Aunt Raven made.  This one had big red polka dots.  She dipped her long wooden spoon into the stock, took a sip, and smiled.  "You've got a good smeller, Lonestar."

"Not as good as Goldy." I soaped my hands, and ran them under the faucet.

"You...prob'ly should...uh...wipe your lipstick off before dinner?" Grandma said.

"Yikes, I forgot," I dried my hands then wiped my mouth with a tissue.

"Did you wear a white satin dress when you got married?" I walked behind her and put the zucchini in the soup pot.  I tried to make my question sound real casual.

"What a question.  You plannin' on havin' a weddin' soon?" She picked up the bar of black tar soap Momma kept on a plate next to the sink and lathered her hands with it to get rid of the onion smells.

"Just curious I guess." I shrugged my shoulders and swallowed hard.

*"E'ne.* Curious. I'm glad it's not make-up to hide who you really are. If it was, your Great-Grandfather would turn over in his grave." Grandma turned on the faucet and playfully flicked water in my direction.

Chapter Twenty-Seven

## WOMEN WORK TOO

"I wanna show you somethin', Lonestar," Momma said after our soup lunch. I followed her into her bedroom. She stood on her tiptoes, pulled down a big brown box from the top shelf of her closet and set it down on her bed.

"Your father and I used to go dancing every Saturday night when we were kids," Momma said. She stood across from me as she untied the string that kept the box-flaps shut. "He was such a good dancer. We even won a prize once." Momma bent over, reached inside the box and pulled out something wrapped in tissue.

I sat down with my back against the pillows, my feet over the side and leaned towards Momma to see what it was. She unwrapped a small, blue, satin ribbon and handed it to me. It smelled musty, like it had been closed away for a long time. I held it carefully in the flat of my hand like a delicate flower. "It says 'Best in the Class,' Momma."

"We were that all right. Your father, Aunt Raven, Uncle Howard and I would go to *Razzamatazz*, a nightclub in downtown Detroit." Momma sounded breathless. Her cheeks flushed red. "We'd dance 'till our feet turned into blocks of cement. The night we won this ribbon your father proposed. *I can't live without you*, he said. *You hang the moon for me.* Momma's face softened. She got a faraway look in her eyes. "He was so handsome then, still is. All the girls used to 'ooh' and 'ahh' when he walked by. I felt special that he chose me."

I handed her back the ribbon. "He's handsome, but you're beautiful Momma. Why wouldn't he choose you?"

"I don't know, Fi...Lonestar. I felt...like a giddy fifteen year-old schoolgirl I guess. Your dad was just seventeen at the time, but he seemed like a man of the world," Momma laughed. "Funny how perspective changes as you get older. Anyway, your dad was so smart he could fix anything mechanical: clocks, cameras, washing machines, car motors. Eventually that's how he got an education. The Ford Motor Company took young men off the streets of Detroit who showed promise and taught them everything that had to do with puttin' an automobile together. They gave every culture, color, and nationality the opportunity of a lifetime." Momma's eyes sparkled with pride

Momma lifted her wedding dress out of the box, carefully pulled away the tissue paper it was wrapped in, and held it across her chest. It wasn't satin. It didn't look like any of the gowns I'd seen at White's. It was a simple cotton dress with tiny pink, yellow, and blue flowers. I was disappointed.

"What do you think, Lonestar?" Momma smiled. Her chin quivered.

"It's sweet, Momma." I tried to hide my feelings.

"I know, it's not what they wear in the movies, or in the weddings we've seen at church, but it was very special for me." Momma ran her long delicate fingers over the heart shaped neckline. "I baby-sat a neighbors three kids for a month. She didn't have money to pay me, but she gave me this dress. It's from *Hudson's Department Store*. Still looks new." Momma stood up, held the dress at her shoulders and twirled around.

I pushed my back deeper into the pillows. "I bet you looked beautiful walking down the aisle." It was good to see Momma so happy.

"We didn't get married in the church." Momma sunk back down onto the bed. Her face flushed with excitement. "Couldn't afford it. We ran away. Eloped." She took a deep breath. "My father died the year before." Her eyes softened with the memory. "That was 1935, I was fourteen. He lost his pipe fitting business during the depression and never really recovered. People couldn't afford to add indoor plumbing during the depression. Broke his heart.    Momma, your Grandma, didn't work of course.    Most women didn't...in...those days."    Momma took a deep breath and shuddered.

"You never talk about your father.  What was he like?"  I reached down, untied the laces and kicked off my shoes.

"You're sure inquisitive today."  Momma brushed her dark brown hair back behind her ears then started to refold her wedding dress.  "My father was tough on all twelve of us."

"Was he tough like my father?"    I crossed my legs underneath me and sat Indian style.

"Worse. Much worse."  Momma's eyes went blank.  Her body got real still.  The only thing moving was a tiny wisp of her brown hair.

I waited like I always did, but I hated it when she disappeared mid-sentence.  It gave me that invisible feeling again.

She shuddered after a while, looked at me and went on like nothing had happened. "None of us were allowed to have lessons of any kind.  Raven wanted to learn piano.  Dawn wanted to have swimming lessons.  I wanted to take dance. *Thare's enuf of yas hare to teach one another,* he'd say in his Scot's brogue.

I laughed at the way Momma imitated her father's accent, but not getting what they wanted wasn't funny.

"So we learned as much as we could on our own." Momma sighed and shook her head back and forth.   "It wasn't the same.   Your Grandma argued with him all the time, but it wasn't any use.  He'd just smack her across the face."

My stomach dropped. The thought of anyone hurting Grandma made me want to hurt them back    "Didn't any of your brothers stop him when he was mean?"

"Bud was the oldest. He tried once, but...your grandfather...well...he was a big man, strong as an ox." Momma wrapped the tissue paper around her dress and put it back in the box.  "And...well...it was a time when men brought home the pay check and women did what they were told."

I thought about what Mr. Jesue taught us in history class. *Twentieth-century America was a woman's country. Women run the schools and the churches. Women spend most of the money. Women build, furnish, and direct activities in the home.*

"Well, it's not that way any more." My words flew out. "Women don't have to do what they're told...they can...be in charge."

Momma looked away. Once her memories were safely tucked away, she put the box back on the high shelf.

Later, at dinner, Momma asked Father. "You have women working at your plant?"

"Got a bit of everything at my plant," Father laughed. "Prob'ly even have some of the Ku Klux Klan." His broad shoulders shook like wild wheat caught in the wind.

*Mr. Jesue talked about the Ku Klux Klan in history class,* I thought. *They were the men who wore white sheets and killed anyone who wasn't white like they were.* I didn't think that was funny, but I didn't say anything. It sounded like Momma wanted to get a job. I look a deep breath and looked across the table at Sean. He raised his eyebrows, then looked away.

"So, they *do* have women?" Momma passed me the rolls.

We were having more of the soup we prepared at lunch. We made enough for a week. I took a roll and put the basket down in front of Brucie. He didn't look up. His eyes stayed fixed on the peas and carrots floating in his bowl. God! how I wished he'd like vegetables. When he didn't eat them, Father got angry.

"Yer no leavin' the table 'till that bowl's clean, Laddie." Father said quickly.

The room got real still. *Here we go again*, I thought. Grandma sat up taller in her seat across the table from Brucie and me. Sean clenched his jaw. Frown lines popped out across Momma's forehead.

"So, what do these women do?" Momma's voice got louder. Her hand shook as she lifted a spoonful of soup to her mouth. She sat opposite Dad, at the other end of our six chair table.

"This'n that." Father clenched and unclenched his jaw. He wasn't laughing anymore.

The phone rang. The shrillness made us all jump. Momma dove towards the small table against the wall and picked up the receiver. "You want Frank MacLean?" Her eyebrows knit together in a surprised expression. "Hold on." She glanced at Father, put the receiver down on the lace doily, walked back to her chair and sat down.

Father hurried to the phone, took a deep breath and picked up the receiver. "Yes, this is Frank what can I do for ya?" After a few seconds he turned his back towards us and whispered, "I'll get it." He hung up the phone and rejoined us at the table.

Momma shook her head. All the color dripped out of her face. "Your gamblin' again, aren't you Frank?" Her words came out low and rumbly.

Father lowered his eyes. His nostrils flared. "How da ya think I bought this here house, Merle?"

"Come and help me in the kitchen," Grandma said to Sean, Brucie and me, as she got up from the table.

We were in trouble again. Those commandments he signed to get Mom back were good and broken.

Chapter Twenty-Eight

## MOMMA GOT A JOB

That next Friday before Father got home, Momma called us all into the living room and sat us down on the sofa. "Well," Momma said looking us each in the eye, one by one, as she paced back and forth in front of us. "You won't believe it but I went and did it." Her usual dark straight hair was layered in curls. Aunt Raven must have given her another permanent.

"Did what? What do you mean? When?" We all called out a question, except Grandma. She was in the kitchen hum-singing.

"I got a job!" Momma stopped pacing and stood tall in the middle of the circle of flowers on our living room rug. The strong scent from her Gardenia perfume made the flowers under her feet seem alive.

"The boss at Koski's Car Sales said I have quick responses." Momma laughed and jumped in the air like something springy inside was making her reach higher. "Mr. Koski didn't care if I finished high school or not."

I blinked my eyes a few times to see if Momma and her good news were going to disappear like some *ciipaa*, but they didn't. "Momma. That's great. Congratulations." We all called out. I gave her a big hug.

When the excitement died down, she lowered her head and sighed. "The only thing is kids, we can't let Father know. Not right now anyways."

Sean clenched his jaw. Brucie nodded. I bit my lower lip. Momma didn't have to ask, nobody was going to say anything.

Grandma pushed open the kitchen door and leaned against the frame. "Come'n get it," she chirped like a happy bird. The front of her polka-dot apron was double dotted with flour.

"Mmmm," we cried as we followed the sweet smell of cake and found our places at the table.

"Oh, oh, oh," Momma cried as she looked at the cake. CONGRATULATIONS, was written in red sugar beads all across the top. "I didn't know getting a job could feel this good."

Grandma stood at the end of the table, cut each of us a piece of cake, then sat down. In between bites I looked up towards the window. Grandma's potato plant was still growing strong.

"Grandma, that potato plant's gonna take over the kitchen soon," I teased. "We'll all end up tangled in its green stringy arms."

"It's found its place in the sun." Grandma laughed then took another bite of cake. Her eyes brightened as she noticed Sean's plate was empty. "More?" She asked. Sean nodded.

"You must be havin' another growth spurt," Momma said looking at Sean. "Pretty soon you'll look like Grandma's potato plant."

I rolled my eyes up, sighed, then stared at Sean. Everything about him was always perfect. He was smart, handsome and growing taller by the second. In magazine pictures, dancers had nice long legs. I wanted to have more of the spurts like Sean had. I pointed my toes under the table and arched my feet as far forward as they would go.

"You're never gonna grow, Lonestar," Sean teased reading my mind. "You'll probably be a little squirt forever." He pulled his shoulders back and stuck out his chest. "I can hold you down with one hand now."

"Don't tease her like that," Momma said. The curls on her head bounced as she shook her head.

"No you can't, Sean." I jumped up from the table and stood on my tip toes.

Sean got up, sauntered over to where I was standing and wrapped one arm around my waist. "Count it out, Brucie."

"One, two, three, go."

I pulled against his arm as hard as I could. When that didn't work, I pushed into his body with all the force I could muster.

"Say UNCLE," Sean ordered. His breath spat out across the top of my head.

"No." I pushed and pulled some more. "Uhhh!" Little gasps flew out of my mouth.

"Say UNCLE," Sean ordered again.

"You'll have to kill me first." There was no way I was going to admit defeat. Sean let go of my waist, grabbed my arm and twisted it until I thought it was going to break. Pain ripped through my body.

"Enough!" Grandma called out. "You don't have to hurt her to prove you're bigger and stronger." Grandma jumped up and forced her way between Sean and me. Sweat beaded on her forehead. Her breath came out strong and hard.

"You should know better than that, Sean." Momma cried. "Why is it you have to ruin my celebration? You're just as bad as your father." Momma turned away in disgust.

My arm was sore the whole next week. I didn't mind the pain as much as having to face the fact that Sean was bigger and stronger. I hated that.

Determined to get stronger, I turned everything around me into a challenge. Yard hedges, fences, boulders, and tree branches all became obstacles to leap over or jump up to touch. I stood on my hands with my feet against the house for twenty minutes. Raced around the block in-between chores 'till Brucie timed it down from fifteen minutes to ten.

"Race ya the rest of the way," I said to Margaret as we headed towards White's Bridal Shop the following Saturday. White's was about ten blocks ahead. Even though she was bigger, I figured with all my training I could best her.

"You're on," Margaret said looking down at me.

"One, two, three, go." Short panting sounds filled the air as our feet hit the pavement. Her long legs made her strides reach farther than mine. After a few blocks, she was in the lead. I stuck my chest out, grabbed at the wind and threw myself forward even harder. A block before White's, Margaret started to slow down. Not a lot, just enough for me to catch up. "Tie," I cried as we both touched the end of the building.

I bent over and forced my breath to slow down. Sharp, burning pains shot through my lungs. Bubbles of perspiration popped out on my arms. It felt good to have a racing partner. Much more fun than running on my own.

I retucked my white cotton shirt into the waist of my flowered capri pants. "Let's stop at the gas station," I said. "I need to freshen up."

Margaret rebelted her black cotton trousers and bent down to tighten the laces on her shoes. As she did, I noticed a bright yellow piece of silk sticking out of her white shirt. One of her buttons had come undone. "What's that?" I asked.

"What's what?" She stood up and looked around. A puzzled look flashed in her eyes.

"That." I tugged on the yellow bit figuring it was something that wasn't supposed to be there. The rest of a small silk kerchief came out in my hand. The end of it was tied to a green one. The green was tied to a blue. The blue to a pink.

"You know what that is!" A tomato red exploded onto her face. She ripped the scarves out of my hand and stuffed them back into the bra under her shirt.

"Sorry." I was so embarrassed. I'd never thought about anyone stuffing their bra before. Margaret turned on her heels and walked away. I felt real stupid.

"You ever stuff your bra with scarves, Mom?" I asked as we stood side by side at the kitchen sink after dinner that night. Grandma worked at cleaning the stove on the far wall.

Momma wrinkled her forehead and shook her head. "What a strange question." She handed me a wet plate.

I looked away, wiped the plate dry, dragged my feet over to the counter on my right and put it on top of the others. The smell of dinner still hung strong in the air. Momma'd made roast beef, gravy and mashed potatoes. I kind of picked at my food. Fighting with Margaret made me lose my appetite.

Light from the full moon splayed through the window, over the potato plant, and onto Momma's face and neck. She turned away from the sink, put her hands on her hips, glanced at the closed door then turned to me. "Lo...uh...Fiona." I saw Grandma nod out of the corner of my eye. She and Momma were up to something.

"Your Grandma and I've been talkin' and...well." Her voice got real soft. "I've been working for a whole week. My first pay's due and...I'd like you to have it." She fingered the bib on her apron nervously. "So you can take those dancing lessons you should've been takin' all along."

I could hardly believe my ears. It was like a fairy landed on my shoulder and blessed me with a wish. I swallowed hard. "Oh." Tears welled up in my eyes and flowed down my face. "Really?" I sniffed.

Momma nodded. Her chin quivered.

"All this time, I...I thought you'd forgotten." My hands started to shake. Luckily I wasn't holding a dish right then, or I'd've dropped it for sure. I looked around to make sure the door was shut so Father couldn't hear, then looked back at Momma. "I love you," I whimpered.

She wiped her hands on her apron, put her arms around my waist, and leaned her head over the top of mine. Her hair smelled fresh. "I want you to have the dancing lessons my father didn't let me have."

Chapter Twenty-Nine

## DANCING'S GOOD FOR THE SOUL

Grandma walked with me across busy Fort Street on Saturday morning at 9:30. "Dancin's good for the soul," she said as we headed for Miss Jackie's Dance Studio. "It's a language all of its own." The fresh morning air was mixed with fumes from the passing cars. "And, now that it's harder for me to move like I used to, I get to watch." She held tight to her canvas bag – it was always filled with leather and beads. "Beadin' keeps my hands busy and my mind at peace," she said as we stepped onto the sidewalk from the curb. I held onto her arm so she wouldn't stumble.

"I hope I won't fall flat on my face, Grandma. The last time I was in class I ended up in bed for three months." I moved from side to side and let my old Hudson's shopping bag swing one way then the other as we headed up the block to Miss Jackie's. The bag was for my shorts and T-shirt. I didn't have a leotard yet. We weren't sure how we were going to get to Capezio's to buy one. That was where everyone went to buy their dance stuff, but it was a long bus ride to downtown Detroit.

"Umm, it's been a while since you got sick and couldn't even walk. But, we've done a fair share of dancin' around the house." Grandma smiled. "You'll be fine."

We walked through the bright yellow door of the dance studio like we were entering a magical kingdom. About five other girls my age were spread out around the room. The first was practicing turns on the wood floor to our left. The second and third were stretching their legs across the long wooden bar between where we stood in the corridor and the dance floor. The fourth and fifth were at the end of the mirror that ran the length of the room doing *arabesques*.  The way they had one leg extended straight behind them, the other firmly on the floor, reminded me of birds getting ready to fly.

The wall on the right was full of framed photographs.  I stopped to look at the first one.  A male dancer held a young woman over his head while she did the splits upside down.

I wondered if I'd ever learn to do anything like that.  It was amazing!  I looked over at Grandma and opened my eyes as big as I could.  She smiled and nodded.

I moved on to the next photograph while still keeping an eye on Grandma.  I wanted to make sure she was okay  She'd been looking a little tired. Grandma walked over to the area that looked like it was set aside for parents to watch the class. It was just to the right of the ballet bar.  She sat down on one of the metal folding chairs, reached into her bag and pulled out a white moccasin, followed by a tube of white beads, a spool of white thread and a needle.  "You go change," she said shaking her head.  "I'm fine."

I took a deep breath, turned and went down the corridor. There were two closed doors, one on the left, marked Office, the second, on the right, marked Changing Room.  I threw my Hudson's bag over my shoulder and went into the second.

"Hi! I'm Georgia," a dark haired girl with a ponytail said as I walked into the changing room.  She wiggled like a snake as she pulled her leotard on.

"I'm Lonestar," I said. "I hope it's okay if I use shorts today.  I don't have a leotard yet." I set my bag down and started to take off my Levis and plaid shirt.

"Talk to Miss Jackie.  She usually has hand-me-downs in her office."

"Okay, thanks." I crossed the hall and knocked on the office door.  A woman opened the door.  "Are you Miss Jackie?" Her face looked a little like the pictures in the photograph, but this woman was...older...not young and willowy.

"I know I don't look like the photos on the walls," she said reading my mind.  "I probably should take 'em down, but they remind me of the good ole days."  She turned and limped back towards her desk. "Oooh," she sighed as she fell into the swivel chair.

Hanging racks of costumes circled the room. Rich smells of sweat and perfume filled the air.

"Georgia said you might have an extra leotard and shoes," I said quickly. "But it's okay." I backed towards the door. She looked like she was in pain.

"I fell." A queer expression flashed across Miss Jackie's face. Her cheeks flushed pink.

I stopped. My breath stuck in my throat. I'd never thought about a dancer falling before.

Miss Jackie's eyes flickered. "Broke my darned leg ten years ago. It never did heal right. So this is all I have left." She lifted her arms up over her head and gracefully opened them to take in the small room filled with costumes.

Her "all" looked like the world to me. Spangly sequins glittered from the edge of a short purple satin costume lined with tooling. A rhinestone tiara, masks of every color and description and faded pink ballet shoes, all dangled on colored ribbons tied to nails above the costume racks.

"Help yourself." She pointed to a large barrel that came up to my waist. "There's just one deal." She shook her finger at me. "When it doesn't fit anymore. You wash it, sew it if needed and put it back."

"Thanks." My breath came out hot and heavy as I carefully dug through the discarded and outgrown leotards, shoes, and skirts.

Miss Jackie pulled her shoulders back, picked up her cane and limped out the door.

The first thing I found was a delicate, flowing black chiffon skirt. As soon as my hands touched the material I knew I wanted to claim it. I carefully pulled the skirt out of the box and held it up to my face. It felt soft, like the butterfly shawl Harriet Helmsly made for Donna and I when we were kids. A gentle shudder moved down my chest and into my stomach as memories of my childhood friend flooded in. I took a deep breath and pushed them away.

After I found the leotard and shoes, I quickly got dressed and rushed to the dance floor. I was the last one there.

"Against the bar," Miss Jackie yelled. "Everybody against the bar." She pounded the floor with her cane until everyone was quiet. "One hand on the bar, one hand extended."

I did what she said and kept my eye on the girls on either side of me as best I could. I figured they'd been there for a while.

"Soften your arm, Lonestar. You're not signaling for a left turn."

I did what she said. Grandma looked up and winked then went back to her beading work. A few other women had joined her on the metal chairs. One was reading a book, another doing crochet, and the others whispered among themselves.

The next week I danced my way everywhere: practiced touching my back leg up against the front one in midair, leapt up at any chance to touch the tallest leaf, raced the cars along Fort, jumped across the concrete squares on the sidewalk, flew up and down our front steps and stretched my body into every pretzel shape I could think of.

When Margaret and I walked to White's, I pointed my toes before taking a step.

"Stop walking that way, Lonestar. You look like you're floating through a cloud," Margaret said as she inched forward. Her new black skirt was so tight she could barely walk. All the girls were wearing their skirts tight now. I hated not being able to run, jump and fly through the air so I wore pants most of the time.

"It makes my ankles stronger," I pointed my toes and stepped forward again.

"Want some lipstick." Margaret used the black glass in front of the bowling alley as a mirror, took out a tube, ran it around her lips then smacked them together.

I looked up and down the block to make sure Father wasn't there. I knew he should be at work, but just to make sure I looked anyway. "Yeah!" I took the lipstick, looked in the glass and carefully turned my mouth from natural to cherry red.

"Makes you look older," Margaret said wiggling her hips from side to side.

"I am older," I said. I held my arms out, slightly rounded at the elbow and lifted my chin as we walked up the street.

The following Saturday I lined up with the other girls just like I had before. "Form is everything," Miss Jackie yelled. "Stand up straight, pull your *derriere* and stomach in, soften your arms and reach the top of your head towards the sky."

I did what she said. It seemed to me I'd grown another inch in just one week. We went through first, second, third, fourth, and fifth positions as a warm up. We slid one leg at a time along the top of the bar, reached the opposite arm up, then folded over.

"Straighten those legs, Lonestar," Miss Jackie yelled from the front of the room. "Work on your extension." She hit the floor hard with her cane. "Not like that. Higher."

Every time I had to pick something up off the floor, I put my feet into fifth position, raised my arms to the side and bent down with straight knees. I dusted the furniture while balancing on one foot. Scrubbed the bathtub while doing an *arabesque*. And practiced sliding on my toes in quick even movements across on the linoleum floor in the kitchen while I helped Momma and Grandma make dinner.

"It's good to see you strong again," Momma said. "That Rheumatic Fever you had last year ... made you so weak ... it was scary."

"I know, Momma." I remembered Momma crying in the hallway after she gave me the shots that helped me get better.

Momma shook her head then dropped some cabbage into the pot on the stove. The smell jumped out of the water as quickly as the cabbage went in. "Ann Marie says if you keep practicin' she can get you a job at the Gaiety Night Club where she sings when you're older. Besides singers, they have a trio of dancers." Momma's eyes twinkled brightly as she threw me a quick smile.  She wiped her fingers across the front of her flowered apron.

Even though we moved away from Jackson Street, Ann Marie was still Momma's friend. She always looked real glamourous whether she was working at the club or not.

"Wow! That would be something." The thought of dancing in a nightclub made me feel special.

I held my head up high, drew my heels into the air, and made my way on the balls of my feet from the sink to the stove. "I'll stir the soup," I offered dropping in the peas I'd just washed and taking the big wooden spoon out of Momma's hand as gracefully as I could.

Chapter Thirty

## GRANDMAS NEVER DIE

The end of April, Georgia, came into dance class all excited. She played Spin the Bottle with a bunch of other kids in her friend's basement. When it was her turn, the bottle pointed at a cute boy named Jack. She held her mouth against Jack's for as long as she could. "I don't know which was worse," she cried, "thinkin' I'd die from lack of oxygen. Or thinkin' I'd die from all the feelings twirlin' inside of me. My heart almost jumped out of my chest. My stomach did flip-flops. And my head felt like a balloon about to burst." We all laughed.

"You have to keep breathing," Jillian said as she pulled her tights up over her long legs.

"Yeah, you turn your head a little so there's room for your nose," blonde Rita added.

Everybody laughed again, but me. The guilt and excitement of Margaret kissing me came back with a vengeance. *Thou shalt not*, rang in my ears.

"Get your *derrieres* out here!" Miss Jackie hollered as she hit her cane against the door like she always did when she wanted us in a hurry.

We rushed out to our places to do our warm-up bar exercises. When we were finished Miss Jackie had us do leaps across the floor. We started in the far corner – took three small running steps – lifted ourselves off the ground – and extended both legs into the splits. I loved the feeling. It was like flying.

"Nice work, Lonestar."

"Thanks Miss Jackie."

"Now hold your chin up and tuck your tummy in while you do it again and again and again." She beat her cane against the wood floor each time she said "again."

Sean came and went, like a man on a mission, between home and the corner hamburger stand. I got so used to his working, it never occurred to me that he was ever interested in anything else, except maybe Goldy. I was practicing my leaps across the back lawn when he came out to give her a quick brushing on the back steps. It was after lunch, so he was probably on a break. When he bent over, I noticed a gold box sticking out of his shirt pocket.

"What's that? I asked walking over to where he sat on the middle step.

"Nothin'." Sean didn't look up, he just kept running the brush through Goldy's hair.

"It's a box. What's in it?" I looked down at our gray shadows on the cement walkway.

Sean's face flushed a bright pink. "It's just a present ... for a girl."

I'd never thought about my brother being interested in girls before. I knew they were interested in him, but not the other way around. "What girl?" The word itself felt like a foreign invader crossing over into what I thought of as my territory.

"Her name's Loretta. She's in my math class." His words came out long and flat.

"Loretta Davich?" I studied the look on Sean's face as I asked. A quick flicker across his eyes told me I was right. All the boys liked Loretta. She was beautiful and curvy. Suddenly I hated her. She was stealing my brother away from me.

Saturday morning, before dance class, Father was picking on Brucie at the breakfast table. He seemed to be mad at one or another of us recently. This morning it was Brucie's turn. "Chew with your mouth shut." Father's eyes narrowed as he peered over the top of his newspaper.

Brucie closed his mouth and chewed, but when he reached for his orange juice the glass slipped out of his hand and crashed to the floor.

Father lifted his hand, ready to swing. "Watch what yer doin'?" he snarled.

"Touch him and I'll call the police," Grandma warned.

"He's just a kid. Ten years old," Momma said jumping up from her seat at the table. She grabbed a rag from the sink and started to mop up the spill and broken glass.

Sean glared at Father, picked up his breakfast plate, rinsed it in the sink and went out the back door. He kept some hand weights and bar bells in the garage out back. Heavy lifting always made him feel better.

"Accidents happen," Grandma said, trying to ease the tension in the room.

Father looked at Momma, then Grandma, then back at Momma. He threw down his paper, pushed away from the table and headed for the door. "You all coddle him like a baby. He's got to learn to be a man."

"He's just in a bad mood, Brucie." I whispered as soon as Father was out of earshot. I tried to sound calm but my insides felt like scrambled eggs.

Momma finished cleaning the floor. Brucie went out to play with Goldy in the yard and I ran upstairs to get my leotard, skirt and ballet shoes. Sean's deep grunts from weight lifting echoed outside my window.

Grandma and I waited at the light to cross the street. It was hard to be patient. Father fighting with Brucie had made us late and I knew Miss Jackie would be mad.

"Well, look who's joining us," Miss Jackie scowled as I hurried onto the dance floor from the dressing room. "Nice of Her Majesty to find time for the rest of us workers."

I took my place at the bar and began to do *pliés* with the other girls.

*Derriere* in, Lonestar. Watch your arms. Soften them at the curve. The bar is not to hold you up you know. It's just a prop." Her eyes flared wildly as she hit the floor with her cane.

I did what she said, pulled in my *derriere*, softened my arm and loosened my grip on the bar.

After warm-ups we moved to the center of the floor. Each girl had to do développé*s*. When it was my turn I wobbled a bit.

"Dancing takes practice, Lonestar. Get that support leg stronger." Miss Jackie stared into my eyes, pursed her lips and said, "or you might as well quit now while you can take up another sport."

She was right. I had to do more. Figure out how to stay balanced and strong. When class was over, I stayed out on the floor ten minutes longer than the other girls. *"Développé,"* I whispered as I centered, found my balance, then lifted one leg slowly up into the air as high as I could. *"Développé,"* I said over and over again as I continued centering, balancing, lifting and extending. My legs shook from the strain of building new muscles.

When I made my way back to the dressing room I felt dizzy from working so hard. I sat down on the bench, put my head down between my legs and forced myself to breathe deeply into my stomach.

"Is your *visitor* here, Lonestar?" Georgia asked as she sat down beside me.

"Well, um ..." I stammered not knowing what to say.

"I always feel tired when I get my *period*," Jillian moaned as she stepped into her jeans.

Wanda came up behind me and patted me on the back. "Try drinking hot milk. It helps."

I nodded to make them think they were right. *Another lie of self preservation,* I thought.

After class Grandma and I went to the park instead of going straight home. Neither one of us said anything as we wandered from one grassy place to another.

"What's wrong, Lonestar?" Grandma's eyes narrowed as she broke our silence.

"Nothin', Grandma." My jaw tightened.

"Your nothin' looks like somethin' to me."

"It's just that, well everybody seems to have their menstrual cycle but me." I turned my head away, trying to disguise my frustration. "Georgia called it her *visitor.* Jillian called it her *period.* And ... I don't know what Wanda calls it, but the point is they all have it. And I don't."

"Having a *visitor* and having a *period* are mighty simple words for something magical, Lonestar." We headed for a nearby bench and sat down. "In *my* grandmother's tribe," Grandma said slowly," they called it *moontime.* It was a mystery." Her eyes softened. "It was a time when women were seen to be very powerful. They held healing energy and could see and understand things that others couldn't."

"I don't care if they could see things, I just want to feel like I'm normal."

Grandma lifted her head and closed her eyes. The wind played with some of the loose gray strands of hair around her face. "It's important that you know. One day you'll be able to pass this information on to your daughter."

I kicked some pebbles under my feet. They went flying across the path.

Grandma continued. "If a man was brought into the council for stealing and he denied it, the council would ask a woman on her *moontime* what she felt. His life depended on her answers."

"That was way back in boon-dock time, Grandma. No one's gonna ask me to make such a big decision."

"Some tribes had women walk over newly seeded fields to make their crops fertile." Grandma looked out at a Maple Tree in the distance.

"Well there aren't any crop fields around here to walk on. It's mostly concrete." *I'd not only missed out on feeling important by a generation or two, I'd missed out because I was never gonna have a moontime,* I thought.

"That's true Lonestar, but sometimes it's nice to remember the way things were. When my grandmother came into her first *moontime*, the women elders built a special *wikiup* ... a small oval hut, made out of twigs and branches ... down by the river. They covered the outside with buffalo skin to keep it warm." Grandma ran the tip of her tongue over her lips and made a smacking sound. "After fasting on fresh juice for a few days the elders led my grandmother to the hut where they talked and shared experiences about what it was like to be a woman. Then, they left her alone to talk to her ancestors. Sometimes they left symbols behind. Symbols to assist in her journey of discovery. The elders wanted my grandmother to remember that she was a part of everything that was around her and that everything was a part of her."

I crossed my arms and scooted down on the bench. *Grandma was trying to make me feel better, but it wasn't working.*

"You've got that nothin' look that looks like somethin' again, Lonestar, what is it?"

I rolled my head back and forth, chewed on the skin inside my cheek, and tapped my foot on the stones all around the bench. *Words'd just make things worse.*

"Lonestar, if you don't put your feelings into words I can't help you," Grandma snapped.

"Don't you see," I snapped back. "I'm never gonna sit in a *wikiup*, share stuff with my elders, celebrate the Earth, fertilize crops or be asked to decide the truth. Not just because we don't do that anymore, but because I'm a freak. Somethin' inside of me is missin'."

"I don't know who planted that idea in your pretty little head." She looked deeply into my face searching for an answer.

"I'm not stupid, Grandma." I looked away.

"No, you're not. But, the truth is much harder to see than the fantasy you've made up." Fire flashed in her eyes.

"And what's this truth?" I looked up into her blazing eyes, sure her truth had nothing to do with me.

Grandma took a deep breath and looked out at the Maple again. "*E'ne.*" She nodded slowly, then turned back to me. "You were born with eggs hidden inside of you. Eggs so small that you'd need a magnifying glass to see'em."

"What are you talkin' about? What eggs?" I beat the tips of my fingers against the tops of my legs.

"You, Fiona Lonestar MacLean, are much more a part of me than you could ever imagine.  When you put yourself down ... you put all women down ... including me."

"What are you talking about?  We're two different people."

Grandma shook her head back and forth and clucked her tongue.  "When I carried your mother in my womb, I also carried you."

"That's not possible.  That would mean Momma and I were twins."  *For a second I thought maybe Father was right. Grandma was crazy.  Or at least her ideas were.*

"Your mother was born with *my* eggs inside of her.  Those eggs, once fertilized, turned into you and your brothers."

I sat still for a long time.  Warmth from the sun covered me like a blanket.  The anger I'd felt fell away and landed on the grass all around me.  New questions danced in my head. *Were these eggs she was talkin' about the reason I felt so close to her?   Did that mean she was a part of her grandmother?   If she was, then I was a part of her grandmother too.  It just went back forever and ever.  Maybe there was something inside of me that knew more than I did and was just taking time to emerge.*

"Grandmas never die, Lonestar.   They just keep bein' reborn over and over again."

I took a deep breath and shivered like Grandma does sometimes. "*E'ne.*"

Grandma put her hand on my leg and patted it. "We all have our seasons.  They just come at different times."

I ran the tips of my fingers along some of the dark lines on the back of Grandma's hands and wondered if I'd have lines like that one day.

"Periods?" She asked with a smile. "Visitors?  Haw!  Now I've heard everything!" She motioned for me to get up.  It was time to head home.

When we turned the corner, a half block from our house, I saw a black Lincoln driving slowly toward us.  It looked like the same one I noticed before.   The one Margaret mentioned seeing outside our house.

"Who's that?" I pointed at the Lincoln. "They seem to be lookin' for someone."

Grandma's face went pale. "They're back." Beads of sweat bubbled out onto her forehead. She pulled out the embroidered handkerchief she always kept up her sleeve and dabbed them away.

Margaret came over in the afternoon to tel me she had to stop going to White's to try on wedding dresses. "Mom's been looking at me strangely," she said. "And asking questions like 'what do you and Lonestar do in downtown Lincoln Park' and 'does Lonestar have a boyfriend?'"

"Jeeze, what did you tell her?" I asked while we sat on my front porch. I picked up the dirty old tennis ball Goldy loved and threw it onto the side lawn. Goldy made some soft happy noises as she scrambled after it. Her breath hard and heavy in the summer heat.

"Umm ... maybe just that we ... kind of hung out, stuff like that," she said quickly.

Goldy brought the ball back. Now, besides being stained, it was wet. I wiped it on my Levis and threw it again. This time Goldy didn't go after it. She just laid down on the sidewalk in front of us. "You tired?" I said in baby talk. Goldy let out a soft growly sigh.

"Momma'd flip out if she knew I was trying on wedding dresses and ready to get married." Margaret scrunched up her face. "She has her mind set on me going to college and being a nurse or a teacher."

Chapter Thirty-One

## EVERYTHING HAS ITS SEASON

By the time school ended – the beginning of June – new flowers continued to pop up around our house. Things we hadn't even planted. "Whoever lived here before was a good gardener," Momma said one Sunday after church as we walked through our back gate. She stopped to bring a lilac branch close to her face. Her blue eyes softened as she breathed in the sweetness of the reddish-purple flowerets. Now that she'd been working at Koski's for a few months, she looked happier than I ever remembered.

Goldy ambled over to us – wagging her tail like she always did when we got home. "Hey there girl!" I scratched her head while she made little happy throat sounds.

Sean found her old chewed up red ball in a clump of grass nearby and threw it twenty-five feet away. "Fetch," he called. Goldy slowly made her way to the ball, picked it up, then sat down on the grass. "She's tired," Sean sighed. "And – gettin' old." He kicked the grass and headed for the back door.

"Miracles of life," Grandma said as she came up behind us. It took her more time to make her way from the back garage than it did the rest of us. She was moving much slower than she used to. "Just when we think somethin's dead, it comes back." Grandma took off her white gloves and ran her fingers over some of the green leaves. *"E'ne*, you are somethin' that's for sure." She spoke to the plant as if it were a little kid.

Father shook his head as he passed by on the way to the back door. "You treat everything like a relative." The car keys made a tinkling sound as he twiddled them in his hand.

Grandma didn't say anything back. Momma glared at Father's back.

"Looks like we've got some invaders here," Momma said quickly as she turned her attention to the back garden. "Dandelions and other weeds are sneakin' up in-between all these rose bushes."

After lunch, Momma dug through Father's tool box and handed Sean, Brucie and me garden trowels. "Start with the dandelion's. Dig'em up and throw 'em out." Her voice was strong – another change since she got her job. "If you let 'em come full circle, they'll multiply and take over."

We headed into the yard armed like hunters out for a kill. Momma wanted the dandelions out first, so that's what we had to do. If it were up to me, I would have let them stay and re-populate. I loved the part Momma hated – the seeds. When a yellow top turned into white fuzzies I'd break it off, make a wish and blow. "Let me be curvy like all the other girls," was my recent wish.

Sean, Brucie and I dug up the dandelions like we were asked and dropped them into the big black trash bin.

Grandma joined us in the yard after she changed into one of her flowered house dresses and an old pair of shoes. "Good job kids." Her dark eyes slowly scanned our work. "Everythin' has it's season." She picked up the end of the hose, turned the water on and pointed it towards the plants we hadn't killed.

"Except me," I mumbled remembering the girls in the dressing room at dance class. I squished up my face, took my spade and jabbed it into the dirt around one of the dandelion's hiding behind a rose bush.

"Everythin'," Grandma threw her shoulders back and nodded in my direction. I stared at the dandelion I'd mutilated. Instead of one proud plant, it looked limp and lifeless in the afternoon sun.

Grandma came up beside me and put her arm around my shoulders. "People like to keep a sense of order, Lonestar. Sometimes we can choose – have some control over what can be and sometimes we can't."

"Sometimes we don't get to choose." I stiffened my back.

"Some things we don't choose and some things are chosen for us." Grandma's eyes narrowed.

Chapter Thirty-Two

## THE SWEET SIXTEEN SINGLES BASH

The next morning, I woke up early. The Big Mommas were going to take the bus to Windsor, Canada. The Metropole Nightclub, was having an afternoon teen dance. The girls all knew how I loved to dance and since it was almost my birthday, they planned a special trip. I wanted to tell Grandma, but I knew if Mom and Dad found out, they'd be furious at her. So, I kept it all to myself. *Yet another lie of self protection,* I thought as I stretched my arms out as far as I could reach, twisted my hips one way, then the other.

Sean's grunts from lifting weights in the back yard sailed through the morning air adding a lower note to the songs of the birds singing. Goldy's playful bark was slower and more growly than before, but it too added its own timbre. The musical sounds bounced against my walls as I sat up in bed with my back against two pillows.

I ran my fingers over the pouch filled with special leaves that Grandma gave me last year. When I could, I still wore it on a string around my neck. *The Kin.ni.kin.nick brings you good luck,* Grandma had said when she gave it to me. I needed some of that luck so I could get to the Metropole and back without getting into trouble.

I brought the tobacco pouch up to my nose. The smell was softer now. But still sweet. Grandma said the Shawnee Indians used tobacco for more than good luck. It carried prayers to the Great Spirit and was a witness to the sincerity of the wish. On minor occasions they put a pinch on the ground, like when Grandma took me into her Sacred Stone Circle for my twelfth birthday present. For major events, like preparation for a hunting trip, or in the olden times, a war party, tobacco was burned. They put it directly in the flames or coals of the sacred fire built for that purpose.

I guess Aunt Dawn's Talisman Stone Readings fall into the major event category because she always drops a pinch of tobacco into the candle flame to help her listen to her inner voices. The voices that help her give the right information to people she wants to help with personal problems.

Still dozy, I wondered if my trip to Canada would be considered major or minor. Unsure, I climbed out of bed, opened my top drawer, took out a candle, set it on a tray on top of my dresser and lit it. The flame was small at first, then a second later, it grew stronger. I took out a pinch of tobacco, dropped it inside and prayed. "God, Great Spirit, *Wakontah*, be with me as I travel with my new friends. It's not eactly a hunting trip, but it is a trip...and it seems major to me." The flames shot higher for a second, then a narrow blackish curl of smoke headed towards the ceiling.

*Shushy,* the wind hummed as it played with the nylon curtains on my French windows. *Bobwhite*, a bird sang out from the backyard below my room. The sounds of the morning seemed to join my prayer and make it even stronger. I blew out the candle and turned to get ready for my big venture.

"See yas," Brucie called out from the back porch on the floor below my room.

"Don't forget to leave Miss Armstrong's local paper," Father called out. His deep voice light and cheerful. He must've been standing at the back door watching Brucie load the last of his canvas newspaper bag for his paper route. "She telephones to complain when you don't."

"I never forget. It's her darned dog. He eats paper like it was steak." At ten years old, Brucie's voice was still high.

"Everybody needs a bit of local gossip, Brucie," Father laughed. "Take two papers. One for her, one for that darned dog."

"You're such a kidder, Frank," Momma called out. Her sweet voice drifted out of the open back door and up through my open window. She was probably sitting at the kitchen table having her morning coffee. I could almost taste its sharpness.

Father was a kidder all right. Sometimes it was hard to know if he was teasing or making up a stupid story.

The phone rang downstairs. "It's okay, Miss Armstrong," Father's voice boomed out. "Brucie's leaving two papers this morning...yep, one for you and one for your dog."

*Poor Brucie,* I thought, *his first job and he has to deal with some grouch.*

I climbed out of bed, pulled on my Levis and rummaged through my drawer for my light blue sweater. Once dressed, I went next door to Grandma's room.

I leaned my head against the door and listened. Her room was quiet. She hadn't been feeling real good lately. I opened the door a crack. "You stay in bed, Grandma. I'll bring you some tea."

I waited 'till it was quiet downstairs. By 9:00 everyone was off to work. Mom to Koski's, Father to Ford Motor Company, Sean to the hamburger stand on the corner, and Brucie on his paper route. I hurried downstairs, made tea for Grandma and put it on a tray along with a few muffins.

"Thank you, Lonestar," Grandma said when I brought the tea in. She was sitting up this time, writing.

I set the tray down on the bed and looked down at her notebook. "What're you writin', Grandma?"

"A few notes." She said with a far-a-way look in her eyes. "Nothin' to talk about for now."

I nodded. "Umm...I'm gonna go out for a while...so...don't worry if I'm late for dinner."

Grandma bit down on her upper lip and studied my face. "*E'ne.*"

"*E'ne,*" I replied. *I wondered if she could see through my head into where I was going.* I went back to my room, grabbed my purse and canvas bag, went down the stairs and out the door. I'd saved some of the dance money Momma gave me for the trip.

By the time I made it to Ernie's Everything Store my heart was doing flip-flops. "I can't breathe," I said to the girls as I hurried up to where they were waiting.

"Hey, Lonestar," British Loraine grinned. "We've been waiting for you." She tucked her white shirt neatly into the waist of her tight red skirt. "Are you ready for The Sweet Sixteen Singles Bash," she clapped her hands and did a little jig.

My jaw dropped. I turned to Margaret. "You didn't tell me it was for 16 year olds."

Margaret smiled. "Relax. We copied *my* birth certificate and changed the first name to Lonestar." She opened her eyes wide and grinned. "Today — we're twins. You're Lonestar Vatroba." Everybody laughed.

"Sixteen?" I questioned. "Who's gonna believe I'm sixteen?"

"Well, you're almost fourteen and by the time we finish with your make-up, you'll look...well...two years older." Margaret turned to the other girls. "Right Big Mommas?"

"Right on," they replied.

Margaret handed me the birth certificate. Lonestar Vatroba was written in white over a black background. Born: March 21, 1936. I stared at the numbers. Sure enough, they made me sixteen. *Six and one make seven*, I thought. *Seven is a spiritual number,* Aunt Dawn had said. *It has many meanings, but the one I use it for is completion.* I hoped the completion wasn't me going to jail for lying about my age."

Cheryl must have seen a worried look on my face. "We'll stand close by," she said. Her red hair was twisted on top of her head in a bun, held in place with bobby pins.

Diane pulled herself up to her full 5'10". "And if you stick close to me ... everybody'll just think you're the shrimp of the group," Diane laughed and straightened her glasses.

We boarded the bus for downtown Detroit a few blocks up from Ernie's, and headed straight to the back corner. I held onto the edge of the window so I wouldn't move too much as Margaret applied my make-up.

"You're going to look great." Margaret leaned over her seat, rubbed her finger into a pot of light blue eye shadow, smudged it over my eye lids, then smoothed it out. She smacked her lips in satisfaction. "And now for a Cleopatra mystique." She waved a black eye liner pencil in the air, then had me look down as she lined my upper lids. Every time the bus jerked forward, she rolled her eyes and shot him a disgusted look.

Cheryl, Diane and Lorraine all sat on the bench next to me. They'd started out with some make-up on, but while Margaret worked on me, they added a few accents. Diane put a black beauty mark on her cheek, just under her glasses. Lorraine drew a black curlycue on the corners of her eyes to make them look bigger. Cheryl covered up her freckles with heavy pancake.

"You bring your lipstick?" Margaret asked. I dug into my purse and handed her my Sweet Lips. She carefully outlined my mouth, leaned back, studied my face and nodded. "Pretty good, heh girls?" Once Margaret finished with me, she took out her mirror and retouched her own make-up.

By the time the Detroit bus dropped us off at the bridge to Canada we figured we all looked very glamorous. Some strangers did too. Two elderly women looked in our direction, then whispered to each other as they passed us by.

We caught the next bus and crossed over the bridge. The river below looked rough. Two ships let out a loud, low honking sound as they passed each other in the distance.

By the time we got to the Metropole it was noon. A line, about half a block long, stretched from the front door out to where we stood in the distance. Gold lights blinked off and on around the sign above the front door. The blinking lights made the club seem even more exciting than I'd imagined.

I stepped out of line to look at the man guarding the entrance. Every once and a while he asked to see someone's birth certificate. *"God,"* I said quickly to myself. *"Wakontah, Great Spirit* don't let him check mine." Even though Margaret made us twins, we looked about as alike as a turtle and a frog. She had dark hair, a long face and brown eyes. I had blonde hair, a pug nose and blue eyes. She was curvy and I was straight up and down.

As we neared the entrance, the girls circled around me and pretended to be in deep conversation with each other. My heart beat like a wild drum. Thumping noises pounded in my head. I straightened my back, lifted my chin...and held my breath as we walked forward. It worked, the guard at the door passed us through.

Once inside, we turned to each other and silently squealed in relief. Margaret opened her eyes wide. Lorraine tightened her jaw. Cheryl wiggled her head. And Diane turned sideways, looked over her shoulder and shuddered.

The floor underneath our feet began to shake. Music blared out through the arched entryway in front of us. Margaret grabbed my hand and pulled me forward onto a giant dance floor. A red, white and blue banner, WELCOME TO THE SWEET SIXTEEN SINGLES BASH, waved over a stage at the far end of the room.

About a hundred girls and boys stood side by side in two circles – one circle inside the other – holding onto the hips of the person in front of them – doing what turned out to be a dance called The Hokey Pokey. *You put your right hip in and your right hip out...your right hip in and you shake it all about...you do the Hokey Pokey and turn yourself around and that's what it's all about...hey!* Everybody was singing as the song blasted through the speakers. They moved their bodies according to the words in the song. By the time they got to the second round, which was *put your right foot in...and your right foot out,* we were ready to join in. We jumped, shook, and shouted the rest of our body parts with the rest of them. By the time the song was over, we were jumping inside as well as outside.

"This is really fun," I squealed. "Sure is." "Man-o-man what a thrill." "This place is hoppin'." And, "I feel like Cinderella at the ball." My friends yelled out loud enough to be heard over the other happy noises in the room.

"In honor of the next dance," a man's voice announced over the loud speaker. "We're gonna dim the lights and turn on those magical florescent lights. So, if you've got anything on that glows...don't think you need new glasses." He laughed as the lights dimmed and the florescent lights beamed into the room from the four corners.

*Glow little glow worm, glimmer, glimmer,* a soft voice purred. *Glow little glow worm...* the song repeated. Some of the boys and girls broke into small groups and took turns winding their way around each other like worms. A scarf here, a belt there and different parts of clothing looked like it was moving on its own. Grandma loves worms. *They're farmers of the Earth,* she says. *They loosen and fertilize for free.*

The four of us formed our own circle. Two older boys joined us, Leroy, a tall lanky blonde and Jonathan, a dark tough looking brunette. I'd noticed them looking in our direction before they came over. Cheryl got all gooey when they introduced themselves.

When it was my turn, I lifted my arms high as if catching the wind with butterfly wings. Those wing like scarves that Donna and I wore at our back-yard powwow years ago. I could feel Donna beside me as I wove in and out of the group. "Right on, Lonestar," Margaret called out. Her words jarred me back to the now.

When I completed the circle Margaret took a turn. Then one by one the others circled around. Since Diane was the tallest and thinnest – she looked the slinkiest when she moved. The fuchsia dots on Lorraine's pink scarf glowed. It looked amazing. When Jonathan wound his way in and out of the circle, he went around Margaret twice. When the dance was over Leroy and Jonathan left, but I saw Jonathan slip Margaret a note. She grinned and quickly put it in her pocket.

After the overhead lights came back on we went from one dance to the other. The entire room did the Bunny Hop where you hold onto the persons hips in front of you and hop, hop, hop. When they put on a polka, everyone moved to the outer rim of the room so two people at a time could hold hands and swoop across the floor. Margaret and I were partners for The Tennessee Waltz. Neither one of us had waltzed before, but after we watched a few girls who seemed to know the movements, we followed along okay. I think I stepped on her foot once, but not too hard. At least she didn't yelp or anything.

I didn't look at my watch until three o'clock. "Yipes," I yelled, "we've gotta go." I didn't want to be too late for dinner. If I was, I'd be grounded for sure. That wasn't as serious as being arrested for a fake i.d., but serious non-the-less.

*If I Knew You Were Comin' I'd've Baked a Cake,* was playing as we walked out through the archway. "Perfect song for you, Lonestar," Lorraine said, "it is almost your birthday." I liked the way she said birthday. Her British accent made it sound special.

We took our make-up off on the bus ride home. Lucky for all of us that Lorraine brought along some tissues and skin cream. It was easier putting make-up on than it was taking it off. I saw the bus driver look back at us once and smile.

When the other girls were busy with each other I turned to Margaret, "What's Ralphy gonna say about you goin' dancing without him?" I whispered.

"We're not gonna tell him, are we?" Margaret said with a wink. She took Jonathan's note out of her pocket and tore it into little bits.

Chapter Thirty-Three

## TROUBLE IN THE HOUSE

When the phone rang the next morning I figured it was Miss Armstrong again. *Father was right,* I thought. *Brucie should start leaving two papers for her.* I glanced at the clock 7:30 a.m. It was time to get moving. I had to get ready for dance class.

"Fiona MacLean, you get down here this instant," Father yelled. His thunder voice boomed up the stairway.

My thoughts scattered like autumn leaves blowing in the wind as I made my way down the stairs two steps at a time. *Did he ask me to do something I'd forgotten?* I wondered. *I vacuumed, dusted, scrubbed the bath tub, changed the beds and swept the front porch a few days ago. Was he upset because I skipped breakfast yesterday? I thought he was too busy to notice. I wasn't late for dinner.*

My knees buckled a bit. *Did someone tell him we took the bus to Canada yesterday to go to a Teen Dance?*

Suddenly a sharp pain pierced my stomach like an arrow. I stopped cold on the landing. *What if Father knew about Momma working? She was always careful about coming and going when he wouldn't notice.* By the time I stepped onto the landing my head throbbed thinking about the maybes.

Father paced back and forth in the living room like he was training for a marathon. Momma sat on the sofa in front of him, a cup of coffee in her hand. Her shoulders bent forward like something heavy was pushing her down. I hated it when she felt bad.

"Yer supposed to watch her," Father said pretending I wasn't standing fifteen feet behind him. His fists opened and closed in rhythm with his feet.

I blinked my eyes a few times while staring at his back. Momma tried to signal me to be calm from where she was sitting. Along with the throbbing, my head went into its cobwebby feeling as I tried to make sense of Dad's craziness.

"She's a good girl, Frank." Momma said softly.

I moved into the room and stood next to Father. Momma nodded and opened her eyes real wide like she did sometimes when something was wrong. It used to make me feel better to get a warning signal. Now, I didn't need one. Father stopped pacing. He turned to face me head on.

"Fi-o-na," Father said dragging each syllable of my name up from the depths of the Earth. "I'm shocked and disappointed in you, Lassie."

"What did I do?" I wasn't going to admit to anything unless I had to.

"You know!" He hissed. "Don't try to pull the wool over my eyes."

My jaw tightened. *Did he know about Canada? Or was it something else? Why didn't he just come out and say what was wrong?* I was not going to step into his snake pit.

"You might as well tell me." I crossed my arms and waited.

"You lied! You know how I feel about lying." His knuckles turned white as he clenched and unclenched his fists.

"I still don't know what you're talking about?" I held my ground like a warrioress. I was tired of following his stupid rules. I had a right to make my own choices.

His nostrils flared. "Margaret's mother just called. She told me what you've been doing." The words came out in slow jerky sounds.

"Just what have I been doing?" I held my warrior stance – feet pressed hard into the carpet – jaw clenched – eyes narrowed.

"*You've* been trying on *wedding* dresses!" Father sneered, shook his head and turned away from me to resume his pacing.

"Trying on wedding dresses?" His words made me dizzy. I bent over, staggered towards Momma on the sofa and plopped down. A swishing sound pulsed through my ears. *I should have been relieved that Father didn't know about Momma working, or my dance lessons. I should have been grateful that he didn't know about The Big Mommas, about us stealing and going to Canada, but I wasn't.*

Fire burned through my chest. *Margaret lied. She was the one who'd been trying on wedding dresses. She was the one who wanted to get married. It was never me.*

"I told him there had to be a mistake but he wouldn't listen to me." Momma patted my knee then ran her hand down the arm of my pajamas.

"Don't try to make me wrong, Merle." Father beat the air with one fist, then the other, like he was in a boxing match with the dust. "I should've seen the writing on the wall." His nostrils flared. "We all know, she must be pregnant."

"Pregnant?" I mumbled. "That's the dumbest thing I've every heard." It was so unfair. I felt like I'd been tied to a stake and set on fire like one of those innocent women Mr. Jesue told us about. The ones who were supposed to be dangerous witches in Salem in the 1600's. Beads of sweat ran down the sides of my face.

Momma's eyes narrowed. Her back stiffened against the sofa.

"Uh, uh, uh." Gasping sounds flew out of my mouth. I stared at this man who didn't even know who I was and shook my head in disbelief. Thoughts pierced my skin like wild cockleburs. *How could he think I'd done something I wasn't even close to thinking about or even capable of? And how could my best friend use me as a sacrifice?*

"*Bas no beatha!* Father's shoulders slumped. "What are we gonna do now?"

"I...didn't do...it." I looked up at Father. Hot tears flooded my eyes.

"It's a tough world." His fists swung out again, this time to the unseen world beyond the front door. He didn't hear me. "People judge. They look for things to attack you for."

I wiped my eyes with the back of my hands and clenched my jaw. There wasn't anything I could do to stop Father's spewing once he got started.

"Each strike against you is another strike against the whole family. Neighbors will stare and point fingers. What kind of life are you gonna have now?" Father shook his head back and forth like a stupid Kewpie doll wobbling on the dash of a car.

His words made me dizzy. Gray clouds moved into the spaces inside my head.

"This'll ruin your chances of ever finding a good husband." His words cut through the clouds in my head like bolts of electricity.

Momma snuck her hand towards mine. Her touch made some of the pain go away. I looked up at her then back at Father.

Father crossed his arms and nodded in my direction. "Stand up, come over here and bend over." Whinnying sounds burst into the room as he filled his barrel chest with air, held it for a few seconds, then let it flow out between his lips.

"No," I yelled. "I didn't do anything." I sat upright.

Momma jumped up and walked over to where Father was standing in the middle of the room. "She's almost fourteen years old." She stood between Father and the sofa where I was sitting. "That's too big to spank."

Father pushed Momma away. She fell. I quickly got up from the sofa, hurried to where she was and bent down to see if she was okay.

"No one's gonna hit anybody in this house ever again." Sean's voice boomed out from the dining room. He must've been watching through the side window. "Not while I'm here." He moved quickly to stand between Father and Momma and me. The muscles in his arms pushed hard against the edges of his sleeves. He was bigger than Father now.

"You wouldn't dare try to stop me," Father said coldly. The corners of his mouth turned up. It was the frozen grin he wore when someone crossed him.

I helped Momma back up and edged her onto the sofa. The insides of her lower arms were red from rug burns.

"Don't tempt him!" Grandma shouted as she came down the stairs from her room. "Or me." She gasped as she stepped down onto the landing. Her left hand squeezed hard against the wooden railing. She must've heard everything that was going on. Loud rattling sounds intermixed with her words. Beads of perspiration popped out on her forehead.

"I told you about hitting Merle or the kids." Grandma's words whizzed through the air like arrows, straight and sure. I liked her standing up for us, but not when she looked so frail. "Move away, Frank," Grandma ordered. Little bulges stuck out around her ankles where elastic bands kept her nylons in place until she rolled them up.

"I can't have my kids telling me what to do." Father cocked his head one way, then the other, clenched his fist, pulled his arm back and swung. Sean kept his feet firm, but leaned his body back, out of the way. Father lost his balance and tripped over Sean's outstretched foot. Father's head made a thwacking sound as it hit against the metal corner of the coffee table. Blood streamed out of the gash above his right eye.

Time stood still for what seemed like an hour, but was probably only five seconds. "Oh my God!" Momma bent down and put her hand over his wound. The blood dripped through her fingers. Father pushed her away, grabbed onto the edge of the coffee table and threw it towards Sean.

Sean jumped back, grabbed the lamp off the side table and raised it over his head, ready to throw it at Father.

"I'm calling the police." Grandma hurried as best as she could to the phone.

Sean dropped the lamp, blinked his eyes, then turned and raced out the back door. He disappeared as quickly as a jackrabbit hopping through the brush. He was probably as surprised as we were.

By the time the two policemen arrived we'd moved Father from the floor to the sofa. Momma had washed her hands and arms, cleaned the blood off Father's head and dabbed it with iodine. Father winced, Iodine burned.

"Want to let me know what happened?" The police officer who looked older asked. Strands of gray hair poked out from the side of his cap. He opened a notebook and took a pen out of his pocket. The handle of a pistol stuck out of a leather holster fastened to his belt.

The younger officer stood next to the first with his back to the wall. He rocked back and forth on the heels of his leather shoes.

Momma looked at me, then over at the older officer. "It was an accident." She pulled down on the sleeves of her flowered dress to hide the rug burns on her arms.

Grandma had gone upstairs to finish getting ready to go with me to dance class. She said that us being out of the house for a while would be a blessing. It'd give Father time to come to his senses. I was worried about her coming out because of her cold and all, but she said she didn't want to miss watching me dance.

"Nothing to report?" The older officer asked gently looking at one of us at a time.

Momma shook her head. The pink ribbon she'd tied in her hair made a rubbing noise.

Father pulled his head up from the pillow. "I'm fine. She's right. Just an accident."

I shook my head no. It wasn't anybody's fault but Father's.

The officers nodded. The older one closed his book and stood up. "Anything come to you, call us back. Okay?" He handed her a card with his name and number on it.

"Thanks," Momma replied softly as she wrapped her long fingers around the card.

"Sure," Dad sighed.

I got up to see the officers out, opened, then closed the front door. I couldn't help but notice the red lights on the police car beaming out for the whole neighborhood to see. "MacLeans in trouble. MacLeans in trouble," it shouted. So much for *secrets*.

When I came back I saw Momma ripping up the card from the policeman. Tears fell down her cheeks, she quickly wiped them away.

## Chapter Thirty-Four

## LIES

"My best friend, Grandma. I can't believe Margaret would lie like that." I clenched and unclenched my jaw. Dust blew in small circles on the pavement as we crossed Fort Street. "I'm never gonna speak to her again. Never!" I held tight to Grandma's arm. Stepping up and down the curbs was still difficult for her.

Grandma was quiet. She just nodded her head up and down as I spoke.

"And Father! Why does he think I'd do something stupid like get pregnant? He doesn't even know who I am." Puffy clouds hung like balls of cotton in the pale blue sky.

"Jeeze, can you believe Sean? I mean I didn't even think he liked me." I got the all-overs just thinking about him standing up for Momma and me.

When we got to dance class I helped Grandma sit in her favorite chair. The gray metal one in the middle of the waiting section, right behind the ballet bar. "Distraction's a good thing sometimes, Lonestar. Takes you away from worries," Grandma said. She smiled as I headed for the dressing room to change. Her breath still sounded wheezy.

"Pay attention, Lonestar," Miss Jackie yelled as she beat her cane on the floor, keeping time with the record on the Victrola. "Extend forward, extend right, extend behind. Change legs."

I stared into the mirror as my reflection made the moves Miss Jackie called out. *Distraction's a good thing sometimes,* Grandma had said. But, I couldn't do it.

Father's voice. Margaret's voice. Miss Jackie's voice. Momma's voice. Sean's voice. Grandma's voice. Sentences whirled together in my brain like the dust in the street. *We all know you must be pregnant.* *Your friend's mother called.* "Point your toes." *You've been trying on wedding dresses.* "Soften your wrists." *No one's going to hit anybody in this house ever again.*

"Well done, Lonestar," a voice called out from the void. I knew someone was talking to me, but I wasn't sure where it came from. A hand touched my shoulder. "You can stop now."

Tiny jerks of air puffed into my lungs. I lowered my arms, put both feet on the ground and stopped – like a wind-up toy that just ran out of tension. Miss Jackie stood in front of me. Her right arm leaned heavily on the crook of her red wooden cane. Worry wrinkles creased the bridge of her nose. It was real quiet. I looked around the floor. Everybody else was gone.

Grandma blinked at my reflection in the mirror. Puffy clouds hung under her eyes. I wished she would have stayed home and rested.

Margaret came over when we got home. "Want to go shopping?" she asked with a smile when I answered the front door. "Shopping?" I said. "After what you did to me."

"Oh!" Margaret's smile faded. "I guess my mom called, huh?"

"Yah, your mom called and said the dumbest thing," I snarled. "She said you told her that I had been shopping for a wedding dress and your mother implied that I was... pregnant."

"I didn't say you were pregnant. I..." Margaret trailed off.

"Go away, all you care about is yourself." I cleared the air between us with a sudden swipe of my arm. "I don't want to have anything to do with you or your stupid group ever again." I slammed the door.

Margaret came back a few hours later. I saw her through the front window. She pushed a letter through the mail slot in the front door, then left. I let the letter lie on the floor while I continued polishing the furniture and vacuuming the carpet.

Once I was finished I stared at the letter. I thought about ripping it up and throwing it away, but instead I took it upstairs and threw it on my bed. I paced the floor and punched the air.

After I'd exhausted myself, I crawled on top of my bed, leaned against the wall, ripped the letter open and read it. "Dear Lonestar, I guess you know I lied. I'm sorry, but I had to. Somebody told my mom they'd seen us go in and out of White's Bridal Shop. She thought I was going to run away and get married. It made her so angry that I didn't know what to do. So, I told her I'd gone to be with you. That you were the one who wanted to buy a wedding dress. I didn't plan on getting you into trouble. It just happened. I don't know who squealed on me but I don't think it was you."

I gave the letter a good shake. "Don't think it was you?" I mumbled. "What kind of friend do you think I am? One like you? A Benedict Arnold. And I used to think being a part of The Big Mommas was cool. Now I can see they're just out for themselves too."

I continued reading the letter. "If you want me to, I'll tell your parents the truth. Maybe they won't say anything to my folks if they know how much trouble I'll get into. I really do love Ralphy and no matter what, we will get married."

"Your best friend (I hope), Margaret."

I folded up the letter and put it under my pillow. I didn't know what to do. What she did hurt a lot of people. One little lie in her house dropped a hornet's nest in mine.

I put a note on my bedroom door, DO NOT DISTURB. It was written in red, like blood. No way was I going to join in our family dinner. I never wanted to see Father's face ever again. Instead I cleaned out all my drawers, folded and refolded my clothes and rearranged my closet.

Momma knocked on my door around seven that night. I'd heard her tiptoe around earlier. She must've read my sign and I'm sure Sean, Brucie and Grandma saw it when they passed in the hall.

"You okay?" Momma asked.

"No, I'm not." I slid Margaret's letter under the door. I heard a slight rustling as Momma picked it up, unfolded it and straightened out the wrinkles. After a minute I heard a sigh of relief, then Momma leaned in closer to the door, "I'll give it to your father," she said. "Maybe it will make him stop to think before he jumps to conclusions."

That night, it was hard to sleep. Father's voice kept repeating in my head. *People judge. They look for things to attack you for.* For what I wondered. I turned toward my window and stared out into the darkness. The wind blew softly, brushing the curtains gently from side to side. Thoughts swirled through my head. They made me dizzy.

When the swirling stopped, I felt heavy, yet strangely relaxed. Then visions came. *I stood in the middle of a large meadow surrounded by evergreen trees. Everything looked peaceful. Green colors flowed into more green. The air smelled fresh and crisp.*

*Suddenly, a gray tombstone, about two feet high, shot up in front of me. It took my breath away. I tried to see what was written on the stone. But, it was hard to do. All I could make out was the year, 1903. I moved forward and ran the tips of my fingers over the etching below the numbers.*

*The Earth started to shake. I looked out across the meadow. Five men, on horseback, looked in my direction. "He, haw!" one yelled. I grabbed onto the tombstone and held tight.*

*The sounds of hooves echoed through the air as the men galloped towards me.*

*"She's mine," one yelled.*

*I stood frozen against the stone. Who were they? Why were they after me?*

*The Earth parted. A woman rose out of the grave and stood on the grass next to me. She looked familiar but I didn't know why. Her dark hair hung over her shoulders and down the front of her long white dress. "Run Tsula, run," she said. "Run away from here. Find somewhere safe."*

*A small boy rose out of the Earth nearby and reached out for my hand. I took it and woke up.*

The vision was gone. I looked around the room to see where I was. My curtains blew in and out of the split in the windows just like they had before I closed my eyes. The clock on top of my dresser glowed in the dark; 2:00 a.m., it read. *Who was that?* I wondered, half asleep. *Did those men kill somebody? Is that why there was a grave? What did Tsula mean?*

Chapter Thirty-Five

## DEATH IS NEVER EASY

It's been over a week and Father hasn't said anything about thinking I was pregnant and trying on wedding dresses. You'd think he'd apologize, but no. He must think if you don't talk about bad stuff then it never happened. I'm sure he read Margaret's note. At least *she* apologized.

The bandage Momma put on Father's head is gone now, but the gash is still red. Momma's arms where she got that rug burn are still pink, but she says they're not sore.

Saturday, when I got home from doing errands, I found Aunt Dawn sitting on the sofa in the living room next to Momma. Two half empty coffee cups sat on the table in front of them. Momma nodded at me when I came in, then quickly turned away. Her eyes were swollen, like she'd been crying. I wondered why she was home. *Had she lost her job? Did she have another fight with Father?* I leaned back against the front door and stared at the two women.

Aunt Dawn lifted one of her arms up and twisted her wrist. The beads on her bracelet clanged together like they always did, her way of saying "hello."

I pushed myself away from the door and sat on the chair across from Momma and Aunt Dawn. My eyes searched from one to the other, as I tried to sense what was going on.

"I know what I saw, Dawn," Momma said. Her chin quivered as she spoke.

"I heard you Merle. A sparrow got stuck in your linen closet, so you know someone's dying and you want *me* to tell you who it is."

I'd heard Momma worry about birds before. They were messengers of doom when they came in the house. When she was seven she found a sparrow under her bed. The next day her sister Diana died from tuberculosis. When Mom was fourteen she found a sparrow in the linen cupboard. The next week her dad died of cancer.

"Dying? Who's dying?" I asked quickly.

"Hurry," Brucie screamed as he rushed into the house. "Come quick."

We ran through the front door. Across the porch. Down the stairs. Onto the lawn. A golden bundle of fur bit the air, coughed, and cried "oooohhhh." It was Goldy. Brucie bent down next to her. Aunt Dawn, Momma and I did the same. Eight hands tried to pat and pet the pain away.

"What happened?" Sean shouted as he ran down the street from the hamburger stand he worked at after school. His face a mass of fear. "What's wrong old girl?" he asked in jagged words as he wrapped his arms around her neck.

Goldy's body quivered. Then stopped. Shrill wails flew into the sky like reversed lightening strikes from Sean, Brucie, Momma, Aunt Dawn and me.

"Don't die," I pleaded. "Please don't die." I stroked her chest, but she still didn't move. "Jesus," I cried lifting my head up to the sky. "You saved people in the Bible. Please save Goldy. I promise I'll be good for the rest of my life if you'll just do this one thing." I squeezed my eyes shut hoping against hope that when I opened them Goldy would breathe again, get up, shake herself off and run to get her ball. I waited for what seemed like a very long time. When I unsqueezed my eyes, Goldy still didn't move.

"I tried to stop her." Brucie wiped his eyes on his shirt sleeve. "When I got back from delivering papers I saw her get some chicken bones out of the garbage and..."

"She was old, Brucie," Sean said slowly opening and closing his fists. "Just old and tired. It was time." Tears rolled down his cheeks. It'd been a long time since he cried. I remember when he said, *nothing's gonna hurt me again.* Father had just gotten his belt out to give us a whipping because I ran away. *Sean was wrong,* I thought. *Some things did hurt him. And us.*

We wrapped her with an old white sheet Momma saved for the bottom of the Christmas tree each year. It was hard to believe Goldy was dead. There was a quiet all around the house, a silence that made me feel hollow inside.

I sat quietly on the sofa next to Momma and Aunt Dawn. Sean and Brucie sat on the floor near the coffee table. Aunt Dawn gave us each feathers and yarn to make Prayer Feathers for Goldy. "Goldy, I love you," I whispered, as I wound the green string around the quill of my feather.

Brucie sat on the floor, on the other side of the coffee table, with his feather and a roll of yellow string. The edge of the collar of his plaid shirt was tucked between his lips. Every once and a while he made a sucking noise. Nobody stopped him this time.

Sean sat quietly. His fingers trembled as he twisted the blue yarn around the quill of his feather. He was the one who took care of Goldy more than the rest of us.

Grandma came downstairs to be with us. She shuffled across the room and slowly made her way to her stuffed chair in the corner. *"Ah-qui-lo-ky,* sick," she said. Her breath loud, raspy. She pulled her embroidered hanky out of her sleeve and blotted the sweat beads popping out on her face. Her long gray hair, usually braided and pinned high on the back of her head, hung loosely over her shoulders like a shawl.

Momma had seen *one* bird. One bird meant *one* death. That was *Goldy.* I swallowed hard, relieved somehow that I didn't have to worry about Grandma.

Grandma gasped, bowed her head and held her breath for a few seconds. Her hands gripped the edges of the stuffed chair. I dropped the feather I was working on. "You want me to make you some special tea, Grandma?" I asked quickly.

"I'm okay, Lonestar. Just a touch of the flu." Grandma leaned her head back. Her feet stretched out onto the printed flowers on the rug. "I'm so sorry about Goldy. She was a good, sweet dog." Grandma loosened the belt around her robe. "We have to give her a funeral. A proper farewell. She's gonna be missed."

Aunt Dawn looked across at Grandma then over at Momma. A look of fear flashed across her face. She picked up one of the feathers from the sack on the table and held it close to her heart.

Momma met Father at the door when he got home from work. "Goldy's dead," she said. Father cocked his head sideways like someone slapped him across the face.

We waited for him to say something about the Prayer Feathers we'd all made, but he didn't. Instead, he fixed his eyes on Sean. "You were real good with her, Laddie."

Sean lowered his chin, looked up at Father and nodded. They hadn't spoken much since their big fight.

"You kids all were." Father sat down next to Momma on the sofa. All the color drifted out of his face. "It's hard when things we love are taken away."

Father changed into his one piece coveralls, and dug a 3 ft. by 4 ft. hole on the side of the house. Sean, Brucie and I lined the hole with stones we gathered from the empty lot across the street. We figured Goldy would like that, it was always her favorite place to discover new smells. By the time we were finished, the last bit of sun dipped over the rooftops leaving us in shadows. A faint sliver of the moon appeared in the sky

Momma and Aunt Dawn helped Grandma walk across the lawn to join us on the side of the house. Sean and Father lifted the sheet with Goldy inside and laid it gently in the middle of the hole. We all crowded in together. Momma handed us each a candle and lit the wicks with a long wooden match, one at a time.

Aunt Dawn shifted her position a bit so Grandma could stand on her own at the head of the grave. "Great Spirit," Grandma cried, as she held the candle out in front of her. "Creator of all things, large and small. Take the sweet spirit of Goldy, and let her run freely in the green meadows of the stars. Give her the joy she has given to us. Give her the strength she has given to us. Let her take the love we hold in our hearts for her as she crosses the bridge leading from this world to the next. She has been a good friend. We will miss her. *Ho*."

## Chapter Thirty-Six

### LOST

Losing Goldy, so quickly, was hard on all of us. Sean started lifting weights even more than he did before. Brucie invented a new invisible friend. A dog with jaws the size of a dinosaur. Momma hummed to herself – to make up for the silence that moved into the spaces Goldy used to fill. Father wanted to play poker with us. He always won. Grandma sat in the garden more. Besides talking to the plants, sometimes I heard her talking to, what sounded like the stars. She'd look up into the sky in the evening and pretend they were friends of hers. *You thought I was gonna be gone a long time, didn't you? But, sixty-four years is not that long.*

I started sitting under the dining room table when Father wasn't home. The sweet doggy scent of Goldy's breath and fur were strongest there. I'd close my eyes and try to feel her with my whole body. That was what Grandma did when she found that *Ciippa* that was following Brucie around at school. I wasn't sure if dogs had a reason to talk to people, but I sure wanted to talk to her.

"What's Lonestar doing under the dining room table, Momma," Violet asked one afternoon when she and Aunt Dawn sat with Momma in the living room chatting and drinking coffee.

"Be polite for a change, Violet," Aunt Dawn hissed, "she's sad because Goldy's dead."

*Nothing was going right for me,* I thought. *Goldy died. Margaret betrayed me. Grandma didn't go to dance class with me anymore, and I still didn't have my Moontime.*

"Momma never complains, but I'm worried. I don't know how much longer her frail body can hold on." Deep sobs separated Momma's last few words.

Momma's momma meant my Grandma! *Had I missed something?* I wondered. *Ah-qui-lo-ky, Grandma had said a few weeks ago. A bit of the flu. I knew she was sick. But, everybody got sick at times. Then, they got better.*

"What's wrong with Grandma?" I asked as I crawled out from under the table and walked through the archway into the living room.

Momma looked up at me with tears in her eyes. "Oh! Lonestar, she's..." Momma shook her head back and forth. "She's not getting better." Steam from her hot coffee drifted up from her cup.

"She's not gonna die," I shouted. "She told me Grandmas never die. *Never.*"

After the rest of us had dinner, I took a tray up to Grandma's room. I breathed in the sweetness of the red rose Brucie'd picked for Grandma from our garden. Momma'd put it in a jelly jar and set it on the tray, next to the Jell-O, the glass of water, and the chicken soup. Soft melodic sounds drifted out of Grandma's room. I leaned my back against the door to listen. She was singing with somebody. I had to tell Momma that she was wrong. Grandma was on an upturn.

*Morn-ing is com-ing. It's time to see the light.* Grandma's words came out slow and jagged. *Morn-ing is com-ing. It's time to see the light.* A stronger, deeper voice repeated.

I waited for a few minutes, when it sounded quiet again I twisted the knob, turned sideways, and walked in, careful not to spill the soup. The deep voice was Johnny Whitefeather's.

"Hi." I held the tray out in front of me and edged the door shut with my shoulder.

"Long time, no see." Johnny got up, took the tray and set it down on the bedside table.

"I'm glad you're visiting," I said. "It sounds like you and my Grandma have been writing a song. Or at least singing one I've never heard before."

"Yep. Your first guess was right," Johnny replied. "We're writin' a new song." He put one of Grandma's extra pillows over her legs – then moved the tray. "That too heavy, Martha?" he asked. Worry lines broke out on his forehead as he studied her face for any sign of discomfort. Grandma shook her head *no*. The corners of her mouth turned up slightly.

"Brucie picked the rose." I stood just inside the door, my back to Grandma's Vanity Dresser, not sure if I should stay or leave.

"It's beautiful." Grandma reached her hand out to touch one of the petals. "And so soft. Just like a newborn baby." Air whooshed out of her lungs as her hand fell back down onto the quilt.

Her movement startled me. She was so weak.

Johnny sat back down on Grandma's right side, careful not to jiggle the bed. She patted one of her quilt patches on her left wanting me to sit too. I eased onto the bed, picked up the spoon from the tray, dipped it into the soup and brought it up to Grandma's mouth. As soon as she swallowed, I brought up another spoonful. *Eating will make her better,* I thought. *The more I can get down her, the stronger she'll get.*

"Your Grandma was telling me what a good dancer you've become, Lonestar." Johnny's eyes shifted between Grandma and me.

"She comes from a long line of dancers. It's in the blood." Grandma sipped another spoonful of soup then shook her head. That meant, *no more.*

I didn't like the "no more". I tilted my head, snorted a bit then set the spoon down.

"I'll say." Johnny's face broke out into a big grin. "I remember a young girl who could dance with the best of' 'em." Johnny lowered his strong jaw and looked at Grandma in a childlike mischievous way. "Why I can almost see her now. White blouse tucked into the waist of a long printed full skirt. Long dark silky hair hangin' down to her waist." Johnny lifted his head and laughed, then shook his head from side to side.

"Eyes that could capture a friend and keep'em in her pocket for eternity."

"My, my, my, Johnny, how you do tell stories," Grandma said with a sigh.

"Tell me," I pleaded. Grandma didn't talk a lot about herself.

"Well, it was called *'Natolekiwekaki'* or 'Go Get 'Em' dance," Johnny looked down at Grandma and grinned. "It's done for fun at *powwows*, special gatherings. We were at the old ceremonial grounds one evening and when the drummin' started and the lead singer called out 'Go get 'em,' I hustled myself in line to be in just the right place to dance with Martha, umm, your Grandma. The boys and girls both formed a long line, one inside the other and moved toward the field next to the singer-drummers. We circled in different directions, sort of like wheels. After one full round, I left the line, put my hands on her shoulders and guided her into my line." Johnny chuckled. His chest moved up and down.

*"E'ne,"* Grandma said. "And we danced all night. I remember my feet hurt the next day something fierce. They felt as hot as the fire we danced around." Grandma licked her lips and pointed to the tray. She needed water. I reached over, picked up her glass and held it while she took a sip.

"I didn't know you were friends when you were kids." I set the glass back on the tray. "I guess I'd always figured you met near Grandma's old house near the forest in Taylor Township."

There was an awkward silence. A silence heavy with buried feelings.

Left all our friends and came to Michigan. My father got a job fitting pipes. That's where I met your grandfather. He was a pipe fitter too." Grandma closed her eyes then opened them again. Her words came out slow, like a sleepy child's. "Life is like a river. It's better to follow the current than to try to swim upstream." Grandma nodded toward the tray. I picked up the glass of water and held it for her again. She took a small sip then wet her lips with her tongue. This time when I set the glass down I pulled the Jell-O bowl forward. "Our Earthwalk always provides opportunities for us to learn how to meet one challenge after another. Some folks call them roadblocks, but they're really opportunities to learn from." Grandma coughed then took a deep breath. "When we get discouraged and think we can't go on, it's good to remember we're never alone. We all have our friends in the Circle of Light."

"What's the Circle of Light, Grandma?" I dipped the spoon under one of the red Jell-O cubes and brought it up to her mouth. She took it in. *Maybe distraction's the answer,* I thought. *If I can keep her busy talking, maybe she'll finish the whole bowl.*

Grandma took a deep breath, deeper than usual. "We all have a circle of friends in the Star World. Even though they're far away, they're always with us, Lonestar. Some are our teachers, some are there for us to teach. We all learn from each other's mistakes. And from the good stuff too." Her voice was soft with a far-a-way feel to it.

I took this opportunity to give her some more Jell-O. She rolled the cube from side to side in her mouth. I reached for the water again figuring maybe she was having a hard time swallowing. She took a sip like she did before. This time, when I put the glass down and dipped the spoon into the Jell-O, she shook her head "no." Defeated, I put the spoon down. I didn't like giving up, but I'd already pushed my luck and gotten her to eat more than she wanted.

I sat on the cement edge of our front steps and stared past our Maple Tree – out over the empty field to my right. It had been one of Goldy's favorite spots. I closed my eyes and tried to feel her soft fur in my hand.

*Suddenly, something wet brushed against my cheek. Goldy's doggy smell fell over my face like an invisible veil.* My eyes shot open. *A dog with gold fur flashed in front of me.* "What?" I turned quickly and looked around. *Was that Goldy?*

"Heh, Lonestar. How's it goin'?" A voice came out of the shadows behind me.

"Uhh!" My heart pounded hard in my ears. I'd been lost in a daydream. I turned quickly to see Margaret standing at the bottom of the steps. We didn't see much of each other now that I'd given up The Big Mommas. "You see anything ...

different?" I brushed my cheek with the back of my hand. *Could she see what I saw?* I wondered.

Margaret turned and looked. "Where?"

"I don't know." I looked around. "Like, maybe on the steps."

"Nope. Nothin'. What do you see?"

"Oh, just something floating in the air." I lied. Grandma always said not to talk about stuff that others couldn't see. Besides, I knew better than to trust Margaret.

Margaret climbed up the steps and sat on the ledge with me. We turned toward the lawn and dangled our legs over the side. "Like my new haircut?" Margaret asked as she fluffed up the edges, letting her long fingers float from curl to curl

Her once shoulder length hair was cut into a short bob. Straight across the back and sides with fringe framing her narrow face. "It looks great!" I said, wondering why I hadn't noticed it right away.

"Notice anything else?" Margaret waved her left hand in the air like she was conducting the birds in the big tree out front. A gold ring with a tiny stone encased her ring finger.

"Is it real?"

"Well, it's a real ring if that's what you mean." She rubbed the stone against her green and white pedal pushers then held it up again. "Mrs. Ralph Dezero," Margaret's words slid off her tongue like honey.

"You're married?" I stared into her dark eyes. *Pools of deception*, I thought.

"Naw." Margaret laughed. "Not married, yet. Just engaged. That's a step closer than bein' engaged to be engaged. My folks'd have a tizzyfit if they knew."

I didn't laugh with her. A few months ago getting married sounded exciting. Now, it didn't. I clicked my heels together and let them fly out and back like I was dancing in the air.

"Your *aunty* come to visit yet?" Margaret leaned in and whispered.

"Which one?" I pretended to not know what she was talking about as I continued to click my heels.

"You know, down there, in Virginia." Margaret pointed towards her crotch then glanced around to see if anyone was listening. Like it was a big stupid secret of some kind.

I pressed my lips together and sighed. "You have to remind me all the time."

"Gads, you're in a bad mood. You still mad at me or something?" She turned sideways and drew her knees into her chest. "I said I was sorry." She held her ring up and watched it sparkle in the sun.

I wasn't mad anymore, just cautious. "Naw," I shrugged my shoulders. "I'm worried about Grandma." I looked down at the lawn. A black beetle was making his way through the tall grass. Every so often he'd sink in between the crevices. Lost in darkness. That's how I felt. A part of me was sinking and I didn't know how to climb back up.

Chapter Thirty-Seven

## GRANDMA'S SONG

As the days went by, Dandelions started to multiply. None of us cared. Old tin cans, bottles, and pieces of paper thrown out by passing cars mixed with the wild flowers in the vacant lot on the corner.

All of our relatives took turns coming over to visit Grandma. It got harder and harder for me to get time with her alone, except while I was feeding her.

I moped around the house. No one could fill the space that Grandma filled.

Then, one late afternoon, two weeks before my birthday, she sent everybody else away and called for me. "Bring me that small pine box in my trunk," Grandma asked, her voice a soft whisper. Momma had propped her up with a pillow so she could lean against the wall.

"Is this what you want?" The box I'd found had small circles burned into the lid.

*"E'ne,"* she nodded.

I sat down on the edge of the bed, careful not to jar it too much, and set the box down.

"Open it." Grandma raised her eyebrows, clenched her thin lips together, and nodded.

I ran my fingers over the circles, lifted the lid and pulled out a bundle of yellowed letters. A strong musty smell flew into the air and mixed with Grandma's usual lavender and sage scent.

"Read to me, Lonestar. I want to revisit the words with your voice." Sips of air fought their way down into her chest.

I carefully untied the faded blue satin ribbon that held the letters together and set it aside. "Any particular one you

237

want?" I ran my fingers over the edges of twenty or thirty letters.

"It doesn't matter." Grandma played with one of her braids.

I picked up the letter on the top of the pile. "Wherever you go, I am there," I read. "Whatever you see is part of me. The moon, the stars, the simple tree, are all a part of you and me." My words came out staggered. The writing was hard to decipher.

"Go on." Grandma looked past my shoulder and out the window. I could feel the warmth of the sun on the back of my neck. My shadow fell across the bed and over part of Grandma.

I set that letter aside and picked up the next. "No one disputes the beauty of a rose. Even with thorns. So, too, you must learn to appreciate all the parts of you."

"More," she said with a deep sigh.

"You are the light of the world. Love this light. Let it shine as brightly as the sun and fall on all of those around you."

"Go on."

"*Kokumthena* sings when you are happy."

We continued on 'till the shadows made it too hard to make out the writing. I retied the letters, put them back into the wooden box and looked over at Grandma. The orange-pink of the sunset made her face look unreal, like a painting.

"That's enough, Lonestar, enough for now," she said patting my hand the way she always did.

"Who wrote all of those things, Grandma? They're very nice."

"My grandmother," Grandma said. "My grandmother wrote them to me when I was a young girl ... like you are now." Her eyes glistened when she mentioned her grandmother.

"You saved them that long!"

*"E'ne.* I saved them for you." Her chin quivered. "Today, I have to leave."

"Leave?" My heart rattled like an old tin can full of pebbles. "Where are you going?"

"It is time for me to go to the Star World to be with my ancestors." Her words came out slow and even, like it was something she'd practiced.

"But, I don't want you to go, Grandma. I need you here, with me." I knew her illness hadn't gotten better; it had gotten worse. But, I didn't *want* to know. Facing that truth was like pounding nails through my hands.

Grandma nodded. "I know ... it's hard," she shuddered a bit.

"You said that Grandma's never die." Tears welled up in my eyes.

"It's true, Lonestar. Grandmas never die. I will live on, inside of you." Grandma fixed her eyes on mine. "In your thoughts, in your dreams, in everything that we've shared. I live in the eggs you were born from and the ones that you will give birth to." Her words pushed their way out of her chest in waves. "I live in that invisible chord that connects our hearts no matter where I go."

"But, I need you here, *now*." I was not going to give up. "I can't live without you."

"My body is tired." Grandma sighed. "It's been fighting off an illness for a very long time. Now my spirit needs to be free."

Tears erupted like molten lava and stung their way down my cheeks. I tried to brush them away, but it was useless. More just kept coming.

That night I slept on top of the bed with Grandma. Dreams came and went like war tribes invading my life. In the last one: *I flew up above the Earth, like I had in other night visions. This time: I didn't stand on a cloud. I didn't stand on anything. All I could see for miles and miles was space.*

I reached for Grandma's hand. It was cold. I sat up and listened for her breath. No sound. I touched her mouth. Nothing moved. I put my ear to her chest. No beat.

Frantically, I made a butterfly with my hands. Flickered my fingers over her chest. Then pushed with all my strength. Nothing. I put my mouth over hers and blew air into her lungs. Still nothing. "God, Great Spirit, *Kokomthena*, where are you?" I sobbed.

Train whistles blew in my ears. I sat up against the wall and looked into her face. Her eyes stared straight ahead at something I couldn't see. The light from the early morning sun, that sun she loved so much, streamed through the window.

Tears rolled down my cheeks. I didn't know what to do. I'd never been with a dead person before. "Grandma, can you hear me?" My voice quivered. "Grandma." I cried. Her name filled the room and ricochet from wall to wall.

"Fiona?" Momma rushed into the room. "Oh, God!" She cried seeing Grandma.

"She's gone," I said looking up. The words clawed their way out of me.

Momma's eyes clouded over. "She told me it was time." Her hands gripped hard to the front of her flowered robe. Slowly, she moved forward, dazed.

I knew how she felt. It was hard to believe someone could be here one day and gone the next. I didn't like it. Grandma said she had to leave, her body was tired. But I still didn't like it. Not one bit. If this was the way the world was set up, then it was stupid.

Momma crawled on top of the bed with me, on the other side of Grandma. She wrapped her arms around Grandma's shoulders, and started to cry. I snuggled down, as close as I could, with my arms across Grandma's lap, and cried with her. Our sobs turned into wails. Deep throbbing painful wails.

Brucie and Sean came into Grandma's room. They too climbed into bed and held onto Grandma. If weight alone could have anchored her to the Earth, we would have won out. But nothing we did, or could do, was enough.

We gave Grandma back to the Earth. I stood at the foot of her grave with my brothers and cousins. Mom, Dad, aunts, uncles, Johnny, and friends of the family, stood on either side. We sang, Amazing Grace how sweet thou art. But, Grace didn't seem sweet to me. Preacher MacNeal led us through a quote from Psalm 23:6, "Surely goodness and mercy shall follow me all the days of my life and I will dwell in the house of the Lord forever." I said the verse along with everybody else.

But I didn't believe it. There wasn't anything merciful about taking my Grandma away.

Johnny stepped forward when the preacher finished. He dropped a pinch of tobacco near some of the roses in the middle of the casket. The red in his shirt stood out like a bright flag against the pale blue sky. "Great Spirit we give you back our sister Martha," he said as he lifted his arms up to the sky. "She has walked among us, proud and wise." His deep voice sailed out over the cemetery like a strong north wind. "Her hand has touched not only those of us here, but all of those that we in turn come in contact with." The feather he always wore flapped against his strong chin. "Let her ride on the back of Golden Eagle, the gatekeeper of the east, to her new home. Let her run with Rabbit, gatekeeper of the south and visit us when she is ready. Let her rest with Black Bear, gatekeeper of the west, so that she may be renewed and find her place in the Circle of Light. And, let her walk proudly with White Buffalo, gatekeeper of the north that she can spread her wisdom to others who call on her for help.

Sean stepped forward, took a pinch of tobacco out of the pouch he now kept in his pocket, and dropped it in the center just like Johnny had.

A cyclone twisted and turned inside my head as I thought about dropping a pinch of tobacco on Grandma's coffin like the others had. *To carry words of prayer to the Creator and serve as a witness*, Grandma had said. The only words of prayer I had were "come back, I need you."

I turned and walked away from the crowd. They could all say goodbye if they wanted. Not me. If I let her go, a part of me would fall into that grave and never come back.

I leaned my shoulder against a tall Pine Tree and watched from the distance. Relatives and friends moved slowly, each saying goodbye in his or her own way. As they did, Johnny set up a drum on a nearby hill. It was about twice the size of the one he'd played at our tent show. Two men joined him.

Johnny and his friends sat in a semicircle on the grass. They began to beat out a soft rhythmic pattern on the drum and chant. *Morn-ing is com-ing. It's time to see the light.*

*Colors of sunrise are breaking through the night. When darkness surrounds me, I"ll know it's time to hide. And wait for the hand that will come to be my guide.*

Something seemed familiar in their words. Something I'd heard before. The memory of standing at Grandma's door flashed into my head. Then the sound of laughter. Hers and ... Johnny's. *A light went on.* It was Grandma's song. I didn't know it at the time, but she and Johnny had been singing her song, the one she had to write before she could die, so she could find her way to the ancestral resting place. I shook my head back and forth. *Why did she have to write that song? Couldn't she have waited?*

"It's time to go home, Lassie," A voice whispered.

I jumped back. It was Father. He put his hand on my shoulder. Tears rolled down his full cheeks. He quickly wiped them away with a handkerchief.

Chapter Thirty-Eight

## FATHER'S HAUNTED PAST

By the time we got home Father was sobbing so hard he could hardly make it from the car to the living room. Sean and Momma walked on either side to hold him up. Brucie and I walked just behind. His tears made me mad. *What right did he have to feel sad?* I thought. *All he ever did was make things harder for Grandma. It was the rest of us who were going to miss her.*

Momma and Sean helped Father sit down on the sofa. "He needs a screwdriver," Momma whispered. "Half orange juice, half vodka." Sean shook his head, "self medication" he mumbled as he headed for the kitchen.

Father leaned forward. He made small jerky movements with his arms and hands as he brought them up to support his head. His shoulders shook like something heavy rested there.

Momma cozied in next to Father and rubbed his back. "You've got to talk," she said. "Tell us what's going on."

Brucie and I sat down in the stuffed chair opposite the sofa. He leaned his head onto my shoulder. Grandma's chair sat empty in the corner. I listened for her footsteps on the stairs. *She should be down any second to join us,* I thought. An ache settled in my stomach a second later when I remembered she was gone.

Sean sat down on the sofa on the opposite side of Father. "Drink," he said holding out the glass. Father nodded. Sat up. Wiped his eyes. Took the glass and sipped. His ruddy face looked older. Frown lines ran across his forehead like claw marks.

"I'm not putting up with this you know." Momma leaned back and crossed her arms over the front of her newest blue dress. "You either run away or clam up when something's wrong and I'm good and tired of it." Her jaw quivered a bit then stayed firm. "We're all sad here.    You're not the only one with sorrows." Yep, she'd had a few sips of something at the funeral too.    I didn't mind them fighting as long as it wasn't about me.    And as long as there wasn't any yelling, pushing, or throwing things.

"I'm sorry," Father said staring straight ahead.    His eyelids were puffed up like protective umbrellas.

"Sorry's not good enough.    We're not leaving this room 'till you've told us what's hidden inside."

"Tick, tock, tick, tock," the clock loudly echoed.    Momma'd spoken for all of us.    And, once more, it didn't sound like she was going to back down.

None of us made a move.

"It's about your mother, isn't it?" Momma prodded after a while.    "Isn't it?"

Father took a big gulp of his drink.    "I thought I'd laid my past to rest."

"No.    You didn't.    That's why you're so hard on us, and especially Fiona."

My head jerked back when she said my name.    What was she talking about?

Father blew hard on his lips.    Air escaped into a flapping sound.    "My mother died, when I was real little." His words came out slowly.    He ran his free hand back and forth over his left thigh then shook his head sideways.    "No, she didn't die. She was killed."

The word "killed" roared through my head like a brush fire.

"And I couldn't help her.    I wanted to.    But, I couldn't.    I was just five, or maybe six. I can't remember." Father's hand shook as he took another gulp of his drink.    "Run *Tsula* run," my mother said. "That's what she called me, Little Fox."

I squeezed Brucie's hand. *Tsula*. That was the name in my dream. The one where the woman cried out to the little boy.

Father ran his fingers through his hair like he was plowing Earth. "It must've been ... 1903. My sister, Dancing Feet, was almost fourteen, Fiona's age. We were playing along the river. I wanted to make the stones skip across the water so I held Momma back. My sister ..." Father stopped, took another swig of his drink, slunk down and stared into the distance.

"Go on," Momma prodded. I'd never seen her so insistent.

Father jerked up. Shivered. Took a deep breath and continued, "was up ahead. She must've hidden in the trees when she heard the men." Father shook his head from side to side. "Five men, raced across the meadow on horseback. *That pretty squaw's here again,* one yelled. *The snobby half-breed,* a second hollered. Others screamed out noises. Words I couldn't understand. Or didn't want to." Father brought his glass up to his forehead and held it there for a minute.

Air got stuck in my throat. I was afraid to breathe. Did father say he was walking with his *mother*? Did he say the men on horseback called her a *squaw* and a *half-breed.* Some of his story I'd seen in visions, like patches in an unfinished quilt. Now they were being sewn together. He was part Indian. We'd all figured that out over the years. But, I didn't think about it being dangerous to be Indian when he was a kid.

Sean clenched his jaw, the veins near his ears ballooned. His chest moved in and out, pushing hard on the buttons of his white dress shirt. He always knew things ahead of me, I wondered if any of this story was new to him.

"Their eyes bulged and faces twisted as they headed right toward us. Momma sent me in one direction while she ran in another. *Get your father,* she cried."

"I stumbled forward unsure of what to do. I wanted to protect her. Do something to stop her from being hurt, but I couldn't. I was too small. My father was gone. Out of town getting supplies for our farm. *Had Momma forgotten?* I wondered. My big sister, Dancing Feet, was the only one who could help. If we got together we could fight off the horsemen. *Where was she? She'd been with us before I stopped to skip stones. How long ago was that?* Thoughts scrambled through my head."

*"Dancing Feet, help,* I screamed. I ran towards the edge of the forest, toward where I thought she might be waiting for us."

It took a second for Father's words to sink in. *Dancing Feet was the name on all those letters in Father's drawer I found a long time ago. That was his sister. She was the one who ran away and left him. Dancing Feet must've ... been a dancer, like me. He's worried I'll run away like she did.*

"The sounds of horses hooves and men yelling whipped through my head like a bad storm. *Run, run, run,* echoed inside of me. I threw my arms from side to side, raced forward as fast as my legs could go. But, I wasn't fast enough."

*Father thought it was his fault. He thought if he could've run faster for help, or if he hadn't stopped to skip rocks his mother wouldn't have been killed.* The floor lamp at the end of the sofa dimmed, then got bright again. This time a woman, dressed in white buckskin walked behind the sofa and stood behind Father. I blinked my eyes several times, but the figure stayed.

"What did your mother look like?" I asked slowly darting my eyes back and forth between Father and the woman. A deep stillness settled inside of me. I vaguely remembered the small photo of a woman I'd seen when I snuck into Father's drawer.

"What?" Father asked mystified. He took another gulp from his drink.

I took a deep breath, blew the air out, and looked over Father's head into the woman's face. Her lips turned up at the edges as she nodded her head. "What ... did your mother look like?" I asked again.

Father shook his head from side to side. "I don't know why you need to know this." He pulled his jacket sleeves down over his hands. "Pretty. She was pretty." Father sounded tired. "With dark hair. Dark eyes. And ..."

"Dark skin," I added looking into the woman's face. "Full cheeks, narrow chin?"

Father's nostrils flared. "Maybe."

"Tell her," Momma prodded. "Tell her the truth."

"What do you think I've been doing?" Father flashed. "Enough already. Enough." He pulled his hands in even further, shrugged his shoulders and tucked his head, turtle style.

Momma stiffened, crossed her arms and leaned back against the sofa.

Sean gave me a sharp look and mouthed, "no".

Brucie squirmed in our shared seat.

There was a fluttering in my ears followed by a message. "'Tsula, Little Fox,'" I said. "Your mother wants you to know that ... you could not ... have saved her. Nothing you could ... have done ... would have saved her. She's telling me that ... people fear what they do not know ... what they can not control." I let the words come out just as I heard them. The woman standing behind Father − my other Grandmother − smiled.

"She spoke to you?" Father's face turned ashen.

"Yes," I said.

Father shook his head and turned away. I didn't care. I was glad that I could see the truth. *Lead her to the light, that her life may be filled with the knowledge that cannot be found in books.* Grandma had prayed for me to see differently than others − and now I could. Tears welled up in my eyes

I wanted to tell Grandma I'd actually seen a *ciipaa*. She was the only one who would've understood what it was like. But, then I remembered, once again, she was gone.

For the next three days, Monday, Tuesday, and Wednesday: Father went to work as usual; Mom snuck off to her job; Sean and Brucie went to school, then work; and I stayed home. I used to get mad at Brucie for making up excuses to not do what he was supposed to do, now it was me. *I'm tired. Sick. Headachy.* I said. I wasn't hungry either. I pretty much stayed in my room and read. Momma brought my dinner up to my room on a tray. I nibbled a bit, then threw the rest out.

Thursday, when I woke up in the morning, a soft light pulsed over the entire top of my bed. It made me feel warm and somehow comforted. I reached up to try to touch it with the tips of my fingers. When I did, it moved down into my body and settled in my stomach area. I waited breathlessly, wondering what the light wanted from me. *Was it another ciippa?* I wondered. But, no one came. Nothing else stirred in my room.

Suddenly, a knowingness burst through my heart. *It was my Moontime.* I sat bolt upright and ran next door to tell Grandma. She'd want to know that I was finally going to be like everybody else. She was right, after all. I wasn't a freak. Those tiny eggs she told me were a gift from her to my mom and then to me, were really there.

"Grandma." I knocked on her door. "Grandma, guess what?" I turned the handle and rushed in. Her fringed maroon shawl hung on a hook next to the door. The flowered robe Aunt Raven made for her lay at the foot of the bed. Slippers tucked underneath, on the floor. The colors in her quilt jumped out at me; it was made from patches cut out of her family's old clothes.

But the bed itself was empty. No one leaned up against the wall smiling at the morning sun. No one said, *congratulations, isn't life amazing!* I turned and looked at the vanity table. No one sat brushing their hair. No hands wove braids in circular movements, twisting and turning, pulling and tightening with just the right tension. No eyes reflected out and held me close in the mirror.

The light through the window dimmed. A cloud passed over the sun. The wind blew hard against the side of the house. I shivered with excitement. *We all have our seasons*, Grandma had said. *They just come at different times.*

I leaned forward and made a hood with my arms. Deep sighs beat their way through the emptiness inside of me. "Grandma I miss you. I miss you so much," I cried

When I could move, I went next door to my room and closed the door. I got out some old pictures of Grandma, spread them out on my bed, then laid down in the middle of them. "Sorry I didn't listen to you, Grandma. I acted like I didn't care when you told me about how important women used to be treated when they got their *Moontime*. I was too into feeling sorry for myself.

I picked up one of the pictures of Grandma and held it out in front of me. She was all dressed up from head to toe. A silver barrette was clipped to the front of her long braided gray hair.

I ran the tips of my fingers over her smiling face. "You said: the women elders built a special *wikiup*, a hut made out of twigs and branches." Tears flowed down my cheeks. I brushed them away with the back of my hand. Slowly everything Grandma had told me flashed through my head.

"Did Fiona come downstairs today?" Father's deep voice carried through the floorboards, beneath my room, from the kitchen.

My head jerked up. Six o'clock, the alarm clock on my dresser read. It was getting dark outside. I must've fallen asleep. I sat up, wiped my face with the arm of my shirt and gathered up the pictures of Grandma I'd spread out on the bed.

"Fiona?" Father knocked on my door. His voice tentative.

I stashed the pictures under my pillow. "Yes," I called back. Father hardly ever came up to my room.

He twisted the knob. Walked in. "It's gloomy in here." He switched on the overhead light.

I blinked a few times as I looked up at Father. My eyeballs felt cat scratched.

"I'm sorry about your Grandma." Father walked to the foot of my bed. His hands pushed hard inside the pockets of his gray jacket. "But you have to get on with your life, Lassie." Father walked over to my bed and sat on the edge.

"You mean get on with the way *you* think my life should be," I snarled.

Father sighed. "I'm just tryin' to do the right thing."

Excuses I thought. Stupid excuses. "Well I don't want to get on with my life. I don't want to pretend that nothin's happened. That my life is the same. I don't want to see other people laugh and look happy. I don't ever want to see anybody, ever again." I crossed my arms over my chest and held tight. The inside of me felt hollow.

"Well, you don't always get to do what *you* want to." His words came out strong, sure, like he could still decide things for me.

"I'm almost fourteen. And, nobody can tell me what to do. Not even you."

"Don't be smart with me." His face reddened like it did when he got upset.

"Well, you can beat me if you like. But, I'm not budging."

Father clenched his fists, grunted and left. A few minutes later he shouted up through the floorboards. "She's got a smart lip, that girl."

"Oh, she's just sad. That's all. And," Momma hesitated. "And, I heard her talking to herself about having her Moontime. She's a woman now."

Saturday morning Momma knocked on my door. "Fiona." I didn't answer. The door swung open. A tray of fresh rolls and a glass of milk entered just ahead of her. "You going back to dance class?" She whispered. She set the tray on top of my dresser, picked one of the rolls up and walked over to the bed. "Here." The corners of her mouth turned up into a half smile.

"I'm not hungry and I'm not going to class. I'm not going anywhere," I blurted out.

"You're not the only one who misses her, you know." Momma snapped, turned on her heels and went out.

Later in the day Father called up from the bottom of the stairs. "You come down here, Fiona. It's time for dinner."

"No!" Food was one of the big three answers for everything. Food, roof, clothes. That was all he seemed to think we needed. Well, I was tired of it. Tired of pretending. Tired of him making decisions for me. I was like one of the butterflies in Grandma's story that we acted out a long time ago. I was not going to get put away in a cave and die. This time I wanted to be free to make my own decisions and I was gonna fight to get them.

Father barged into my room without knocking. "You have to eat."

"I don't *have* to do anything." I pushed my back against the wall behind my bed and melted into the plaster. The wood, insulation, plumbing, all became a part of me.

"What is the matter with *you*?" He flung his hands forward in a challenging gesture.

I sat up tall. "Me?" I retorted. "What's the matter with *me*? What's the matter with *you* that you could not let me know about my heritage. You've hidden pieces of me away like old bones Goldy used to hide in the yard. You treated my Grandma like she was crazy, and you ask *me* what's the matter with *me*?"

"I did it for your own good." Father growled.

"What good was that?"

"People look differently at you when they know you're from a mixed heritage." Father swallowed hard. The adam's apple in his throat went up and down. "Damn it Fiona, it's safer to be white. I wanted you to be full Scots, that way you'd be accepted anywhere you went in the world. You're blond, blue eyed, not too dark, nobody could tell."

"I don't want to be accepted if it's a lie." Tears shot up into the corners of my eyes. This time I couldn't blink them away. "Besides people should be accepted as who they are. Isn't that what being American is all about. Isn't everybody a half-breed, quarter-breed or mismatch of one thing or another?"

"You're impossible."

"Well I'm not coming out of my room until you accept me as who I am and not as somebody you made up." I cocked my head from one side to the other like Father did sometimes.

"I do accept you as who you are."

"I ... I want a Puberty Ceremony." The words choked their way out of me. "I want to walk in the footsteps of my ... Grandma's grandmother and ... yours." My chin shook so hard it was difficult to talk. "And I ... want to use my full name, Fiona Lonestar McClean.

Father's hand slammed across my face so fast I didn't see it coming. Blood dripped onto my shirt. I held my hand up to catch it but it dripped between my fingers. "Go ahead slap me again," I cried. "I'm not giving in."

Father stomped away. His shoulder slammed against the door and banged it into the wall.

He was good and mad, but I didn't care. *When you want something you have to figure out what work to do to get it,* Grandma said. I was doing that figuring now.

"Calm down." Momma's voice drifted up into my room from the kitchen below.

"How can I calm down? She's impossible. There's no way in heaven I can get through to her. Why doesn't she understand that it's a dog eat dog world out there?" Father's voice boomed out.

"What's that on your shirt?" Momma's voice dropped. "And the back of your hand?"

There was a scuffling of feet across the linoleum floor followed by clinking glass. Father was probably pouring himself a drink. A screwdriver more than likely. His self prescribed medication. *Good for what ails ya,* he'd say.

"Did you hit her?" Momma shouted. "I heard her yelling, but ... you said you wouldn't hit her ever again. You promised." Momma's words came out in little spurts. "Oh my God. It's blood isn't it? Fiona's blood."

My back stiffened. Was Father gonna get mad at Momma now?

"She wants a Puberty Ceremony for her birthday, Frank. Is that such a terrible thing?" Momma cried.

"It's ... not as simple as all that, Merle," Father snapped.

"Fiona's not your mother. She's not your sister or anybody from your past. I know your father didn't let you talk about your mother after she was killed. It was dangerous. They took Indian children away from their families. They forbade them to practice their religion or speak their native language. Don't you think I felt some of that loss too? But, right now I'm proud of who I am, and I'm good and tired of having you treat us all as if we've got something to hide." There was more scuffling on the floor. This time it went out to the hall and into their bedroom. "Wham." The sound of their door slamming rattled the clock on my dresser.

"Merle, open this door," Father pounded his hands against the wood a few times. But, as far as I could hear, the door stayed shut.

Chapter Thirty-Nine

## THE PUBERTY CEREMONY

The next day, Momma called Johnny Whitefeather. He came over with a small forest in his truck. "Your Grandma would've wanted you to have this," he said as he set about making my *wikiup*.

Momma and I held hands as we sat side by side on the back porch and watched.

Johnny sang as he bent some of the larger branches to form an oval hut, then filled in the open spaces with leaves to enclose the sides. The top was left open.

Sean found an old red rug for the door. Brucie dug some army blankets out of the garage for the floor. Father poked his head out every now and then, but didn't say anything.

When it was all finished, Johnny sprinkled blue corn around the *wikiup*. "To help you on your journey," he said.

It was amazing! By the evening our backyard had been transformed into a sacred space. It would've been better to have my ceremony near Grandma's Stone Circle, but having a ceremony at all was the most important thing. It meant that the part of me I'd been having to hide could finally come out into the open.

"Great Spirit," Aunt Dawn said lifting her arms toward the sky as Momma, Aunt Dawn, Aunt Raven, Ann Marie, Violet and I sat in a circle inside the *wikiup*. "Mystery of all life. Be with us now as we welcome Fiona Lonestar MacLean into womanhood." Aunt Dawn's voice sailed out through the open roof and up towards the stars. "*Kokumthena*, you who sit nearest to the Great Spirit, we ask you to look down and bless this ceremony. Guide us with your wisdom and knowledge. Circle us with your divine light. Be with us now, as we honor this special life passage of Moontime. Ho." The pungent smell of *kin.ni.kin.nick* mixed with the crisp scent of the leaves and other outdoor smells in the damp night air.

Aunt Dawn nodded towards Momma, Aunt Raven, Violet and Ann Marie. "We welcome you into womanhood," they chanted seven times as we sat shoulder to shoulder in a tight circle on top of the army blankets. *Seven, the number of completion. Everything has a beginning - middle - and end,* I thought.

The power of their words along with Aunt Dawn's prayer made me light headed. It was hard to believe what was happening was really happening and not just a dream. My ceremony was to last until the following morning. Not as long as Grandma's ancestors, but at least it was a start.

As we sat in the hut, a strong yellowish beam from the lantern flared out between us. It whispered over our bodies and onto the white leather bundle Aunt Dawn laid out in front of her. She untied the string holding it together. It opened, revealing several objects. She picked one up. It was a ball of red clay, about the size of a baby's fist. Her dark eyes fixed on mine. "Our ancestors were formed from the richness of the Earth. Part of your passage is to acknowledge them." She cradled the ball of clay next to her heart then set it back down on top of the white leather.

Aunt Dawn then picked up a few small corn kernels. "Life's possibilities lie protected within your body like these seeds. You must guard these future children with strength and courage. When you are ready, you may give birth through love and conscious action." She closed her hands over the seeds, brought them to her heart, and like before, set them back down.

It was a powerful feeling to know that I had a choice about bringing a child into the world. I wasn't ready yet. But, one day I would be.

"This is from a mountain." Aunt Dawn said as she picked up a small grey stone and held it in the middle of her hand. It was my birthday stone. I wondered how she found it. "This stone belongs to something larger and more powerful than itself." She continued. "Part of your ceremony is to understand that you too are connected to something beyond what you are aware of right now." She enclosed the hand holding my birthday stone with the other, brought it to her heart, then, set it down on the leather as she had the others.

I brushed the hair out of my eyes and stared out at the ball of clay, kernels of corn, and my birthday stone. Powerful symbols to help me in my ceremony. I swallowed hard and pulled down on the bottom of my long white dress. Aunt Raven made it for the ceremony. The sleeves flared out at the elbows and the neckline gathered together with a ribbon. It made me feel very special.

"The knowledge of the ages lives through your mind, body and spirit." Aunt Dawn said. "There are spiritual forces within that emerge when you pray. Have an intention. Let the knowledge flow through you. Answers will come. We all have an intuition, a wisdom. It is a gift from the Great Spirit. As a child we know this connection. As we grow, it fades. We must give it attention, treat it as a friend, for it to return."

"What if I ask and nothing happens?" I broke in.

Aunt Dawn touched her finger to her lips. "Then ask again. And again. Until it does. This knowledge is so powerful that it is beyond words." She clapped three times and nodded again to the others.

Momma reached her hands towards me. "I'm very proud of you, Fiona Lonestar MacLean." Tears sprang up in her eyes. A warm, tingly feeling shot through me as our hands touched.

Aunt Dawn pushed on the red rug over the doorway, stepped outside, held it open for everybody else to crawl out, then closed it again.

That was it. Whatever was going to happen next in my Puberty Ceremony was going to be up to me. I wanted to turn to Grandma. She always had the right words to help me. But she was gone.

I spread out full length on top of the blankets and looked up. Tiny pieces of dust twisted and turned in the yellow lantern beam. They looked like miniature people.

I picked up the round piece of clay, held it close, then switched off the light. "God, Great Spirit, *Kokumthena*, help me tap into that knowledge of the ages that lives in me. Help me acknowledge my ancestors," I prayed softly.

After some time, visions came. *I began to feel as if I was inching my way inside a huge cave. I couldn't see anything. But I could touch the cold surface and smell the dampness.*

*I continued to move forward but nothing changed. It was still dark. I needed some light. A flicker or a beam of some kind to reveal where I was. I pushed my backside into the wall and slid to the ground. There was no way to see inside the cave.*

I opened my eyes. My breath caught in my throat. " I can't see," I cried out. A sense of failure fell heavily across my chest.

It was still dark outside, but not as dark as in my dream. I held tight to the clay ball, crawled over to the door, pushed the flap back and stepped out. A cool breeze brushed across my body.

The vision was scary. It seemed impossible to find my way through the cave and connect to the knowledge of the ages. Aunt Dawn said if I didn't get an answer at first, to ask until I did.

The smell of the air was wildly fresh. I looked up at the sky. The Milky Way was overhead. *It's where the souls of children wait to be reborn,* Grandma said a long time ago. *Maybe one day, one of them would be mine,* I thought.

I walked over to the *wikiup*, pulled back the red flap and crawled into the center. I picked up the round piece of red clay and held it in my lap. As the stars shined brightly overhead, I closed my eyes and prayed again. "God, Great Spirit, *Kokumthena*, help me tap into that knowledge of the ages that lives in me. Help me acknowledge my ancestors." I waited a few minutes. When it didn't answer, I asked again.

And again. Dogs barked in the distance. Cars honked. Still I sat.

*Imagine starlight moving gracefully over the outside of your body, then filling every cell inside as you pray,* a voice whispered softly inside my head.

I didn't know that voice, but it was worth a try. I had nothing to lose. I closed my eyes. I imagined starlight flowing down from the sky, over my head and neck, along my shoulders and arms, across my spine and down my legs, then up the front of my body. About the seventh time of imagining the circuit, the me I knew disappeared. Thoughts faded. Something beyond words took over.

*I was inside some kind of energy, like a light droplet that's part of a star. It was oval and radiated a gold glow. The light wasn't stagnant. It was in a constant state of change. Narrow circles of it whirled around me. As it whirled, the circles got bigger and reached out farther. It felt wonderful and safe. Shivers ran up my spine. I found the missing light.*

"Help me acknowledge my ancestors," I asked again. This time the words felt heavy, like anchors docking a ship. It took all my strength to lift them out. All I wanted to do was sink inside the gold glow. As I stayed with my intention and allowed the relaxation to be there at the same time, visions came.

*I flew up into the sky. Weightless, I did cartwheels and flips. "I can fly," I sighed. "Like an eagle"*

*The higher I flew, the smaller I felt. My body was tiny. A piece of dust. The Earth became a giant ball in the distance. Blue oceans cradled rich green pieces of land. A brilliant light flashed all around me and circled the Earth. This time I saw lines of people making their way towards my* wikiup. *They came over the hills in thousands, down valleys, across oceans on boats, through deserts, past forests, and around lakes. Nothing seemed to stop them in their move. And, there were so many. I'd never thought of family beyond my parents and grandparents. Now, I saw that my bloodline was endless.*

*I'd also never thought beyond being part Scots and Indian. After I'd seen how many people I had descended from, the light energy moved me even closer. Black, yellow, red and white; tall and short; blonde, brunette and redheaded. Every size and color imaginable moved towards my hut. They couldn't see me as I floated along, in and out of some of the groups. No one looked up or showed any kind of awareness about what was happening. They just kept walking.*

*Nobody needed to tell me they were my relatives. I could feel their magnetic connection move through my veins. It was an Intuition. A wisdom. Something beyond words. I, Fiona Lonestar MacLean, was connected to so much more than I ever thought possible.*

I opened my eyes. *Strong, courageous warriors live in your blood,* Grandma said a long time ago. I didn't understand what she was talking about then. It was almost unbelievable. How could I tell my friends they came from every color there ever was? Or that they were surrounded by a protective light like a part of the sun?

*Ceremonies are experiences that don't translate into words*, Grandma said. How many other things did she say to me that I didn't, couldn't understand before now?

I set the ball of clay back down on the leather. Stretched out on top of the blankets. Brought my knees up to my chest. Twisted one way, then the other. It felt good to stretch. It felt good just to be me. I rolled the tip of my tongue across my lips. They were dry. After having such an amazing journey, I was thirsty.

Something shiny, over by the door flap, caught my eye. I blinked a few times to make sure I wasn't seeing another vision. It was an orange metal cup. I sat up, reached over and picked it up. It was filled with water. I took a sip. Coolness flowed down my throat. Someone must've been looking out for me. *Was it Father?* Earlier on, I thought I heard heavy footsteps walk past my *wikiup* and latch the back gate.

I reached for the corn seeds and held them loosely in my right hand. Johnny Whitefeather had spread blue corn on the outside of the *wikiup. To help you on your journey*, he had said. Grandma's ancestors always carried corn because it stayed fresh. It was a sacred plant.

I sat up and crossed my legs. "God, Great Spirit, *Kokumthena*, help me to understand how to guard the seeds in me," I asked. I was beginning to trust those forces Aunt Dawn said would be present for me.

*Soon, I was drifting along inside the cozy protection of my light again. This time it took me to a garden. Lush green grass spread out all around me. Purple, lavender, white, and scarlet flowers in every size and shape imaginable lined the edges. Some were in trees, others on bushes, and yet more stood alone. Birds, butterflies and bees flew in and out of their petals and leaves carrying pollen and seeds from one tree, bush or flower to the next. Their wings fluttered gracefully as they glided from plant to plant, bush to bush, tree to tree in never ending movements.*

*Fox, deer, rabbits and other four legged cousins came forward to eat, play and multiply. Bluebirds, Robins, Ravens, and other feathered relatives flew overhead and nested in the trees. Soon, every animal I'd ever seen filled the meadow in a never ending dance of birth and rebirth.*

*Suddenly it dawned on me. Some parts of the Earth don't have choices about creating new life. But I do. I'm the part of the Earth that can walk, think about consequences and make choices. An incredible sense of power pulsed through my veins. Deep inside me, hidden from view, were seeds that I would guard with my life.*

My eyes opened. Guarding my future children was a gift. Guarding myself and my treasures was also a gift. Gifts that somehow had been passed on to me by the great mystery of creation. It was something I would never take for granted.

I stood up and stretched my arms towards the sky. The tips of my fingers reached through the opening in the top of my hut. I'd been sitting inside a small space, yet the visions had taken me outside where space seemed endless. It was like living in two worlds.

I sat down, put the seeds back down on top of the leather and picked up my birthday stone. *This is from a mountain,* Aunt Dawn had said. *It belongs to something mightier than itself. Part of your ceremony is to understand that you too are connected to something beyond what you are aware of right now.*

I closed my eyes and prayed just like I had before. Having had two different visions, I let go of what this one might be.

A warmth moved down my throat as my breath made its way into my chest and stomach. I imagined the rays of light flowing down from the sky just like before. Soon the feeling of being inside the light energy came back. I sank deeper and deeper into its gentle rays. "God, Great Spirit, *Kokumthena*, help me to understand that I am connected to something beyond what I am aware of right now," I asked.

*The stone was part of a mountain,* I thought. *Since I was holding the stone, did that mean it was now a part of me? Or was I a part of it? Does something carry me along like I carry the stone?*

Questions pushed against the top of my head like wild seeds looking for fertile soil. "Calm down," I said. "Calm down." I was trying to think my way into the message from the stone rather than just letting go and allowing visions come like they had before. *When answers don't come, ask again and again,* Aunt Dawn had said. I took a deep breath and imagined the light rays once more. "God, Great Spirit, *Kokumthena*, help me to understand that I am connected to something beyond what I am aware of right now," I asked.

After a while, I heard a voice. *See the lights in the sunrise, they are all a part of you.* It was Grandma's voice. *You'll see them one day.*

*A hand came out of nowhere, reached through a fuzzy thin wall, and pulled me through. "Don't be afraid," she said. The voice was light, that of a young woman.*

*"I'm not," I answered. I tried to see what the woman looked like but as soon as I was through the wall we entered a dark tunnel. It was peaceful this time. Quiet. Our feet edged forward in silence.*

*At the end of the tunnel, we stepped out onto something hard. I looked around. We were at the top of a high mountain. A soft misty glow stretched out for miles all around us. The* moon hung overhead.  Colors shot up in a zigzagged pattern out of the stone.

"Beautiful isn't it?" The woman said. Her voice a soft whisper. The fringe on the sleeves of her white buckskin dress swayed with her movements.

I turned to face her head on. Now that we were out of the tunnel, I could see a little. Not as clearly as daylight, but enough.  She was just a few inches taller than I was.  And not too old. Maybe Momma's age, thirty-ish. Thin lines broke out around the edge of her dark eyes.  Her coffee-cream colored cheeks widened. An aura of confidence and peace radiated around her like a thin veil.

"Come." She brushed some black wisps of hair away from her face and tucked them behind her ears. A path led from where we were towards the center of the mountain. We followed it.

We walked together, side by side, hand in hand, as if we were old friends.  Something about her made me feel at ease. It was hard to say what that was.  Maybe just the soft way she spoke, or the movement of her body.  The colors continued to dance all around us. When a big flare occurred, I stopped to watch.  Awestruck each time.  My new friend waited patiently. It felt good not to be rushed.

Ho ya ne ho ya ne ho. Ho ya ne a.  Chanting sounds rang out in the distance. I looked over at my friend.  She nodded and smiled. A mischievous look in her eyes.

As we got closer I could see that the singing was coming from a group of eleven women circled around a small fire. They were dressed in white buckskin, just like my new friend. Some were young, about my age. Most seemed older, maybe forty. The woman at the far end had white hair, so she was probably sixty or so.

"E'ne. In the Star World we get to be any age we want.  We can even change shape."

She read my mind!  E'ne was a word Grandma used.  "Do I know you?"

*She stepped in front of me. Her dark eyes held me in their gaze. Endless waves of love poured out. A scent of lavender and sage drifted through the air.*

*My heart thumped loudly in my ears. The women's chants reverberated down my spine. I swallowed hard and blinked. Maybe I was making all this up. Maybe I have too much imagination like Momma says. When I stopped blinking, my new friend was still there. She just kept right on holding me with her eyes. Then I knew who she was. Tears rolled down my cheeks. A soft wind buzzed in my ears.*

*"Grandma!" I staggered forward and wrapped her in my arms, careful not to let go of my stone. "Oh! Grandma. It really is you. You're so young. I didn't recognize you."*

*"This is my little piece of Heaven, Paradise. I've been waiting for you to visit."*

*"I've missed you so much, Grandma. So much." Joy fuzzed up inside of me. It flew into the air and caught on the current like dandelion seeds. "I wanted you to be at my Puberty Ceremony." I studied her face for a sign of recognition. "Did you know I'm having one? Just like you said your grandmother did." I twisted from side to side. "Of course it's not exactly the same. It's in my back yard, not down by the river. It's one night not four, and ..."*

*Grandma pinched her mouth together and shook her head. "I know Lonestar. From time to time I visit your world. Ceremonies, rituals, are not about where they are, or how long they last, but about creating a sacred space inside of you. You did that, Lonestar. Now, we're going to celebrate."*

*"What about the last part. The stone is from a mountain. I have to understand I'm connected to something beyond what I'm aware of right now?"*

*Grandma laughed. "Each vision has moved you closer to where you are right now. This is the mountain. And you brought the stone with you?"*

*"Yes, I did." I opened my hand. The stone had been snuggled safely inside.*

Grandma brought the tips of her fingers to her lips and nodded. "That is good, Lonestar. The stone will be happy here." She led me inside the circle.

The women stood, brought their hands together at their chests and bowed.

"Who are these women," I asked.

Everyone on Earth has a connection to a group of some kind. These women are my group. We call ourselves The Circle of Light." Grandma tilted her head from side to side. Her long dark hair moved from shoulder to shoulder. "This is no ordinary group of women, Lonestar. Each is powerful in her own way. We send you visions and dreams to help you on your Earthwalk."

"We?" I squeezed the stone tightly in my hand and touched it against my lips a few times. "But, you are my teacher. You're the one who always understood me. The one I always turned to."

"E'ne. And my voice will live on, in your thoughts, and your heart. But, sometimes you will need more than I can give."

I nodded slowly as if I understood, but I couldn't imagine others more powerful than Grandma.

She reached for my hand again. We walked clockwise around the circle. No one looked surprised to see me. Each put one hand on her heart and one on mine as a way of greeting. No one spoke. The only sounds were those coming from our shifting feet on the ground, our skirts swaying, and a song that played inside my head.

The melody and words were faint at first. With each touch they grew louder. After the last woman put one hand on her heart and one on mine, the full verse erupted deep inside me. Ho ya ne ho ya ne ho. Ho ya ne a. Ho ya ne ho ya ne ho. It was the song I'd heard earlier in the distance, now it was a live thing, singing in my bones.

Grandma led me to the fire. She pulled out a tiny box, opened it, and dropped some of her special Kin.ni.kin.nick into the flames. I took a pinch of tobacco out of the pouch I wore around my neck and dropped it in as well. The burning leaves *sizzled, then reached their fingers upwards. The sweet pungent smell I knew so well filled my lungs. Grandma smiled.*

*I unclenched my small stone, held it above the fire, and dropped it in as well. The ground under our feet began to shake. I jumped back. Grandma laughed. "Our mountain is saying 'I gwi yen.'"*

*My light energy started to expand. I could feel it reach out. A growth spurt of another kind. Colors leapt out of my body. Red, yellow, orange, and purple flames shot up. Its lights joined with those in the fireworks all around me. Everything swirled and turned along with everything else. "I am the fire," I cried. "I am the light."*

*Yes," Grandma laughed. "Now you know."*

My breath caught in my chest. I opened my eyes. It was dark outside. My vision had been so filled with light that it took me a minute to be able to focus. I was back inside my *wikiup* The cool air brushed across my cheeks and down my body, but I wasn't cold. The fire burning inside of me was warm, soothing. I touched the ground. I had gone from this world to another and come back. Happiness raced through every cell inside my body. "I found my Grandma," I muttered over and over again. I leaned back and clicked my heels.

The sense of being the fire and the light was intoxicating. No worries. No fears. Only peace.

A soft *pa dum, pa dum, pa dum,* vibrated through the air. The magical sounds of a drum. I pulled back the red flap, stepped into my slippers and looked around. Candles lit up the edges of the back porch steps and the back of the house. Four figures sat around a large drum below the kitchen window. Their hands beat out a slow rhythm. The candlelight flickered over the shoulders of Sean, Brucie, Johnny Whitefeather and...Father. My breath caught in my throat. Father was wearing his kilts. He looked up and grinned. *"Bas no beatha, Tsula,"* I said knowing all of our connections.

Momma, Aunt Dawn, Violet, Ann Marie and Aunt Raven opened the back door, stepped onto the back porch and walked down the stairs. They each wore a shawl of a different color. Shawls like Grandma used to wear. The fringe whispered gently as they walked. *The Earth is my ma-a-ther.* They sang. *The sky is my fa-a-ther.*

Momma had on a blue shawl. Her favorite color. It matched her middle name, Blue eyes. As she moved closer to where I was standing on the lawn I could see that she had another one in her hands. It was maroon. My stomach tightened. Grandma's shawl! As she put it around my shoulders the smell of sage and lavender once again drifted into my nose. I picked up the corner of the shawl and rubbed it over my cheek.

We circled the *wikiup* in a dance. One that Grandma had taught us a long time ago. *Toe-heel, toe-heel, step turn.* I threw myself into the sounds coming from the drum. An umbrella of stars flickered over our heads like a twin world hoping to be noticed, wanting to join the party. Momma laughed as we turned toward each other, then away in the ritual movements. Our long skirts swept the ground. Everyone seemed so happy. Aunt Dawn's prophecy had come true in a way that I hadn't thought about. We were all dancers – connected to the rhythms of the Universe.

A faint early morning light changed the dark into a deep blue. The stars faded. Faces began to appear beyond our circle. They moved through the gate in a long endless procession and joined us in our dance. My stomach tightened. They were the lines of people I'd seen in my vision. And they were actually here. I wasn't sure if anybody else could see them. But, I could.

The yard expanded with each new arrival. Some brought musical instruments. Fiddles, bagpipes, flutes, banjos, tambourines, sticks, and some things I didn't recognize joined the *pa dum* of the drum. The sounds, different than a regular orchestra, brought a rich harmony to our celebration.

Grandma stepped forward with my ... grandfather. They joined hands with Momma and me. Then Father walked across the damp grass with his mom, dad and Dancing Feet. Just when I thought everyone who could possibly arrive was with me, I saw a speck in the distance. As it got closer, I could see it was a young girl ... with dark braids .... she smiled and waved at me as if we were best friends. It was Donna. Even though she wasn't a relative, somehow she'd gotten through to join the party. It was a miracle. The crack I felt in my heart before came back. This time it was a chasm. I forced myself to breathe deeply over and over again.

We all danced together as if those who had left the Earth plane had never been gone. The sun came up over the edge of the houses. I watched the colors do their famous light show: deep blue turned to lavender, orange, pink, and finally a softer blue. I turned to look at Grandma. I wanted to share the awesome arrival of the sun with her. Something she always looked forward to. But, she was gone. My hands were empty. The crowds of ancestors began to fade as well. The bagpipes, fiddles, and other instruments got softer and softer. Only the sounds of the drum stayed the same as we continued to dance.

I looked up at the sky. Hidden worlds lived and breathed behind the morning light. Sometimes those who left Earth came back to visit. Sometimes we could visit them. The Universe was a continual expansion of something beyond words. A beautiful, amazing place that I had just begun to explore.

A flash of light beamed down from the sky and surrounded me like a cocoon. "I'll always be with you Lonestar," Grandma's voice whispered inside my head. "I live in your thoughts, in your dreams and in your heart."

*Ho ya ne ho ya ne ho. Ho ya ne a. Ho ya ne ho ya ne ho.* Chants rang out in the distance followed by a song. *Life is a circle. A circle never ends.* I reached out for Momma's hand, then Father's. "No wa si," Father said, I nodded. It was good. It was the best birthday I'd ever had.

# QUESTIONS FOR DISCUSSION

1. Fiona runs away in frustration when her father forgets her birthday and her parents fight. What do you feel when you are upset by your parents behavior?

2. Grandma tells Fiona that Father's anger may not be about her. It could be about him. Do you think this is true?

3. When someone does something wrong in Fiona's family all the children are hit with a belt, something that is against the law today. How do you think children should be disciplined?

4. Father is against Grandma and Aunt Dawn teaching Fiona Native American Rituals and Ceremonies. Do you think family ceremonies and rituals are important? Why or why not?

5. Fiona is quarantined with a disease. That meant no contact, no television and no telephones. How would you react to being separated from your friends for a long period of time?

6. Dancing is important to Fiona. It gives her a sense of accomplishment. What do you do that makes you feel good about yourself?

7. In families where one or both of the parents suffer from alcoholism, drugs, gambling or other addictions there is often a great deal of chaos. Sometimes promises are broken, angry outbursts occur and children are forced to take on a sense of responsibility that is beyond their years. What else might occur in a family where there is an addiction?

8. Fiona's brother is hurt by a bully on the playground. Has anyone ever bullied you?  Have you ever bullied anyone else? What choices could you make when you get angry or someone is angry at you?

9. Clubs can be important. They often teach skills, good conduct and help to develop an awareness of others among additional positive outcomes. What do you think of The Big Mommas, the club Fiona joined?

10. Fiona had difficulty making friends at her new school. What do you think is the best way to make a friend? What is the best way to be a good friend?

11. Margaret lied about herself and blamed Fiona for being the one trying on wedding gowns. Have you ever had anyone lie about you? Have you ever lied about someone else? What was the outcome of that lie?

12. Have you ever experienced the loss of a person or pet that you loved? If so, how did you grieve that loss? How did you find comfort?  Did anyone help you?

13. Have you gone through puberty yet? If not, what are your thoughts and feelings about all the changes that are coming?  If yes, what was your experience with the changes?

14. What way could you honor those changes? You can write about it or draw it, or just think about it.

15. Fiona's Ceremony is also about learning to listen to her Inner Wisdom (that part inside of us that lets us know what's right or wrong through body signals). What happens to you when you tune into your Inner Wisdom? It can be as simple as knowing who's calling you on the phone before you answer it, or having an inner sense about someone else's feelings without asking.

# GLOSSARY

**Ballet Terms:** *Arabesque* (one straight leg lifts back while supported by the other). *Balancé* (rock from side to side). *Bourrée* (gliding quick movements). *Chaînés* (rolling turns). *Detourné* (turned aside). *Développé* (draw one leg up to the knee, move it into the air, then down to the ground). *Glissade* (glide). *Plié (bent knees).*

**Bas no Beatha** (death or life): During the 16th and 17th centuries the MacLeans were one of the most important Scots clans in the Western Isles. This was their war cry.

**Benedict Arnold V:** 1741-1801. A general during the American Revolutionary War who later defected to the British Army.

**Ceilidh:** A Scots gathering that usually includes singing and storytelling.

**Go Get 'em Dance:** A dance for amusement where the men circle behind a cluster of women and choose one at a time to be part of their circle.

**Indian words:** *Ene* (yes). *Haw* (hello). *I gwi yen* (I am grateful). *Wa-chi-tah* (intended). Niawe (I thank you). *Ciipaa* (ghost). *Ni-neem-e* (I see it). *Tsula (*fox). *No wa si* (it is good).

**Kin.ni.kin.nick:** A mixture of bark, dried leaves and tobacco. Tobacco is usually put on the ground for minor occasions and burned for major events as a prayer for rain, or preparations for a war party or hunting trip. Shawnee do not generally use tobacco in pipes but place it directly in the flames or on the coals of the sacred fire built for that purpose. The smoke from burning tobacco carries words of prayer to the Creator and at the same time serves as a witness to the sincerity of the wish.

**Kokumthena:** According to Shawnee myth, the idea of creation came from the Great Spirit (Moneto), but the actual work of creation was performed by Kokumthena. She is the most important figure in Shawnee religion. She lives in a home in the sky and, in addition to Shawnee and other Native American languages, speaks her own non-Shawnee language that can only be understood by children under age four who forget it as soon as they begin to learn Shawnee.

**Powwow:** A Native American gathering that usually includes food, singing and dancing.

**Talisman**: A stone, ring, or other object, supposed to possess occult powers and worn as an amulet or charm.

**Tecumseh**: 1768-1813. Revered as the greatest Shawnee Chief. His dream was to unite the tribes into a great Indian confederacy and occupy a separate Indian state.

**Tenskwatawa:** 1768–1834. Also called Open Door or The Prophet. Tecumseh's brother and a Shawnee Warrior.

**Turtle**: Shawnee believe they originated from an island balanced on the back of a giant turtle.

Made in the USA
Charleston, SC
14 December 2011